I0818882

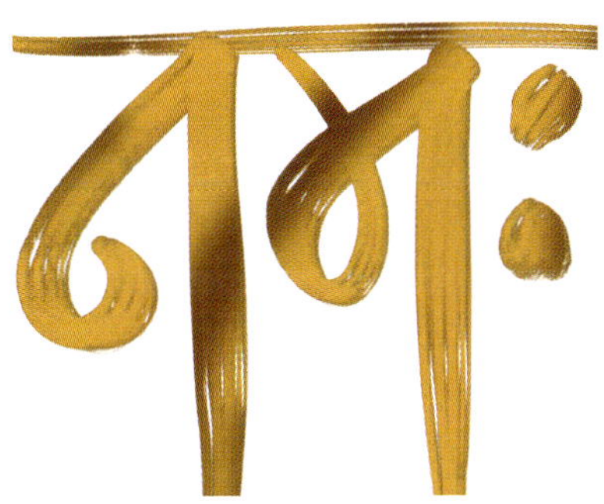

NAMAHA

STORIES FROM THE LAND OF GODS AND GODDESSES

ABHISHEK SINGH

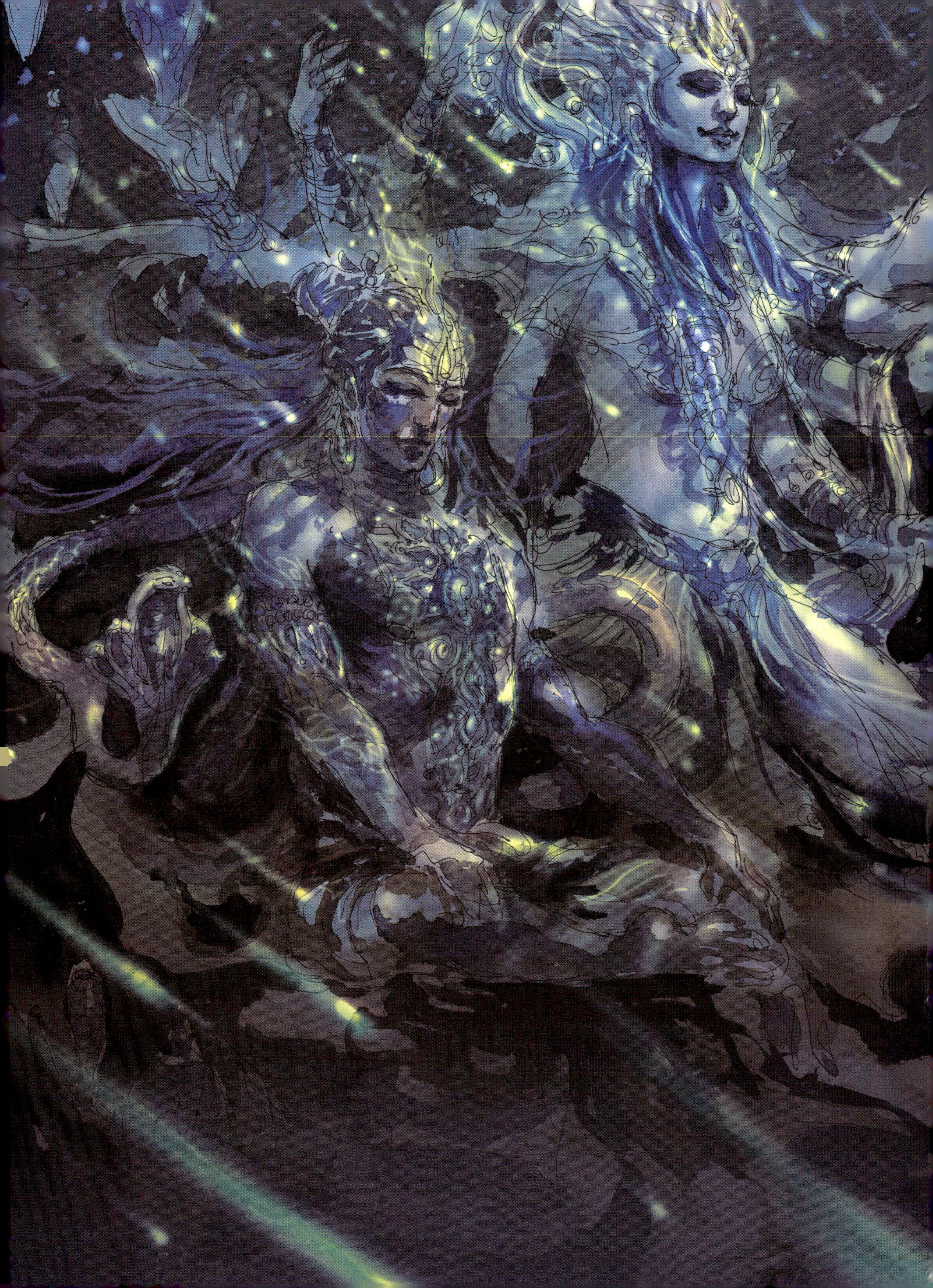

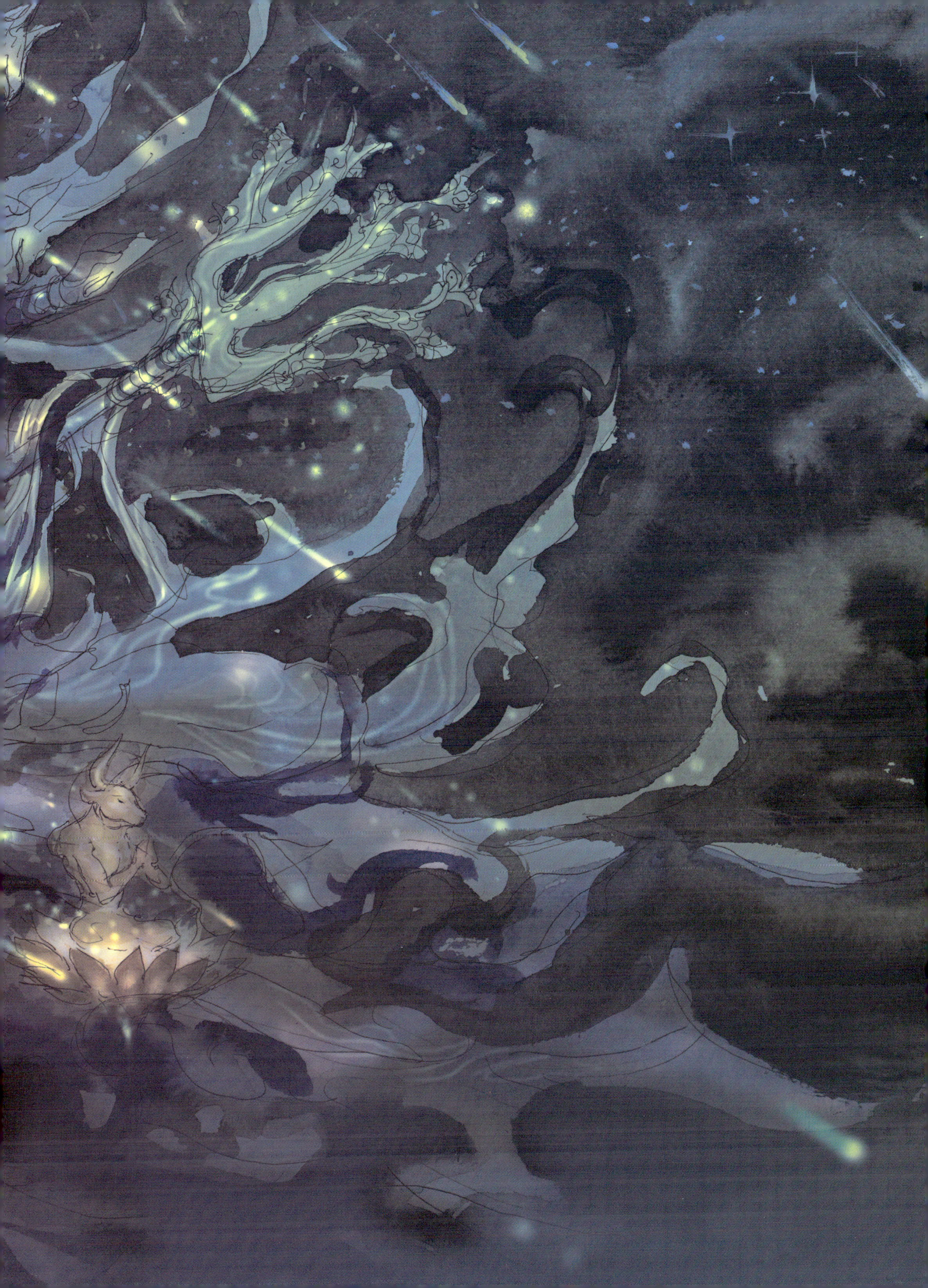

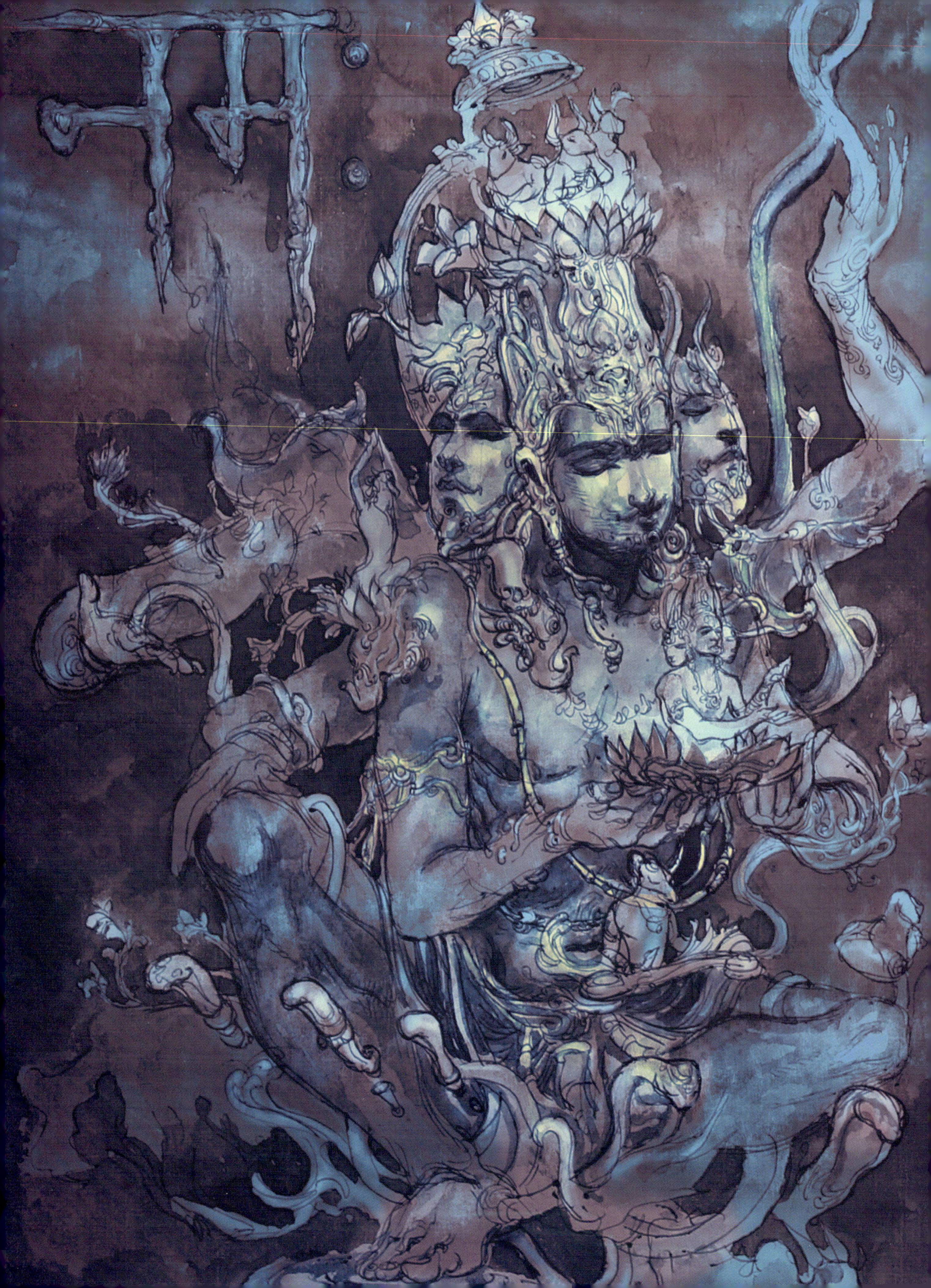

Dedicated To Mother Earth

Shanti, Krishna, Girvar, Naresh, Tripti, Vidhyut

Kim, Snow, Maze, Batty

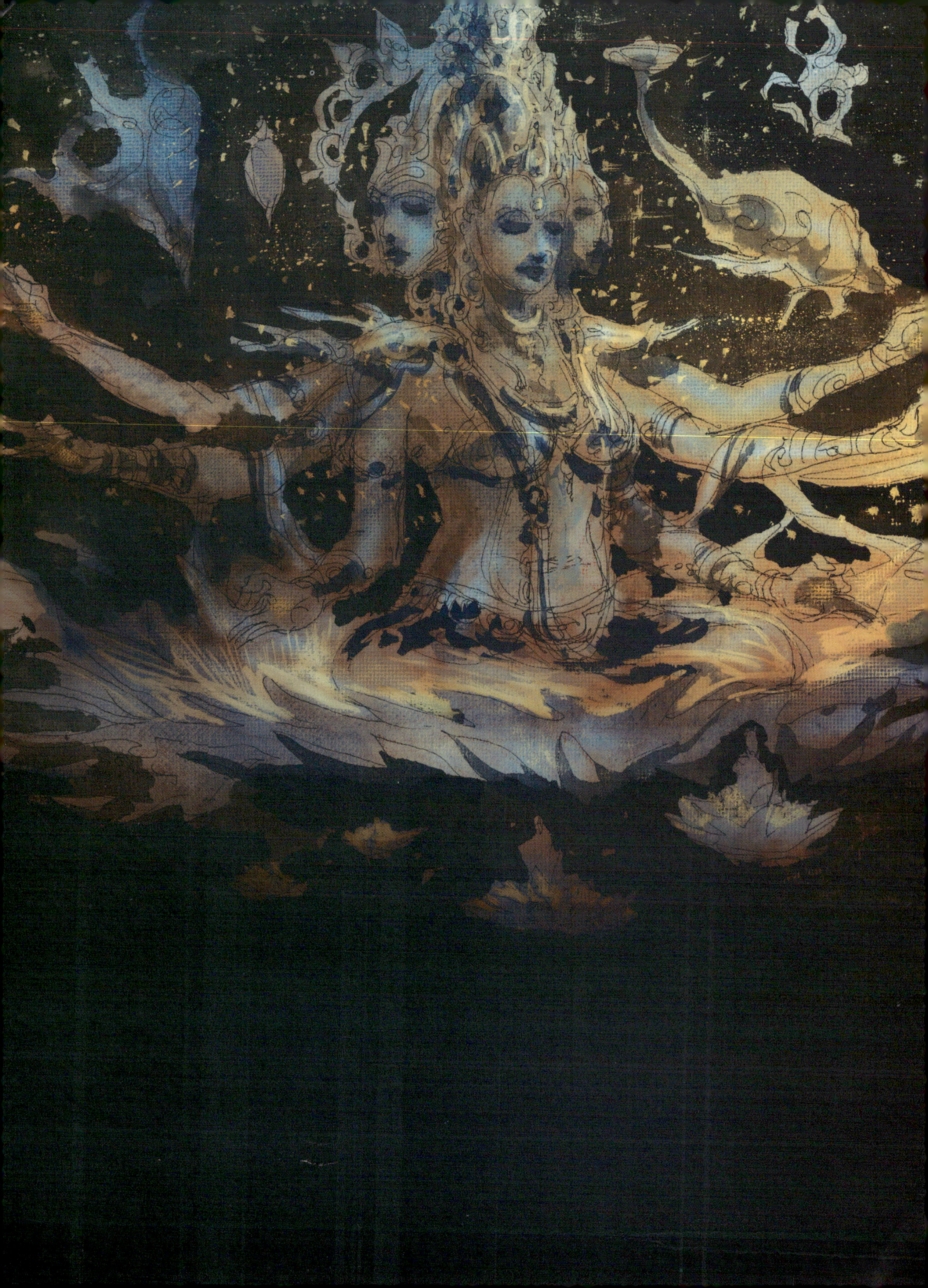

STORIES

01 / NAMAHA

02 / ANSUYA

03 / TOUCHING THE SUN

04 / LITTLE DROPLET AND A THOUSAND RAINBOWS

05 / DESCENT OF THE GANGA – GANGA AVTARAN

06 / THE KNOWER OF SOLITUDE *KEVALYA*

07 / THE YUJ

08 / THE PILLAR OF LIGHT

09 / HALAHALA

10 / THE CREATION OF THE SUN

11 / ISANA

12 / GRI – INVOKED

13 / BLOOM

14 / PASHYANTI – THAT WHICH IS WITNESSED

15 / ADI-YOGI

16 / FOURTEEN SOUNDS, ONE OUTCAST

17 / THE FLUTE

18 / UNMANI

"Mother, bless me to become Shanti (peace)

To become Daya (compassion)

To become Shunya (emptiness)

To become Sattva (illuminated)

Oh Mother, bless me to become

a tendril of your love unbound."

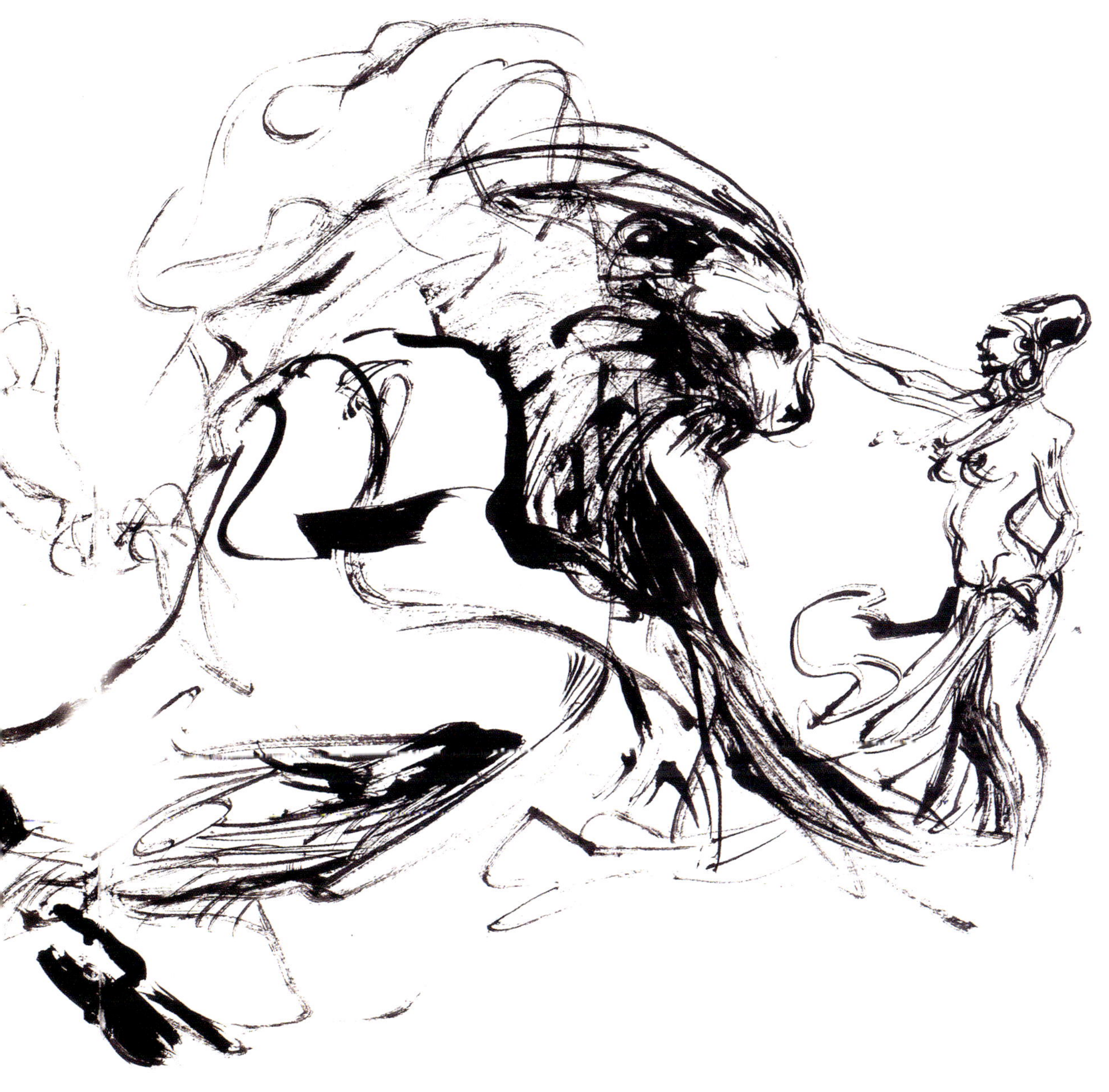

NAMAHA

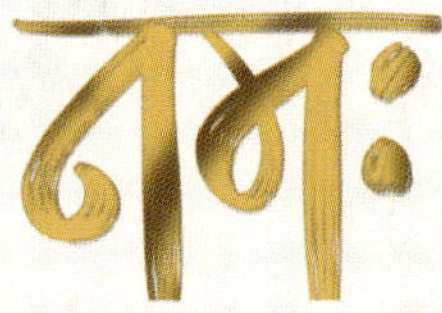

Am I born of the many beginnings? If I am, do they still reside in me?

Beings decay in the realm of time; will my body, mind
and spirit decay too?

Will they have different endings?

Am I the finite body I am given or the infinite mind in it?

If the spirit is truly eternal, why does it dwell in a temporal body?

Who am I in this grand design?

(asked Atri, one of the seven great sages, who meditated amongst the stars)

A sound ripple sent by a distant nebula hummed in Atri's anahata and, he spoke embodying this astral message

"Om" is the sound of the universe, the Birth.

Shivay is the point of dissolution, where creation blends into the silence of nothingness, the End.

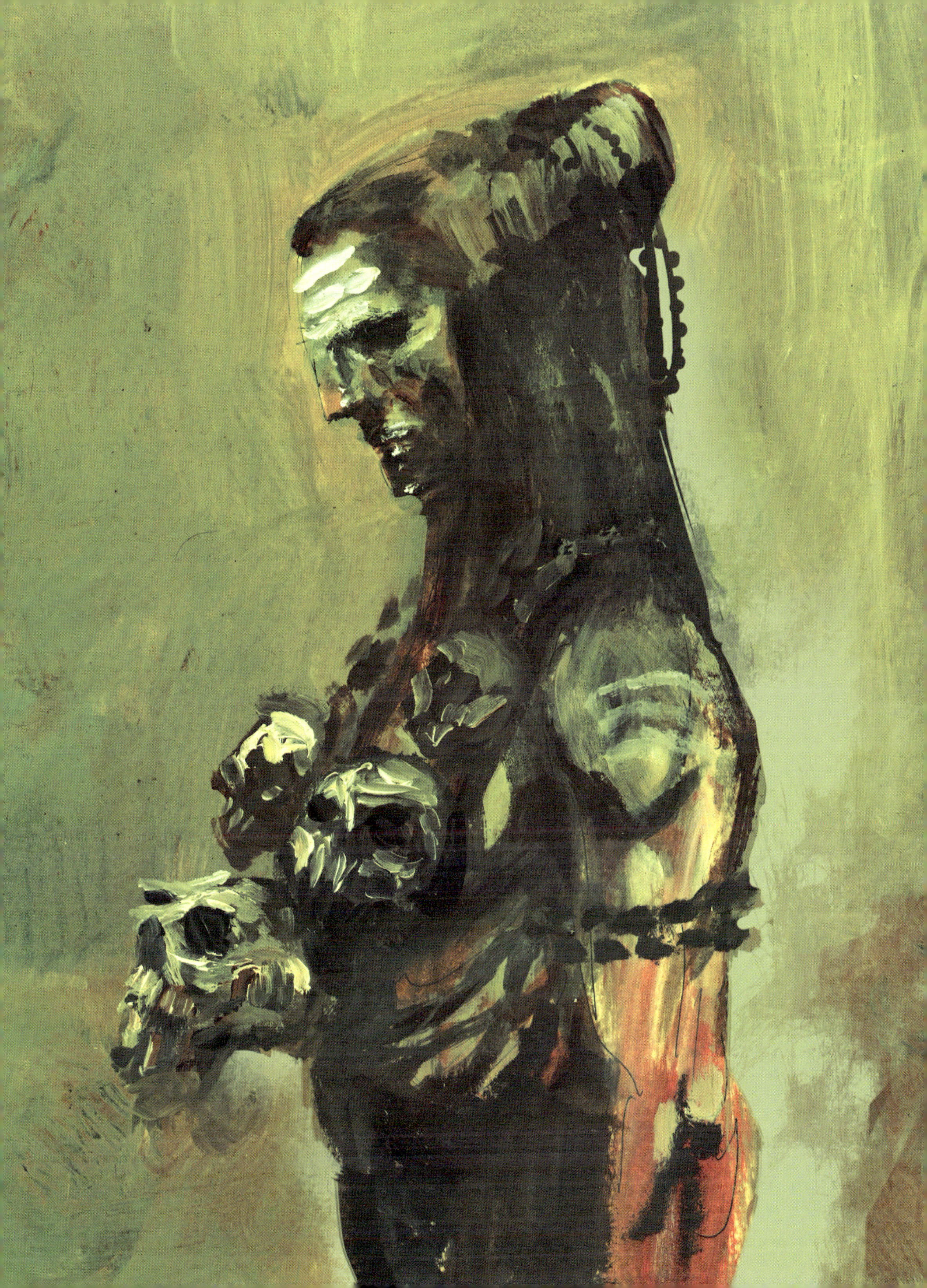

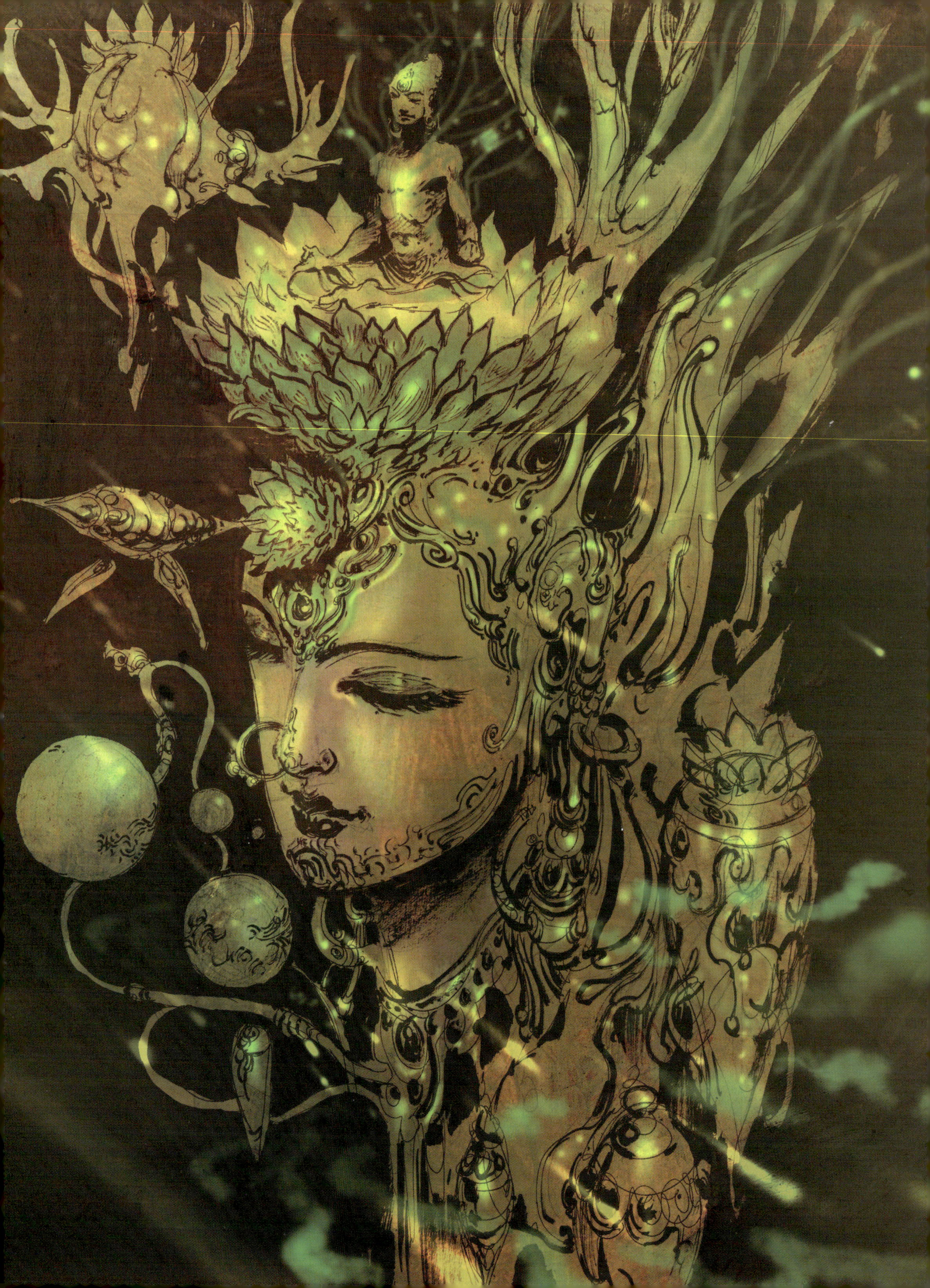

"Namaha" is everything in between.

The bridge between the mysterious origins of the beginning and the inevitable absolution.

It's where the seeker lives, wading through the many paths.

Experiencing the fleeting eternity through the in-between spaces, locked and tired in this transient life.

A place where all the beginnings you are born with,
bleed into a palpable substance called "Life";
Where the mind has both the illusionary coverings and
the "Will" to breach it.

It'll show you the distance between your intent and destiny.

You are the intent.

Exploring the searing terrains between dream and reality.
You will be the seasons of life and the in-between transitions.

You will be made aware of the deeper imprint you share with the cosmos and the majestic Earth.

Try and be one with it.

Hold onto as much "life" as you can
against all insurmountable odds.

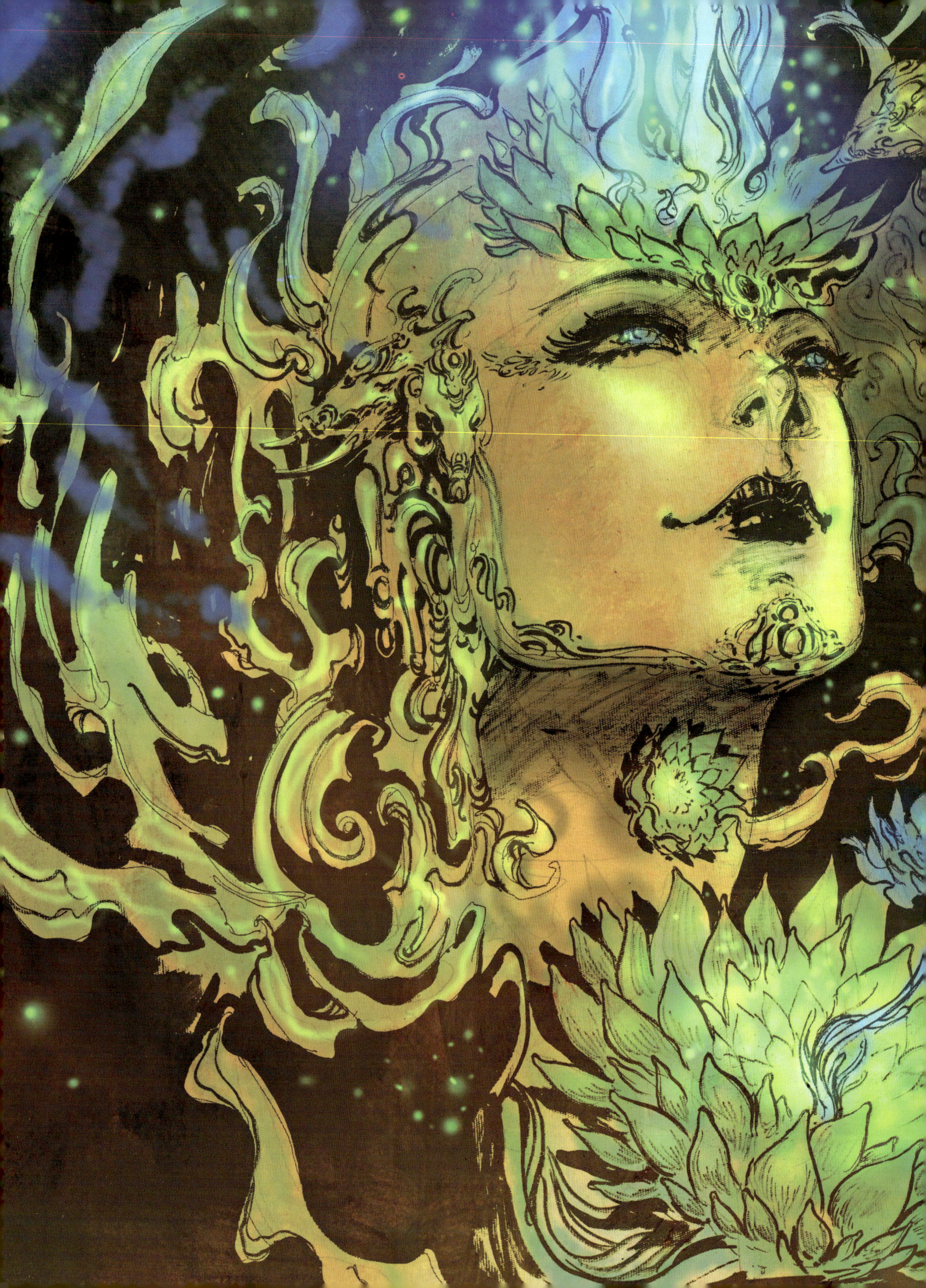

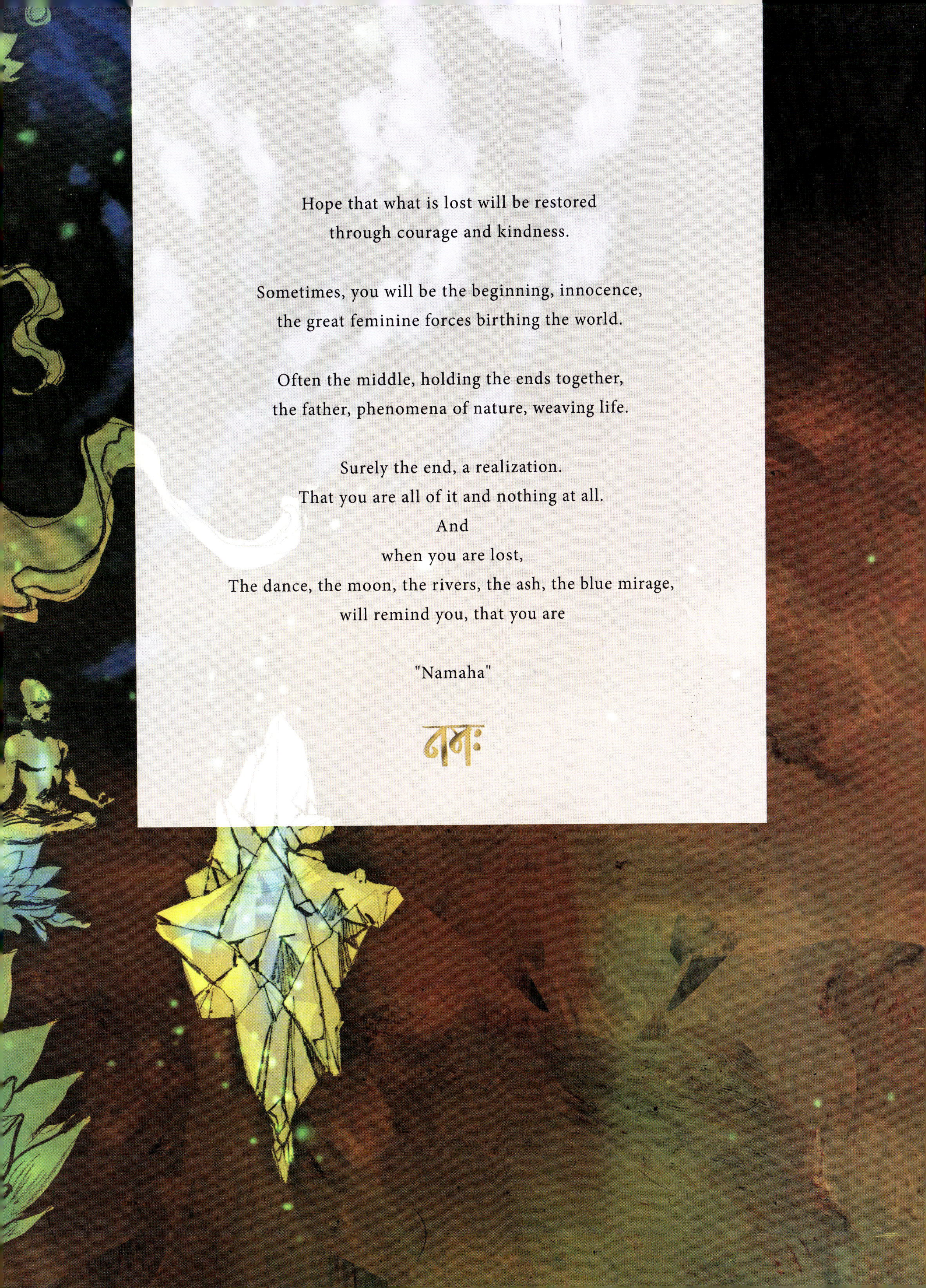

Hope that what is lost will be restored
through courage and kindness.

Sometimes, you will be the beginning, innocence,
the great feminine forces birthing the world.

Often the middle, holding the ends together,
the father, phenomena of nature, weaving life.

Surely the end, a realization.
That you are all of it and nothing at all.
And
when you are lost,
The dance, the moon, the rivers, the ash, the blue mirage,
will remind you, that you are

"Namaha"

नमः

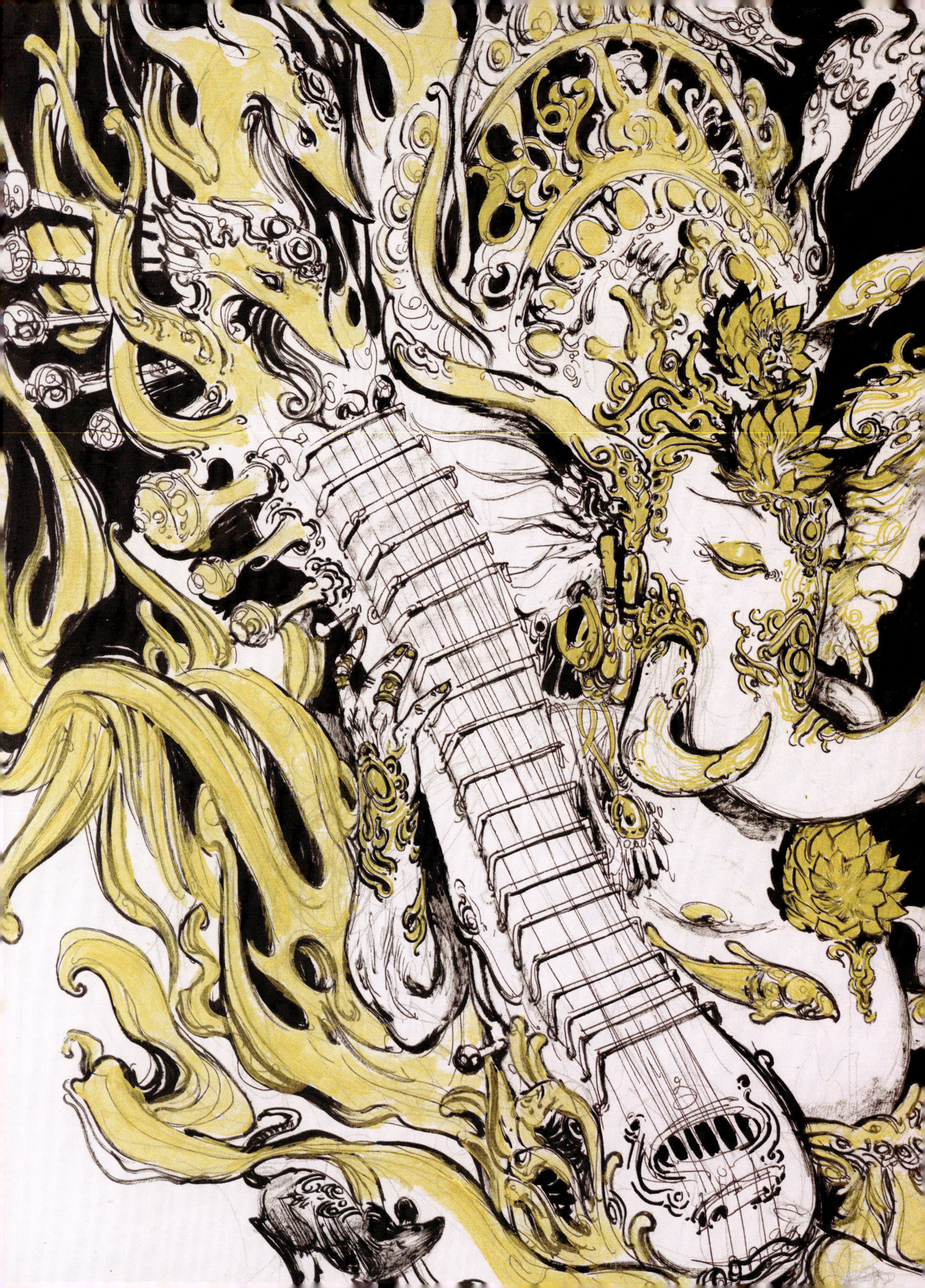

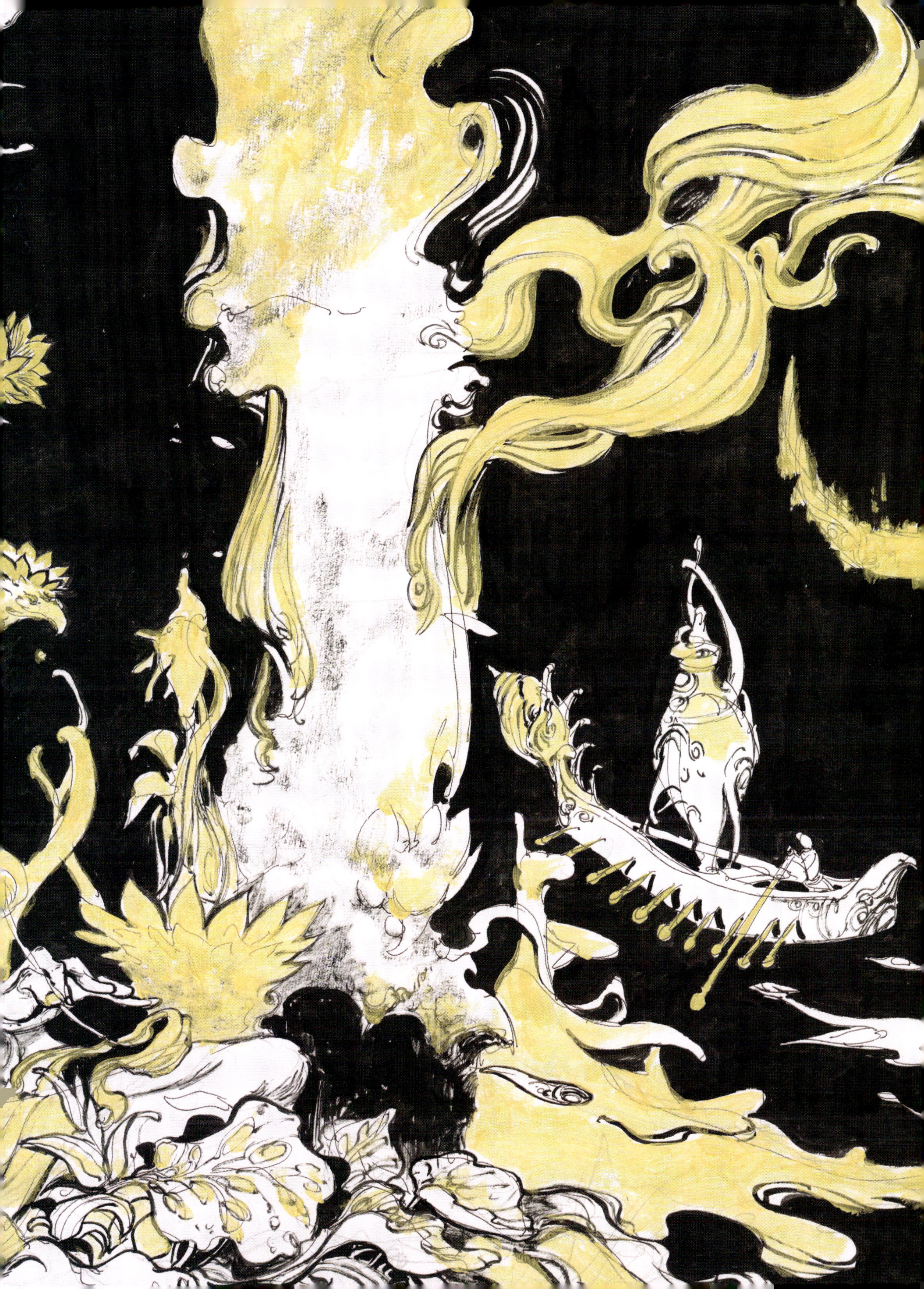

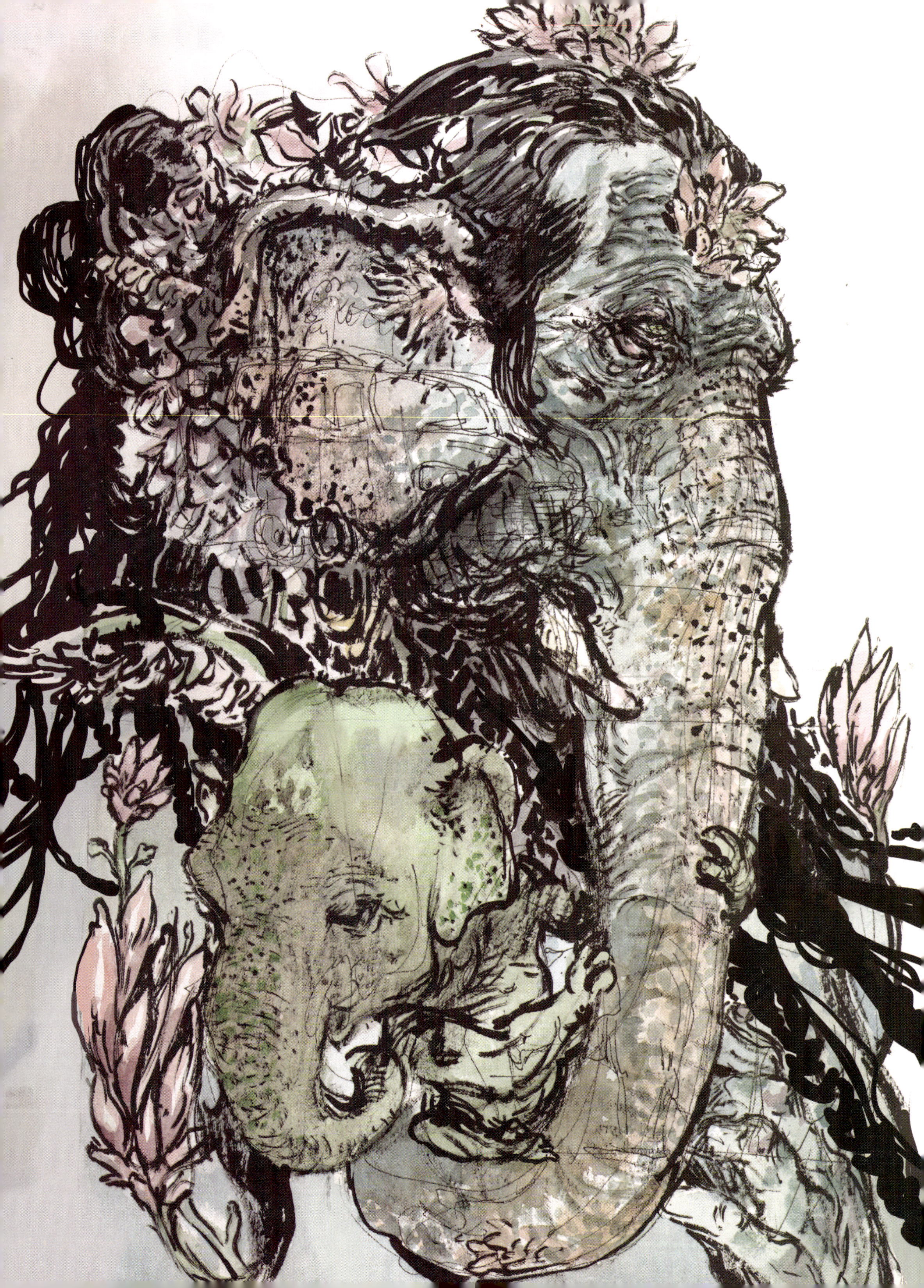

ANSUYA

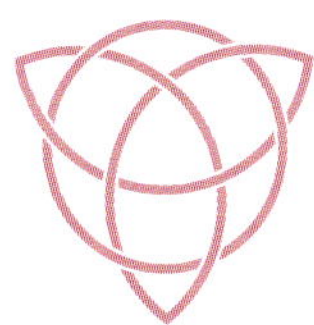

Mother, without you, how will I find a place of happiness in this world of broken spirits?

Wait for the night. That is when everything blends as one. Don't be afraid, just imagine you are inside the womb again.

The stream will sync its sounds to the falling stars and the night will eventually perch them like sea pearls. Join them and make shapes, maybe one such shape will be your guide.

I'm there in the shapes now.

A Nakshatra, a constellation will guide you but remember, whether to keep up with the journey or not, is your choice.

Don't be afraid of the night. It takes away the worldly forms of division and bias.

It makes everything one, so there will be no separation between you, the sky, the mountains or the stars.

You will become all of it, one big breath when the night dawns.

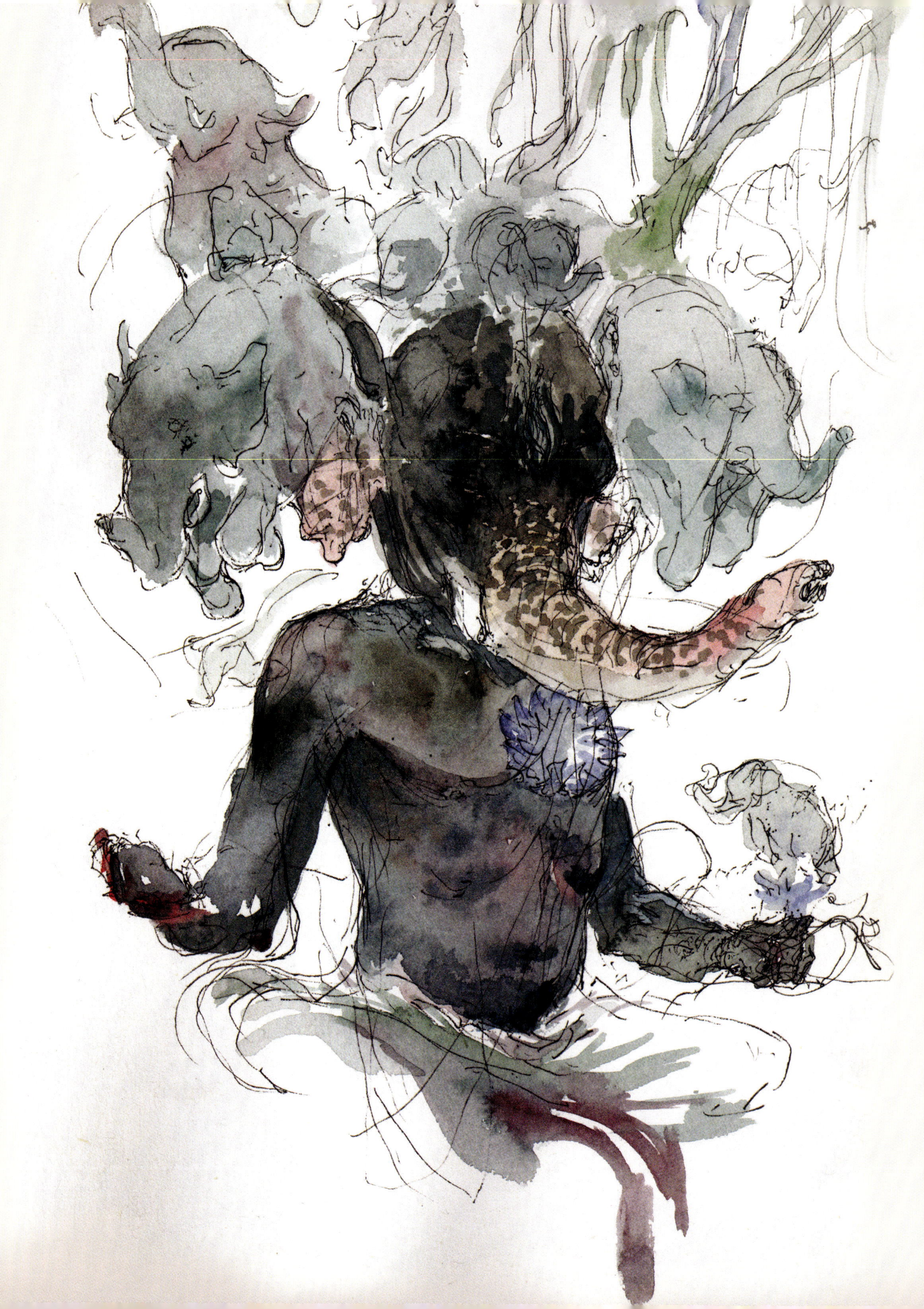

Remember that you have come from the night, inside the womb of this universe which is dark.

Within this womb, lives the light. You are that light.

Know that by shutting your senses, you can truly glimpse the greater beyond.

The harmony, the breath of all as one.

But remember Son, happiness does not mend broken spirits, it's the journey that does.

Trust the journey, that you will find me in every one who will remind you of the forgiving force of Earth, the fragrance of kindness, the courage of love and the grace of endurance.

You'll stagger and endure.

You'll embrace the storms and they shall whisper a lesson, far greater than the trial itself.

I'll be there in them, inside that heart of life.

Looking out for you, Son.

Always.

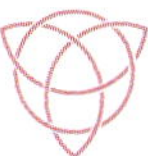

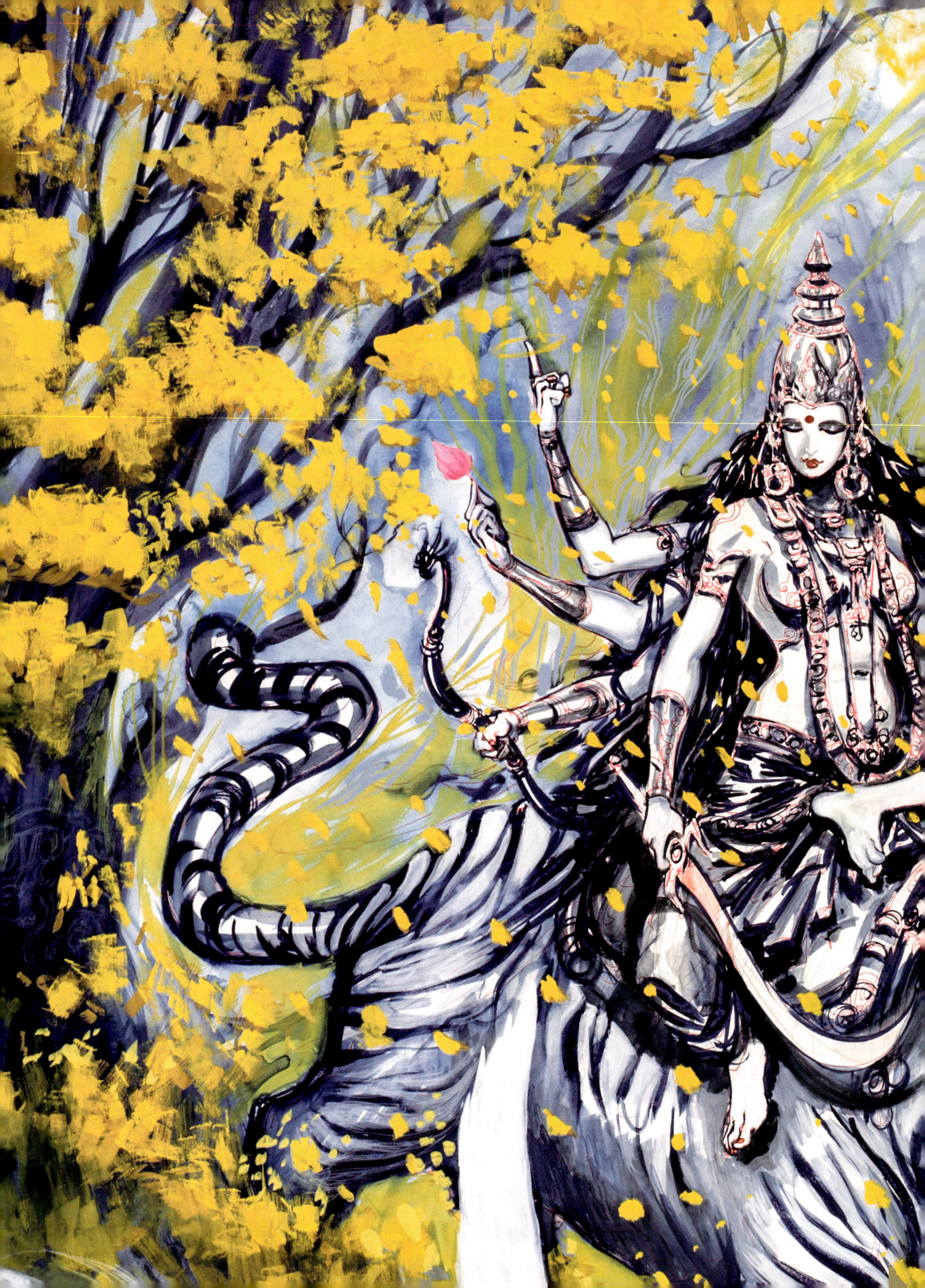

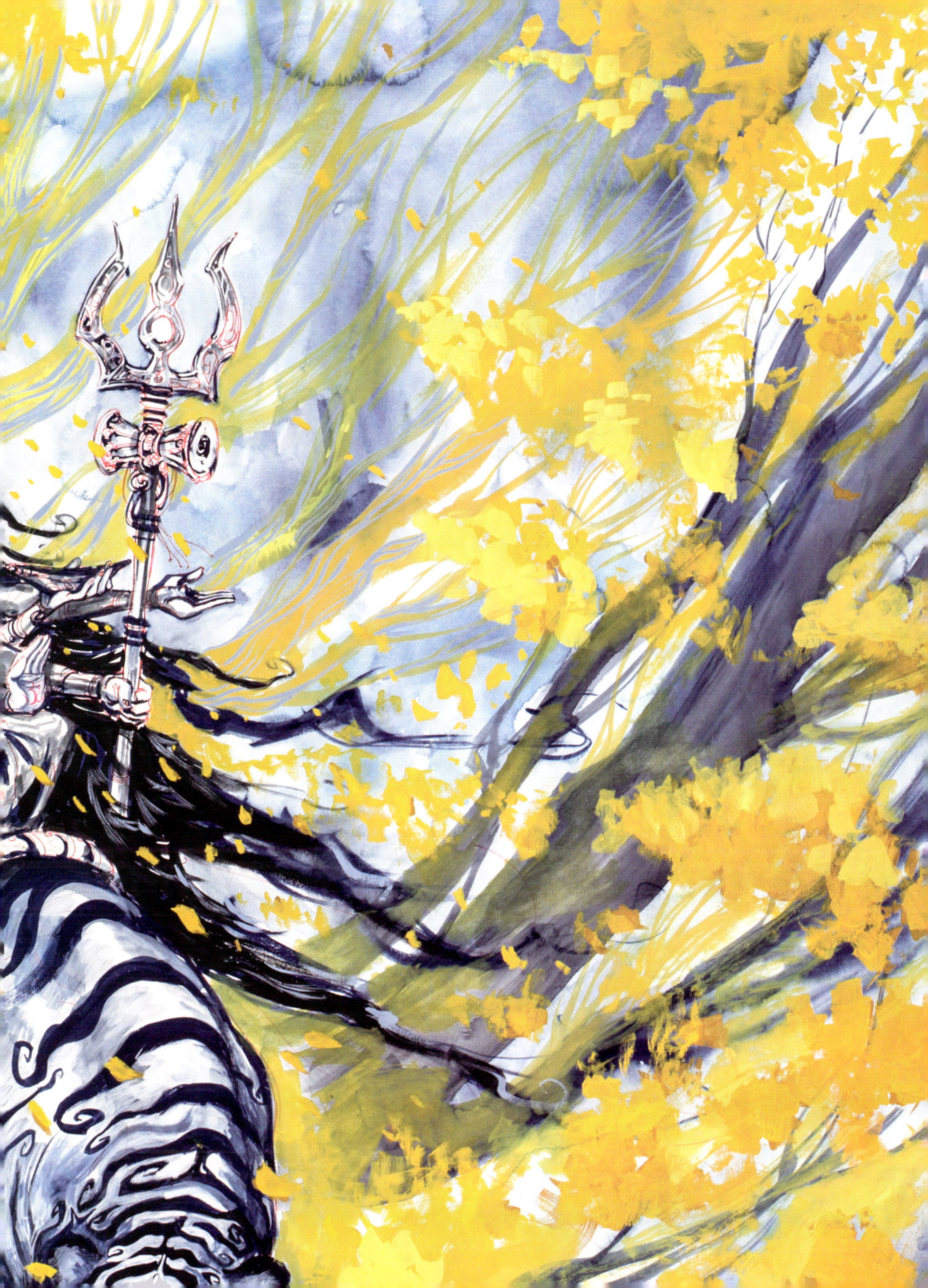

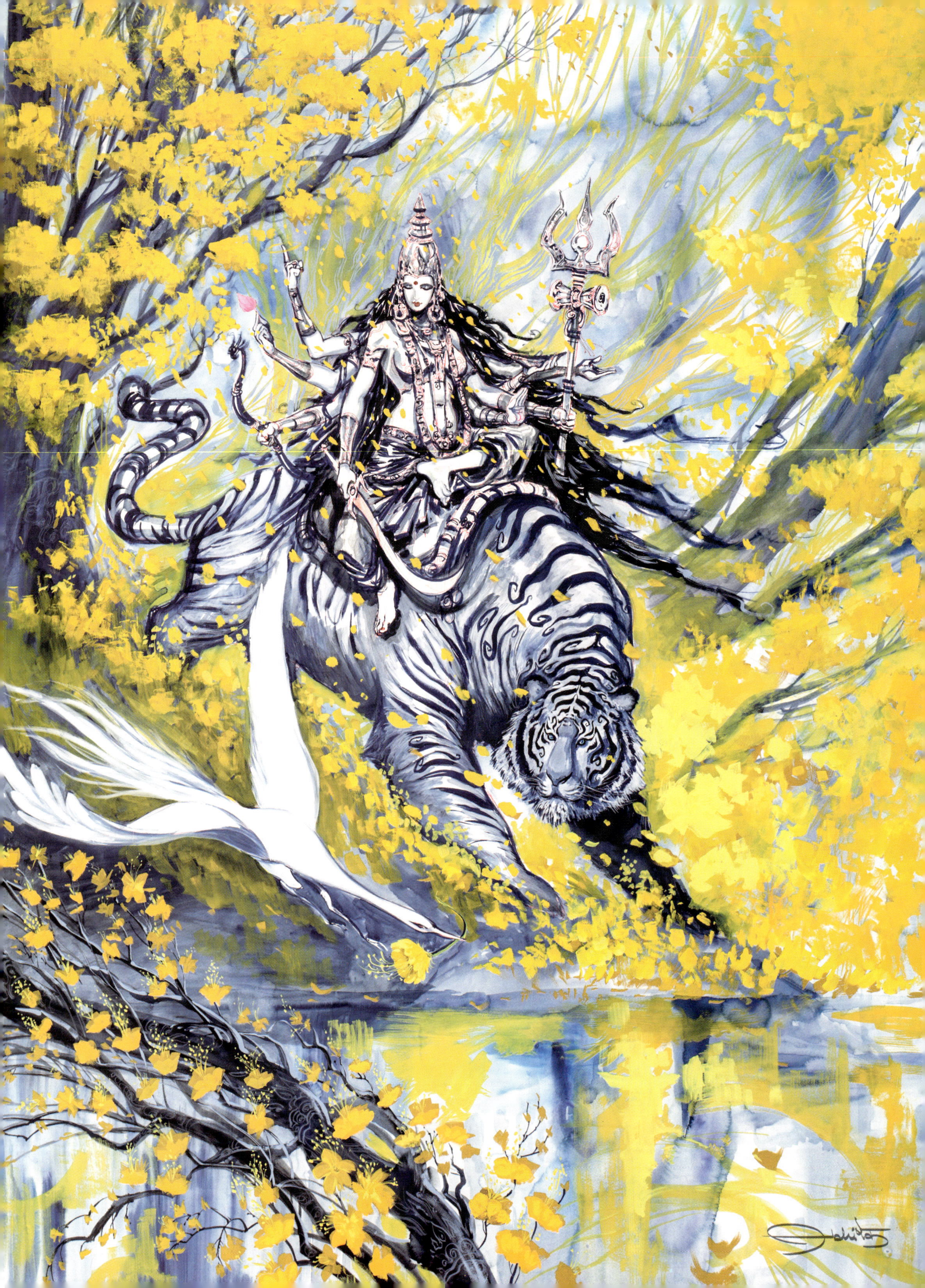

TOUCHING THE SUN

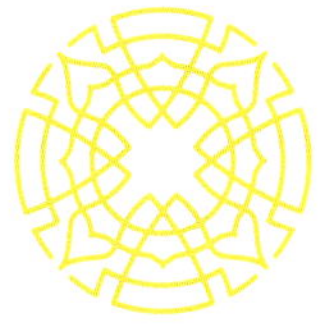

Jiva: "Can one touch the sun without burning one's fingers?"

Devi: "The seed consumes the sunlight to become a fruit. When we eat the fruit, we also consume the same sunlight.

Often we become indulgent and take in more than what we require. This greed starts to burn us back, creating stress, unhappiness and suffering.

When you are kind and start giving this energy to others, you can feel the sun from where the sunlight is coming.

That's when you know you have touched the sun within, without burning your fingers.

Then the swan, which was the Jivatma, took a flight with the sunflower of truth held in its beak, across the pond of life."

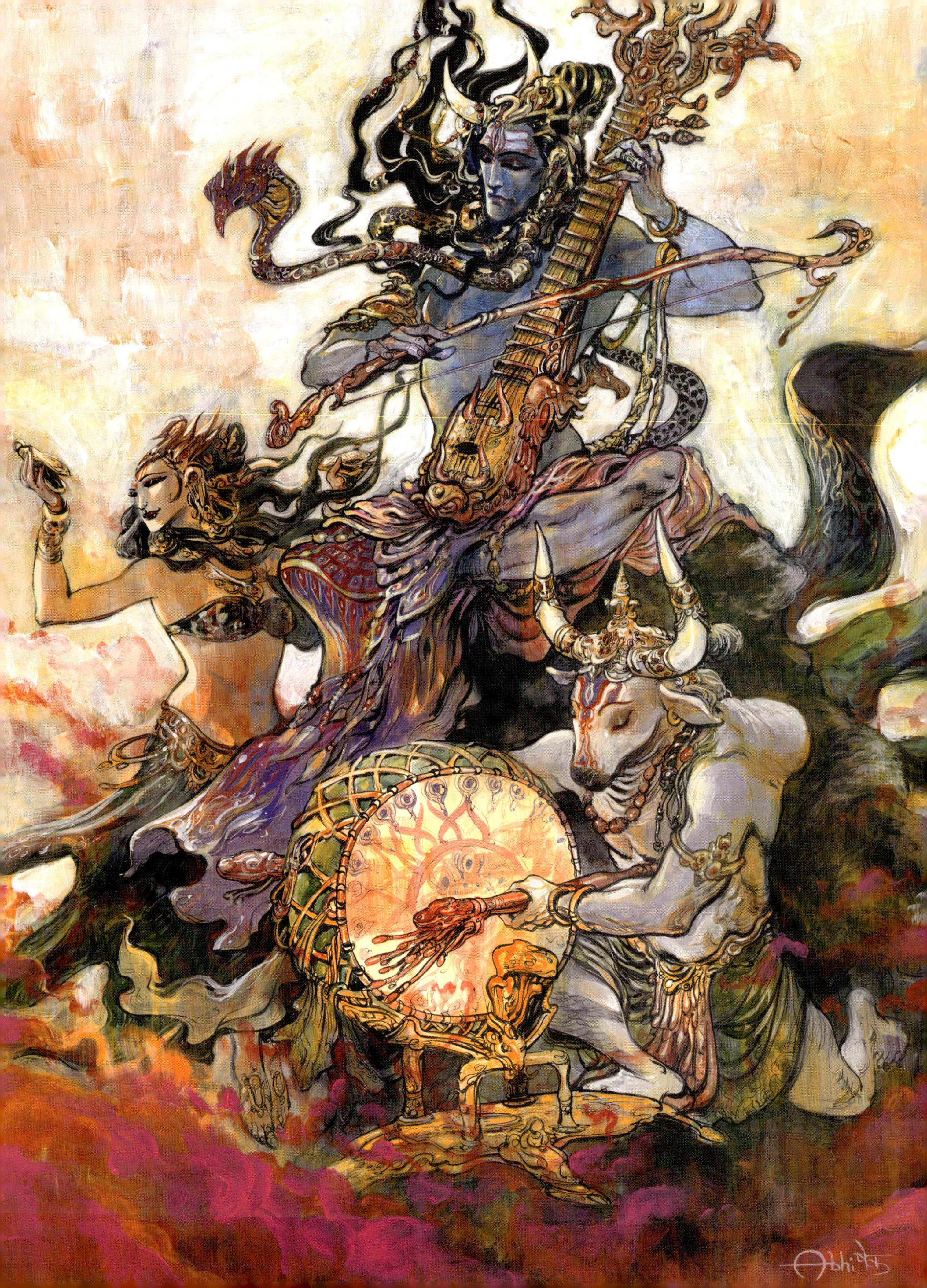

"Sing to the barren sky, like rain does to a famished tree.

Be the sound that lives humbly between the murmur of leaves and chirping of birds.

Become the song which dwells in the silence of listening and in braving the storms."

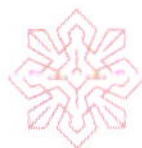

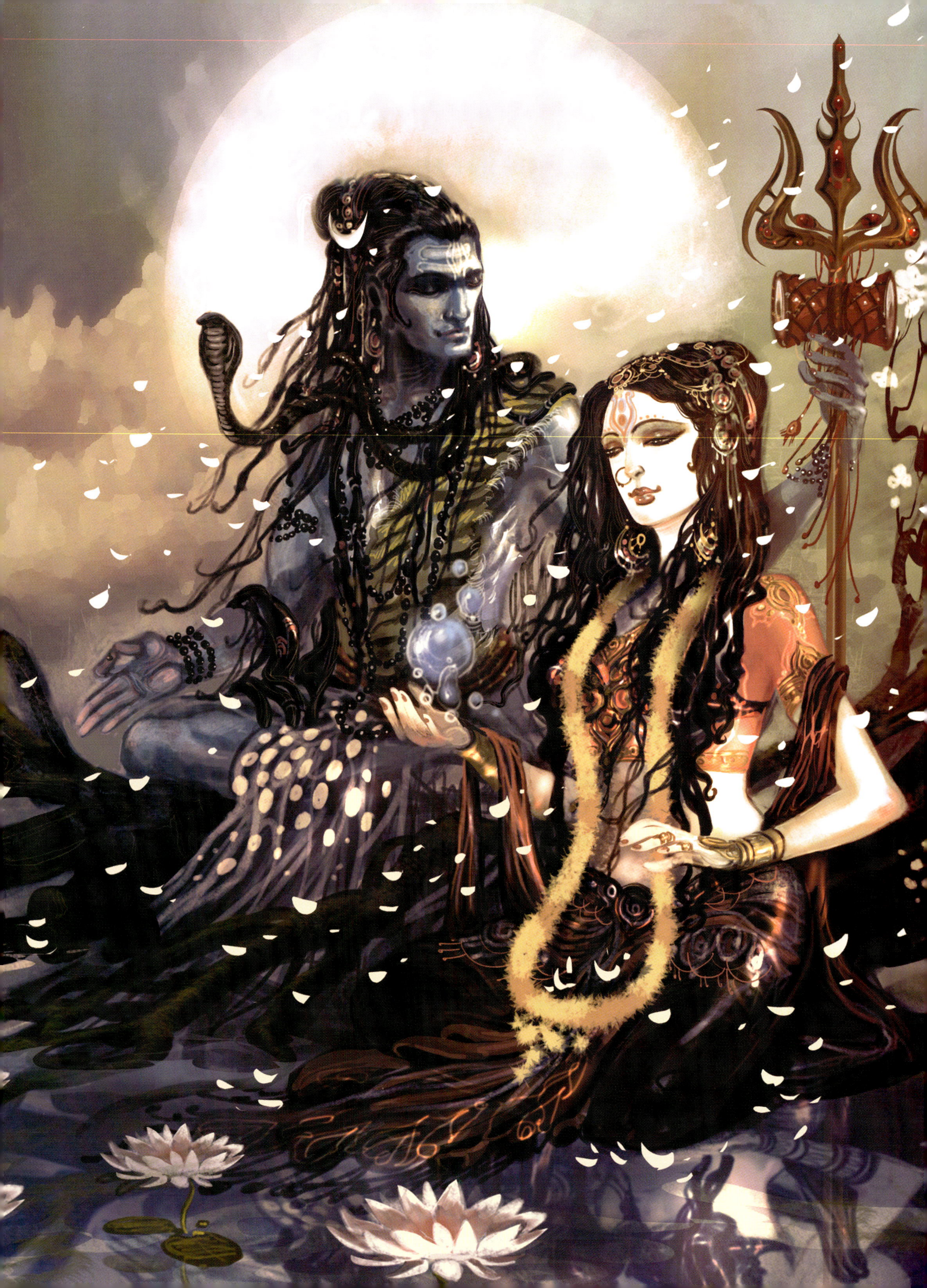

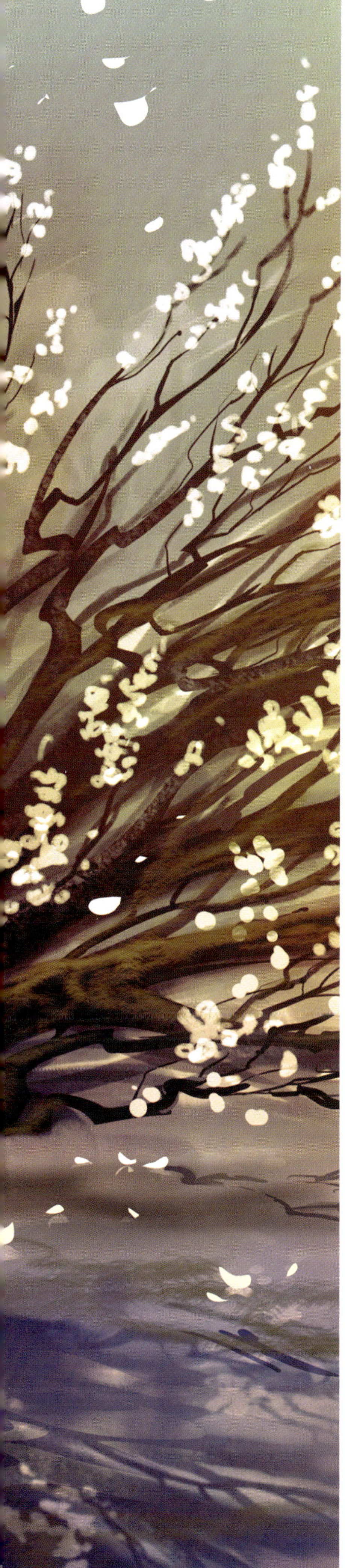

LITTLE DROPLET AND A THOUSAND RAINBOWS

Little droplet: "Where is the way to the rain?"

Parvati: "Before you reach there, the sun will scorch you or the birds will drink you up. You are safe here in my palms."

Drop: "But I have a feeling in my heart that I must make my way to the 'rain'. I don't even know if that's what adrift drops must do."

Parvati: "Well if that's what you wish for, little wanderer, here's a morning ray coming towards you. Go catch it, it'll take you with it. Journey well, little drop, one day you may become what you are seeking."

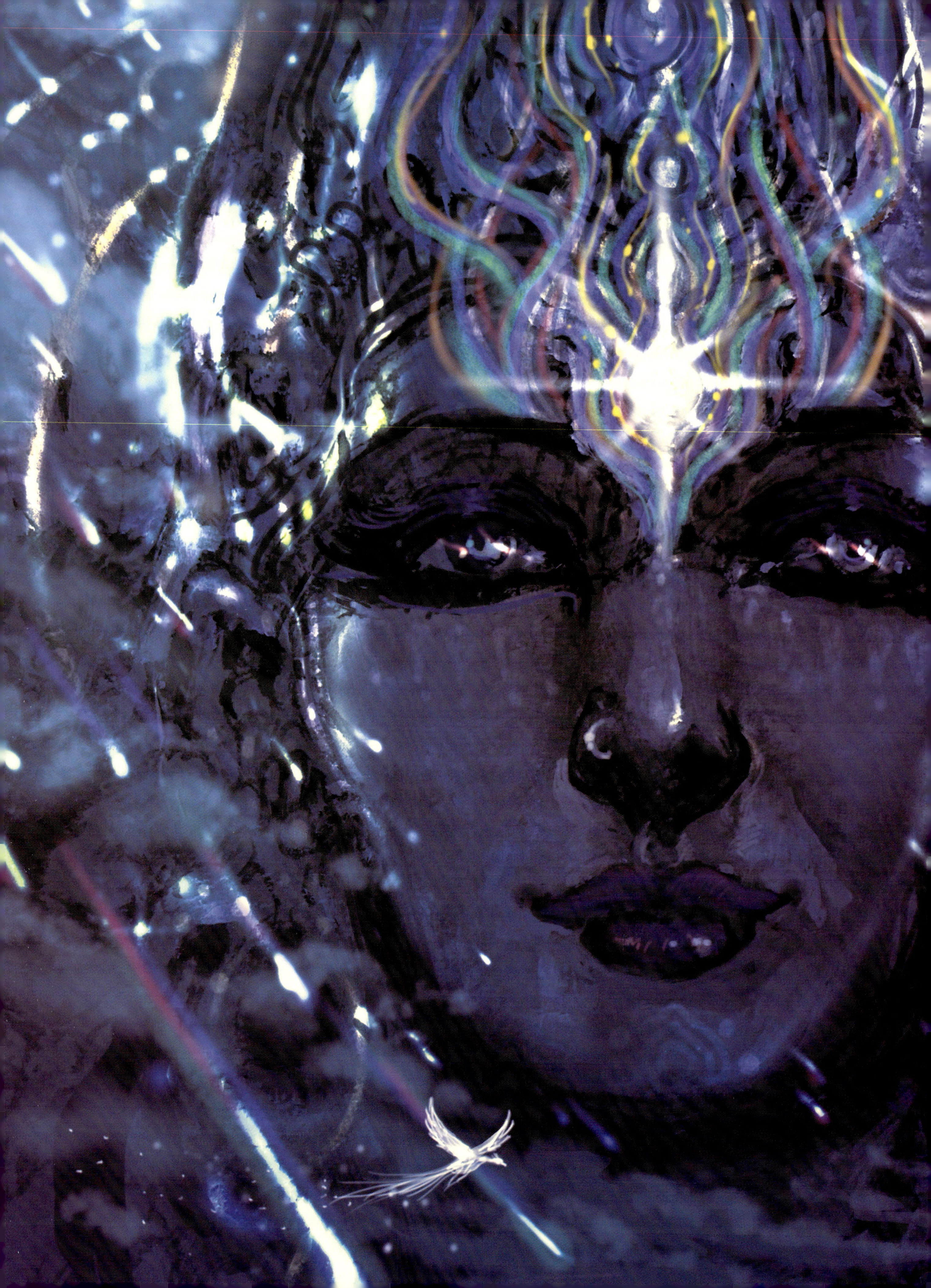

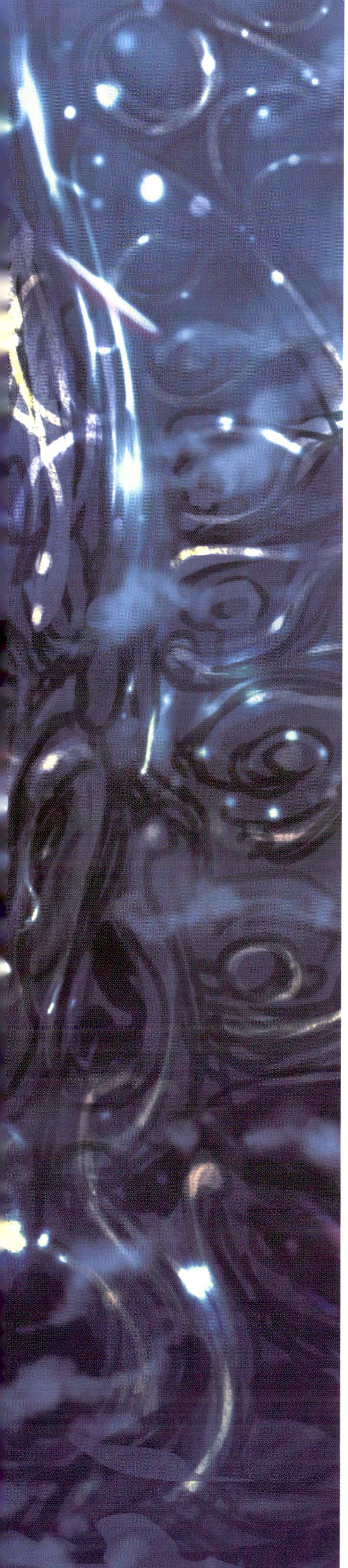

With that, the little drop caught the dazzling ray, radiating all its seven colors onto the sky.

When it reached the doors to the cloud castle, it saw an old bird lying with it beak damaged, collapsing. It surely needed water to revive itself.

Without any hesitation, the little drop gave itself away to the bird.

The ocean saw this and wept through Uma's eyes.

From where did the little droplet learn to be so giving, so selfless?

"By being in your gentle and giving palms, Mother," the drop said.

Uma could still feel his presence in her.

A blue hand gently lifted her chin, wiped her tears lovingly and gestured her to look at the sky.

There was a rainbow! The bird was a test. The droplet was happily dancing in front of all the other raindrops, lurching them to make rain happen.

The ocean stretched her palms again, hoping that the droplet would now land in them.

In that moment, a thousand rainbows appeared as she opened her heart, a rainbow for each droplet.

And this is how "Love" was reborn into the world.

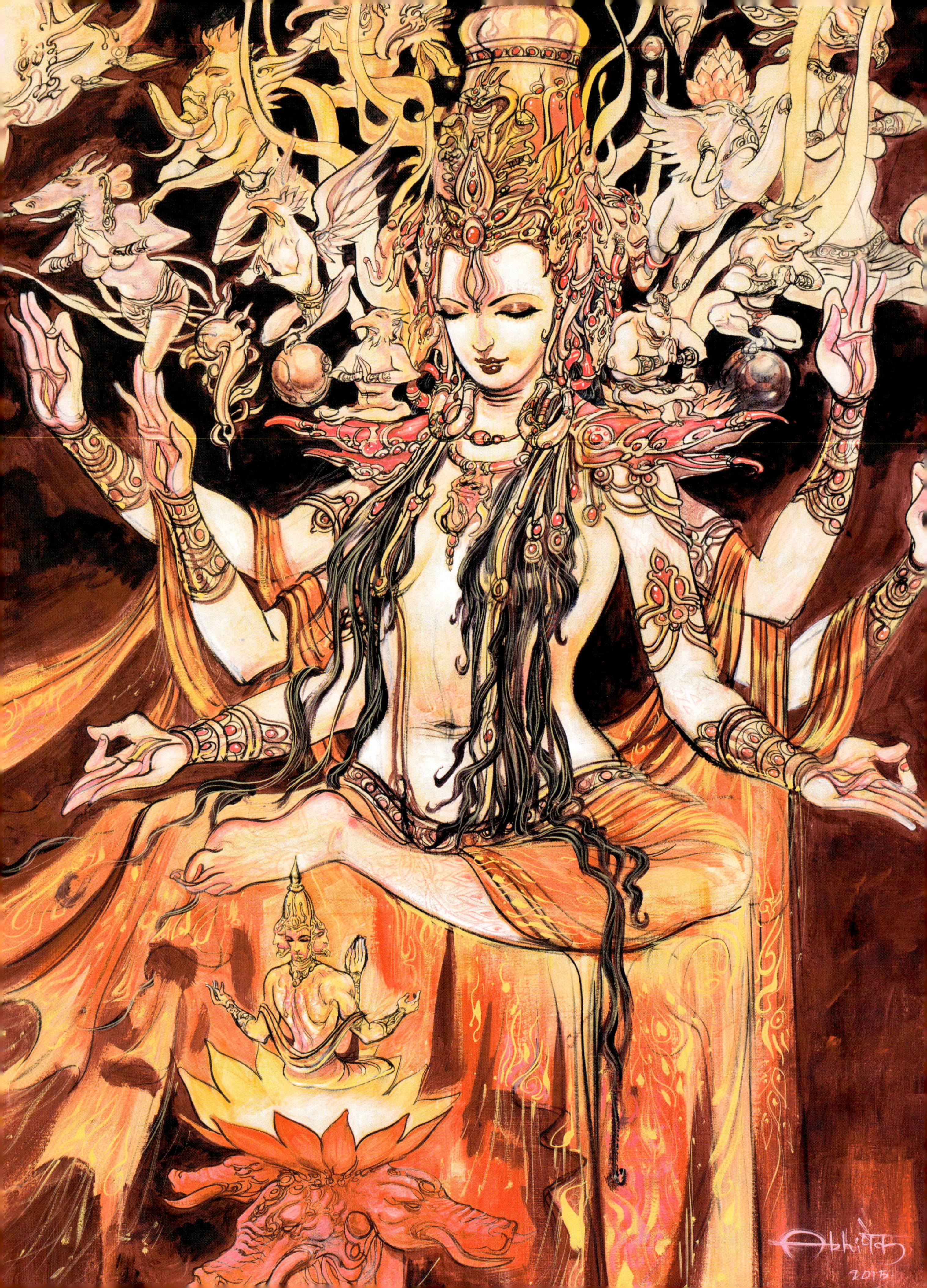

"Every atom a teacher, each Universe a seeker."

Adi Shakti imparting Brahm gyana knowledge of the energy universe to Brahma.

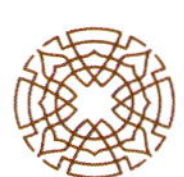

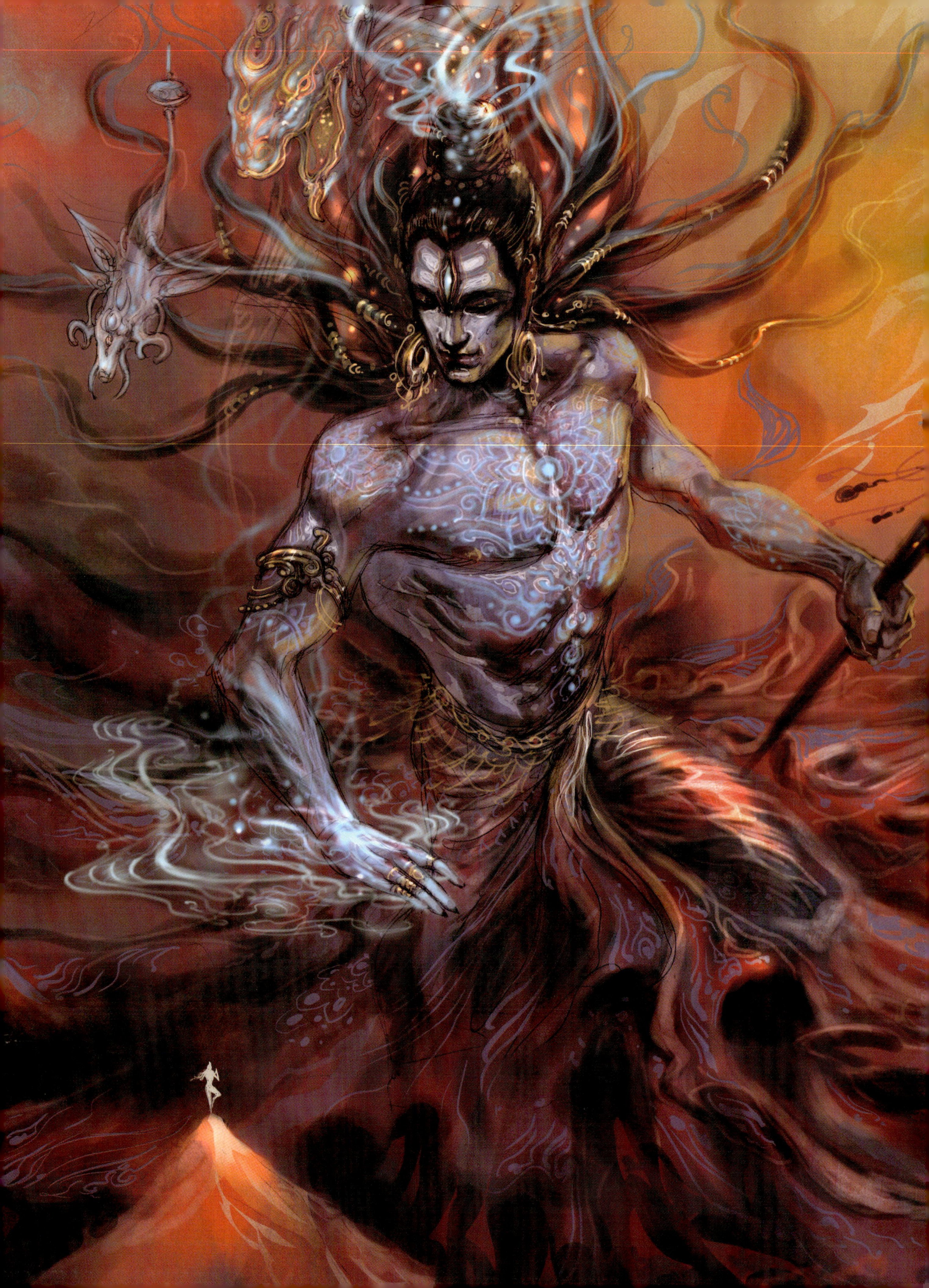

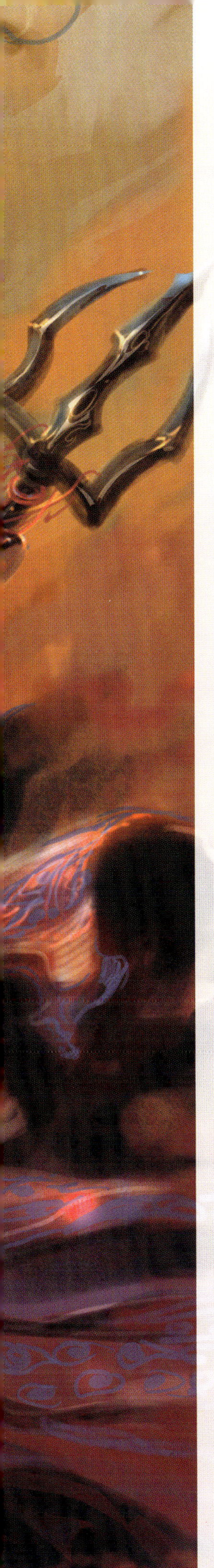

DESCENT OF THE GANGA -GANGA AVTARAN

"A river in the sky was invoked."

King Sagar and his sixty thousand sons were incinerated by Sage Kapila for their foolish mistake.

The kind-hearted sage told the king that the only way he could purge it was by bringing a river down from the heavens.
This task ran across generations of kings who withered in the hopes of witnessing it.

Sagar passed it to his earnest grandson Anshuman, who left it in the hands of his famed son, King Dileep.
The arduous penance consumed Dileep's life, and in those bleak circumstances, he passed the burden onto his son Bhagiratha.
The river responded compassionately to Bhagiratha's penance.

His penance symbolizes rebirth and the descent of light as a journey of enlightenment for a yogi.

(The river Ganges was a river of light when it descended from the heavens. It gave away all its energy to nourish the world and heal its burnt souls. Some of the ancestral souls turned themselves into river beings and stayed immersed in the Ganges to maintain the natural equilibrium.)

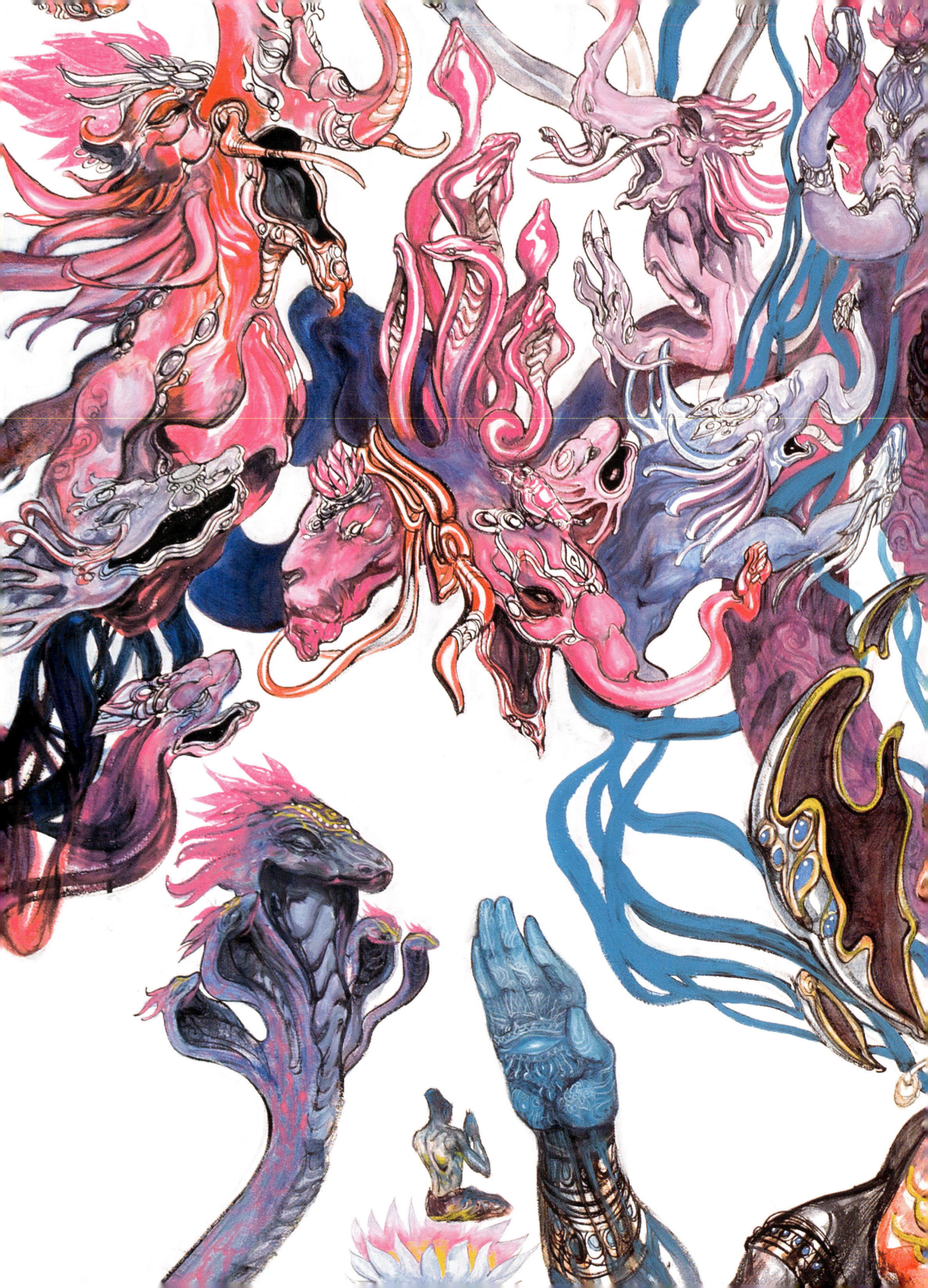

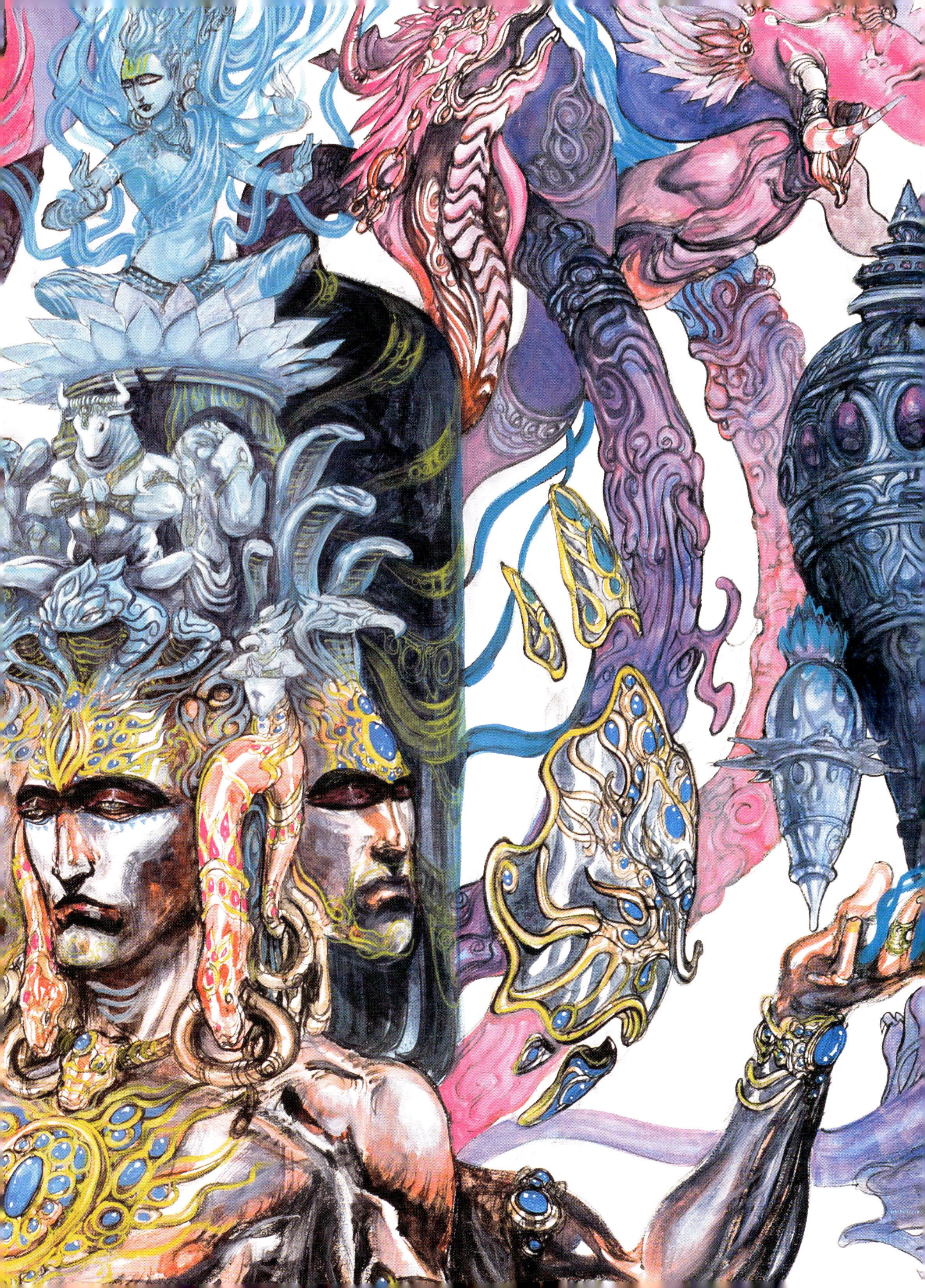

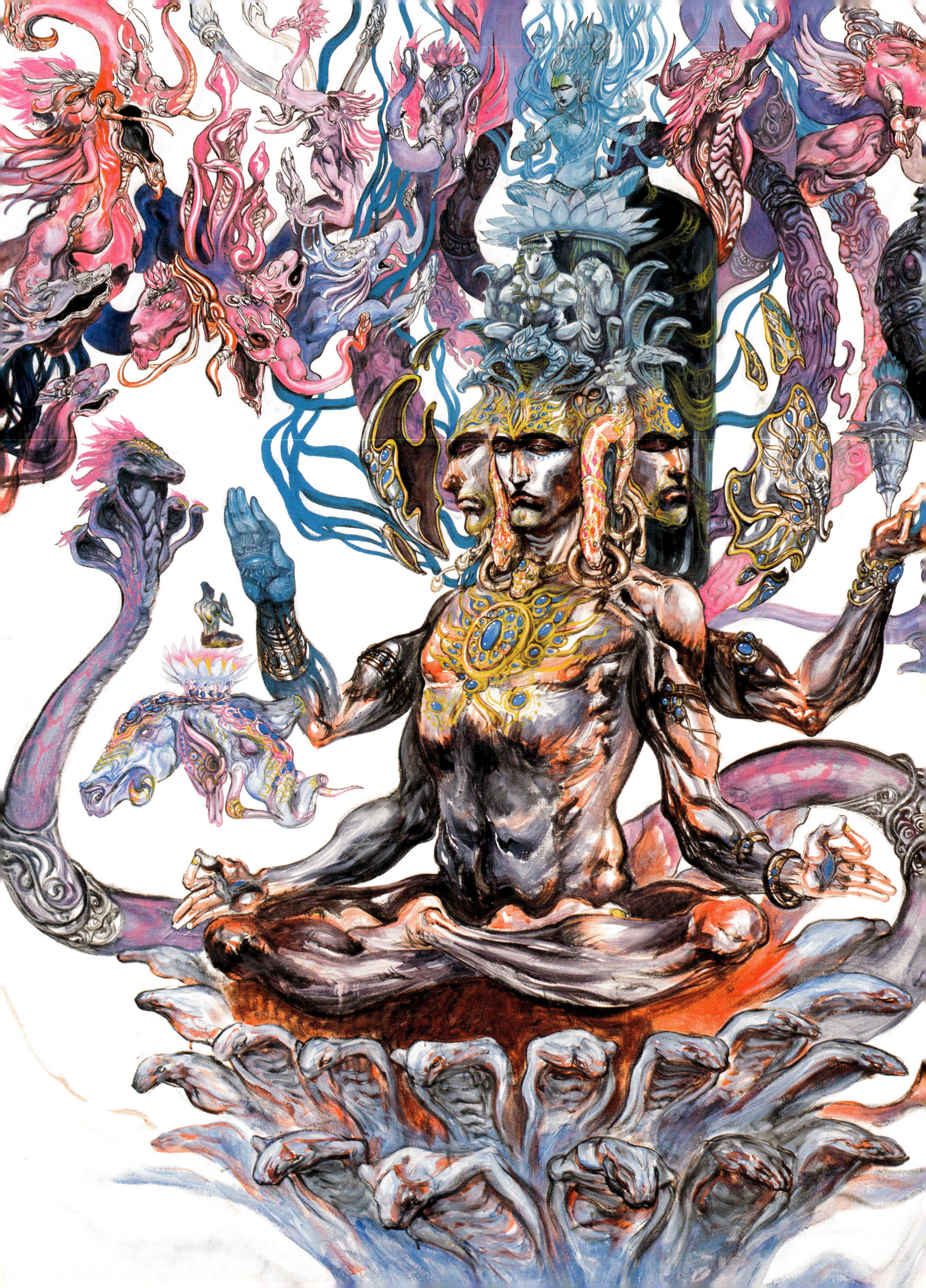

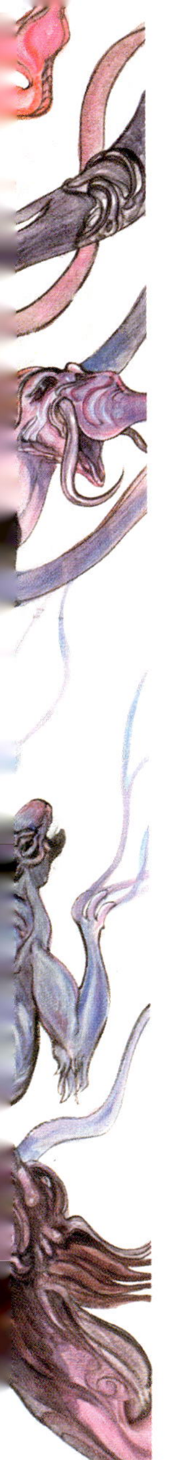

THE KNOWER OF SOLITUDE

kevalya

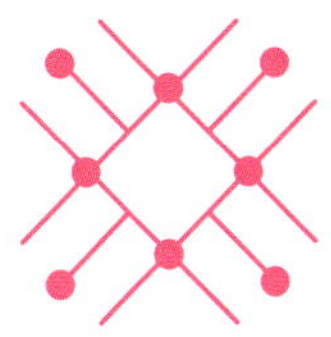

"What is 'Kevalya', this 'solitude' you've become?", asked Bhagiratha?

"Is it to get away from people and places of clamor? Go into the forest or inside the water if one can hold his or her breath?
Is it to drive away desires from one's mind and rest in a place of non-materialism? Or is it to take oneself away from the burning greed and wants of comfort?

Oh *Rishikesha*, lord of all senses, what is it?

Is it to take the body and mind into the five *Yamas* away from the distracting habits? To immerse in *Ahimsa* (non-violence), infused with *Satya* (truthfulness).

Is it to restrain *Muladhara* and find center in the all-pervading presence of *Brahman* and channeling it in our daily conduct (*brahmcharya)* to be as giving as nature, to be *Apari-graha* (non-aversive)?
Is it to be non-possessive of our own good thoughts and let them manifest through our actions for others?"

Bhagiratha continued, "Oh *Niranjana*, the unblemished one!
Is this what solitude is?

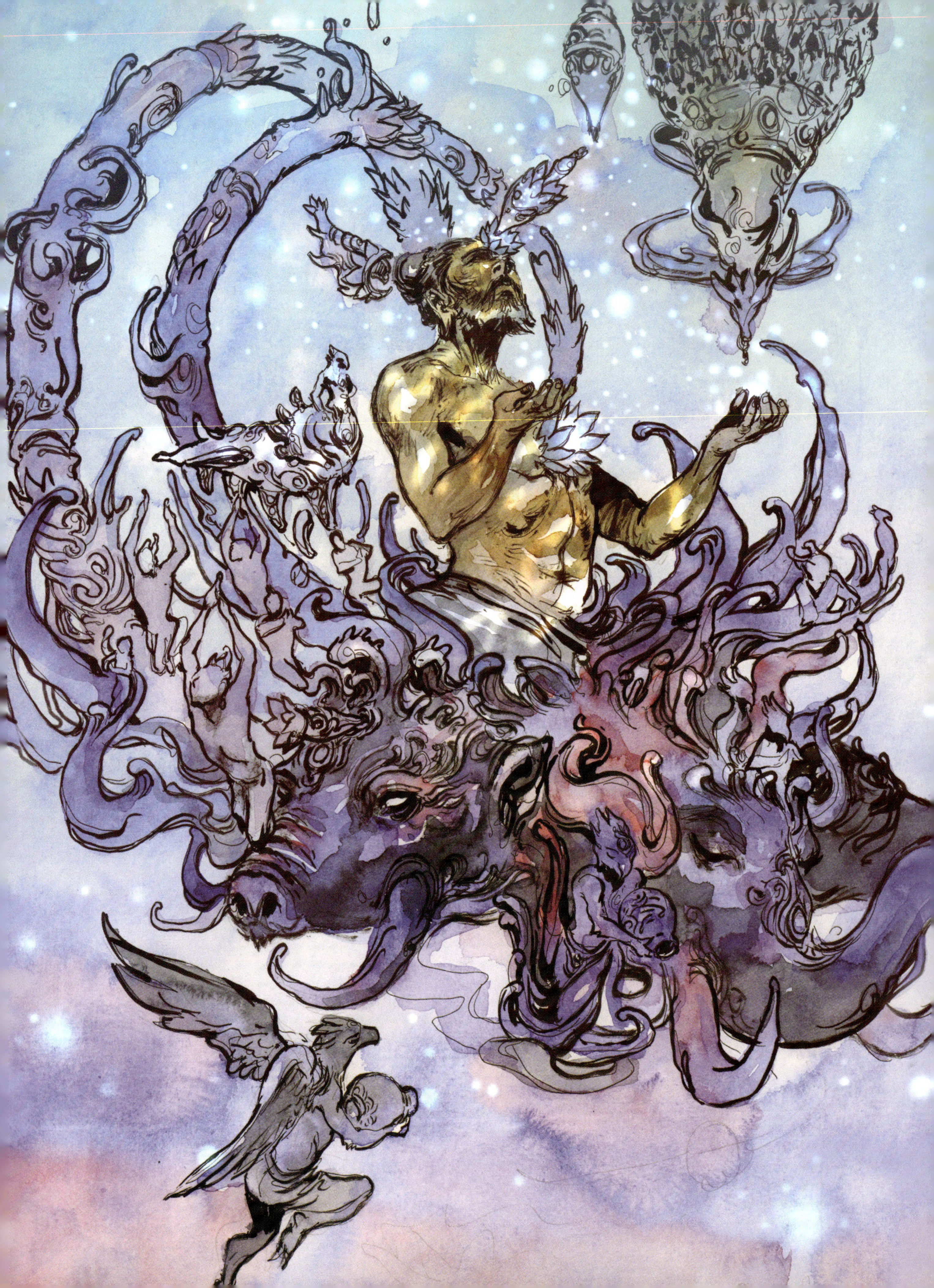

Is it to understand *Kshama* (forgiveness), to own one's mistakes and to channel *Krodha* (anger) as *Karuna*?

Is it to see *Daya* (compassion) in oneself as a reflection of others?

Oh *Ishadeva*, Lord of the nature, what is *Kevalya*?

Is it to find control over *Niyamas* to clean one's mind of temptations, ego and malicious strands?

To be *Santosha* (content)?
To contemplate the nature of things and find that we are nothing but a part of one universal self aligned by *tapa*, the collective radiating energy.

Is it to know this and then give away this energy to everything around, following in the footsteps of the ever-giving *Prakriti* (Mother nature)?

Is it to know through this energy that there is a vibrational language in things around and within?

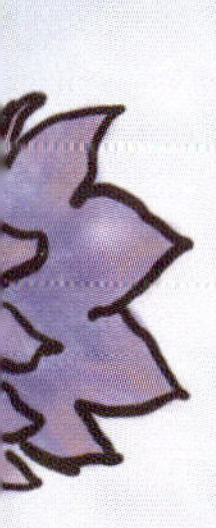

Is it to feel this in one's heart and express it in silence that emanates love?

Is it to reconcile with time and death, to overcome the fear of decaying?

Knowing that the divine vibration will live on.

Is it to create in one's mind *Huta* (a ceremony of soul fire) and observe *vrata* where one understands resolve and sacrifice?"

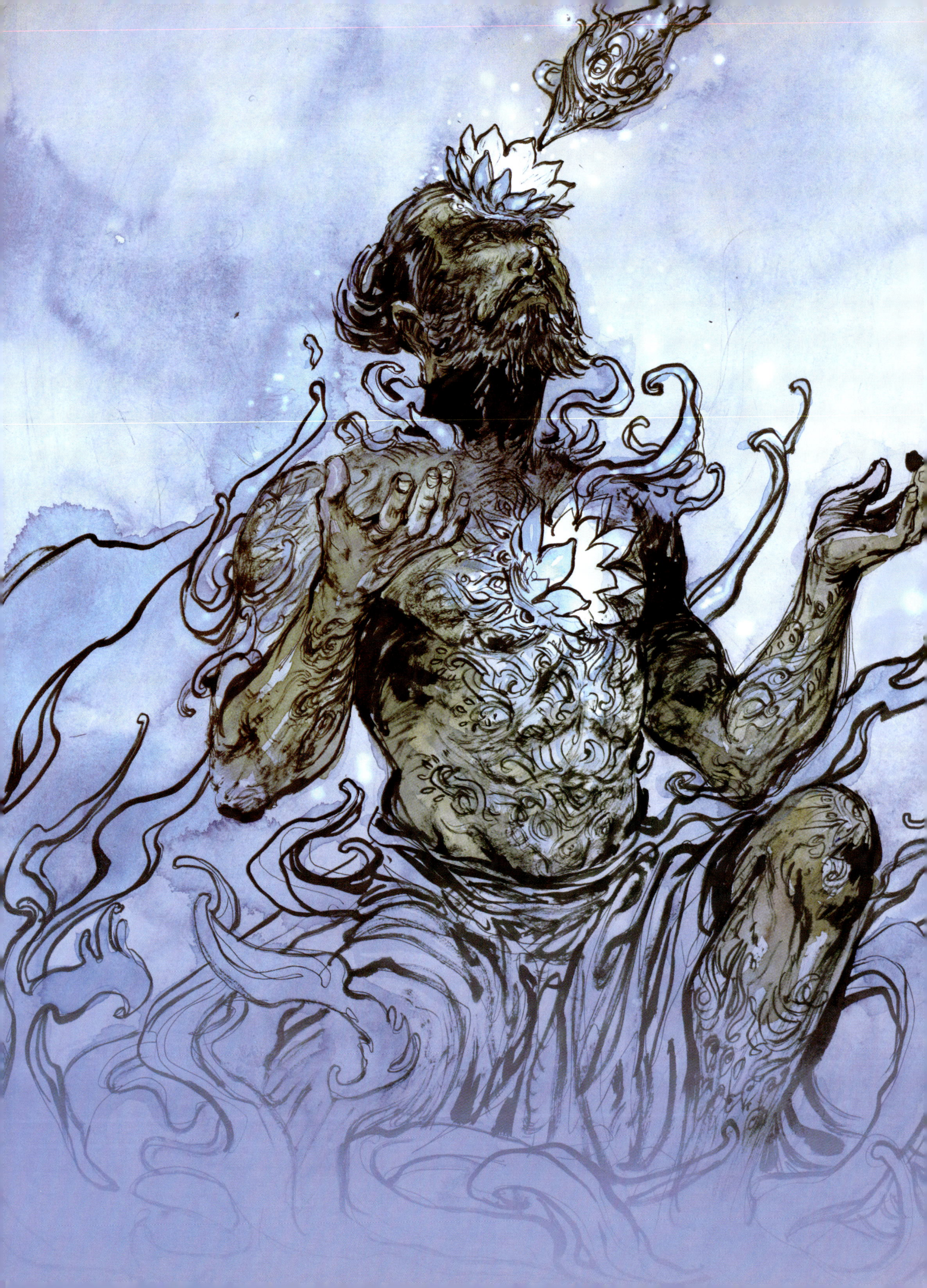

Is it to observe *Mita-hara* (moderation in consuming) and master the *Siddhasna* of one's mind, to keep it steady against any difficulty?

Oh *Matangadeva*, the lord of premonitions, what is this solitude?

Is it to know that *Asana* is not about holding the posture of the body alone but of the mind?

To stay with the steadiness of the thought and let it flow.

Is it to know the *vrittis* (the waves of the mind) and to be in tandem with the *laya* and *parlay* (the resonance and the dissolution)?

Is it to know that *pranayama* is the ultimate prayer, to acknowledge that we are all tied by the etheric fields, inhaling and exhaling the unknowable divinity?

To know that each breath is a pearl we are creating inside the ocean of time, a rosary in accord with all things around.

Is it to acknowledge this universal connection we share through our breath?

Oh *Nirguna*, the one without any material properties, what is *Kevalya,* this solitude you have become?

Is it *pratyahara*, to go away to a place in ether to bring back the lost awareness to our minds?

Is it *Dharana*, to be introspective while still embodying the world and its beings?

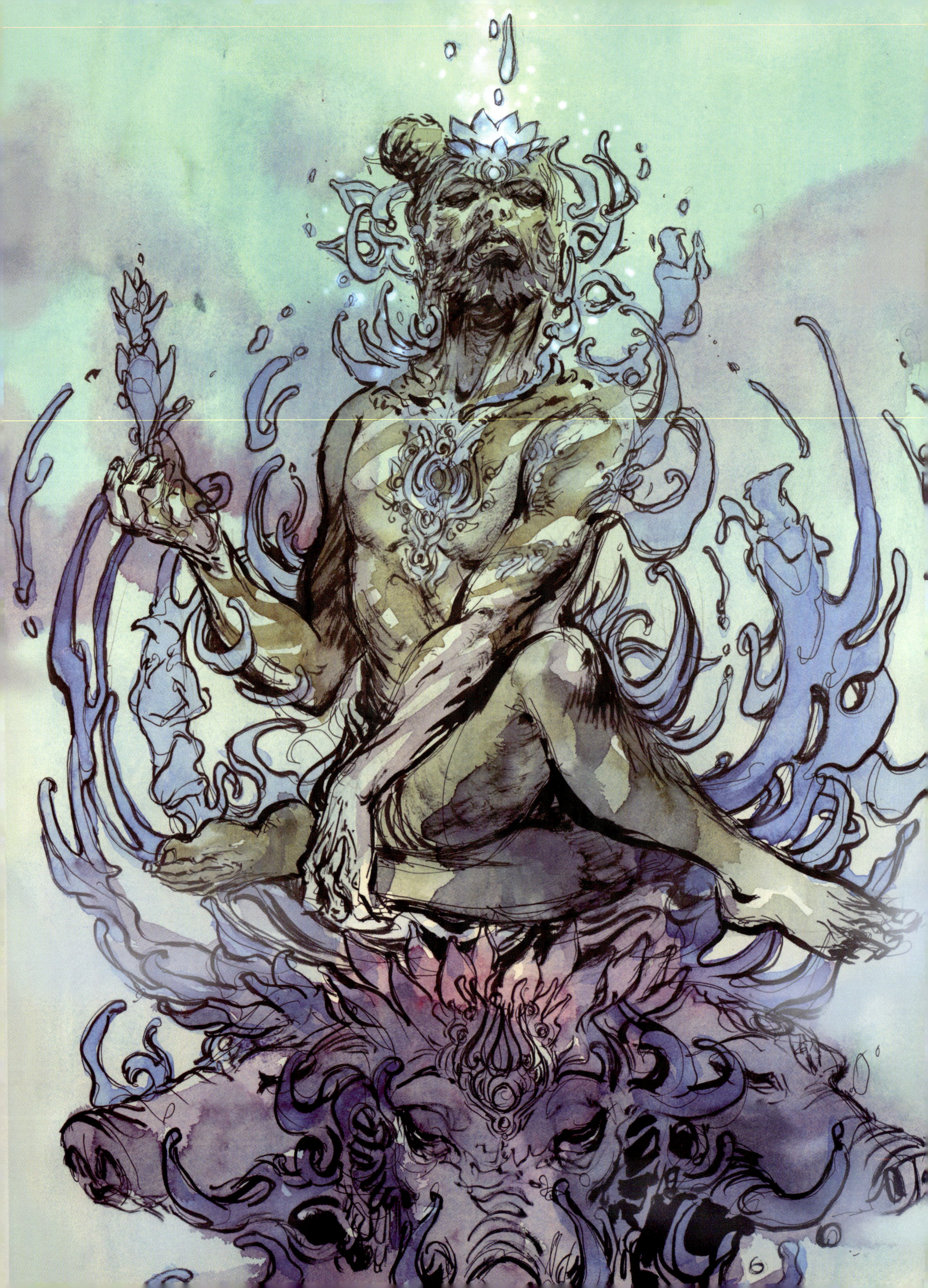

Is it to be *leen,* immersed in *Dhyana*, a place of universal harmony; to align its ebbs and flows and to exude that radiance to everyone around just like the sun does?

Is it to understand that *Jivan* and *Mrityu* are cyclic and that they are but two medians intersecting in this world of existence?

That we all are part of one sentient being.

Is it to melt away into the all pervading *Brahman*; give back the *shakti* (energy) to its source, so it can be emitted back into new worlds and beings?

Is it to give,
My body to earth.
My mind to ether.
My life to fire.
My colors to water.
My flight to sky.
My deeds to humility.
My love to courage.
My sight to innocence.
My memories to love.
Myself to Being."

With that, Bhagiratha was draped in silence.

The blue one hadn't spoken a word yet, or maybe he spoke through Bhagiratha's unblemished intent.

The river of the light was seeping through his palms, glinting off the blue hued beings, like waves crashing onto the stones of time.

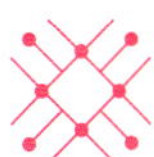

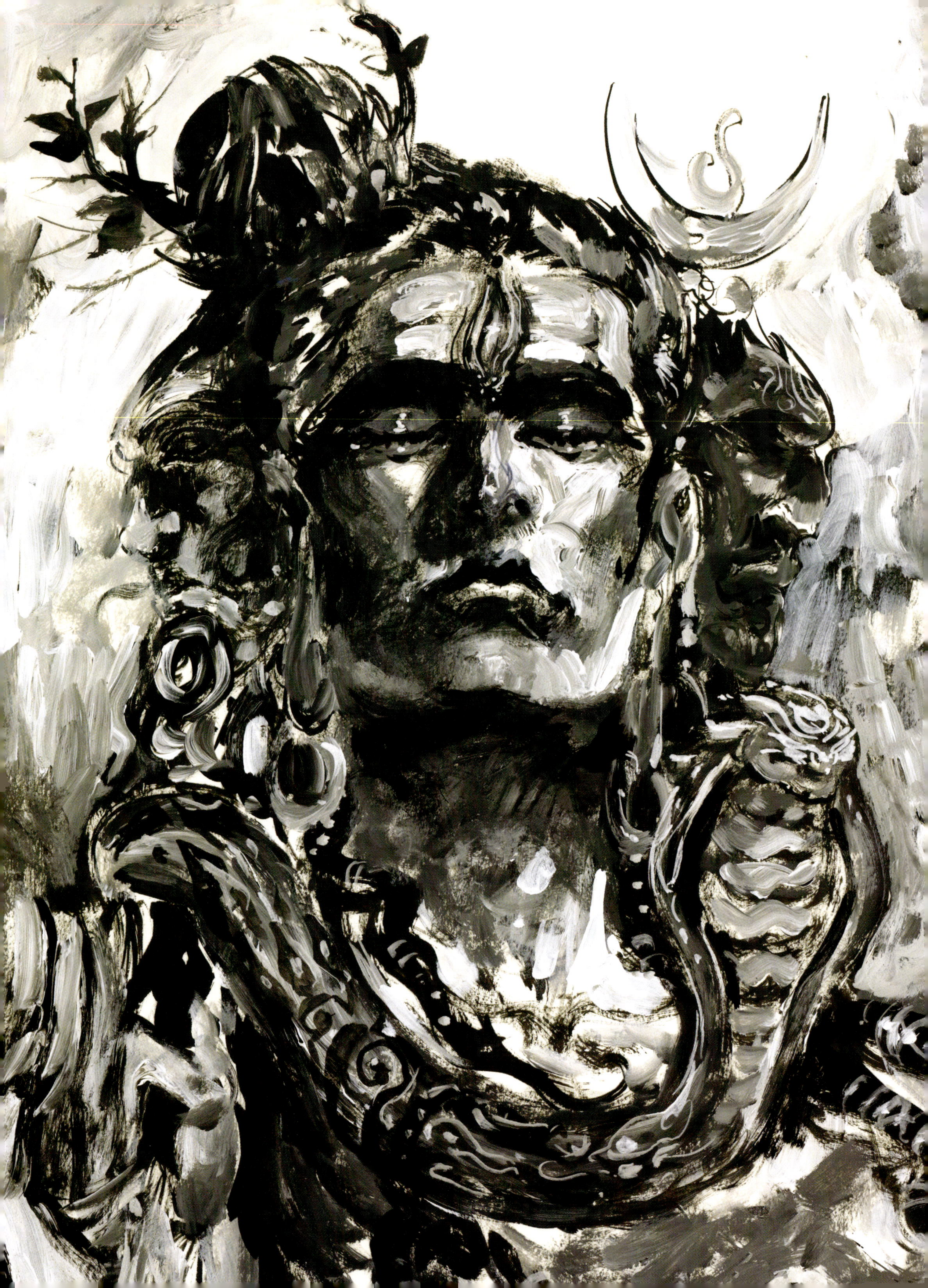

THE YUJ

Shiva: "What saddens you, my son?"

Nandi: "Oh Adiguru of Yuj. You have sat in *dhyana* in the most acute *padmasana* for eons, you contort your body as if it were malleable, made of clay. Each time I try to physically master this art, I fail. My *asanas* look blunt. Will I ever be able to become a good yogi?"

Shiva smiled and said, "Nandi, I love it when you sing.

Do you know, when we sing with joy, it is 'Vaikari yoga'.

When we subtly hum a song, it is 'Madhyama yoga'.

When we let the song echo in our minds and let it fill the expanse, it is 'Pushyanti yoga'.

When the song goes back to its original sounds and resonates in silence as a chant with our being, it is 'Para yoga'.

What is not yoga, oh master of bulls, my son.

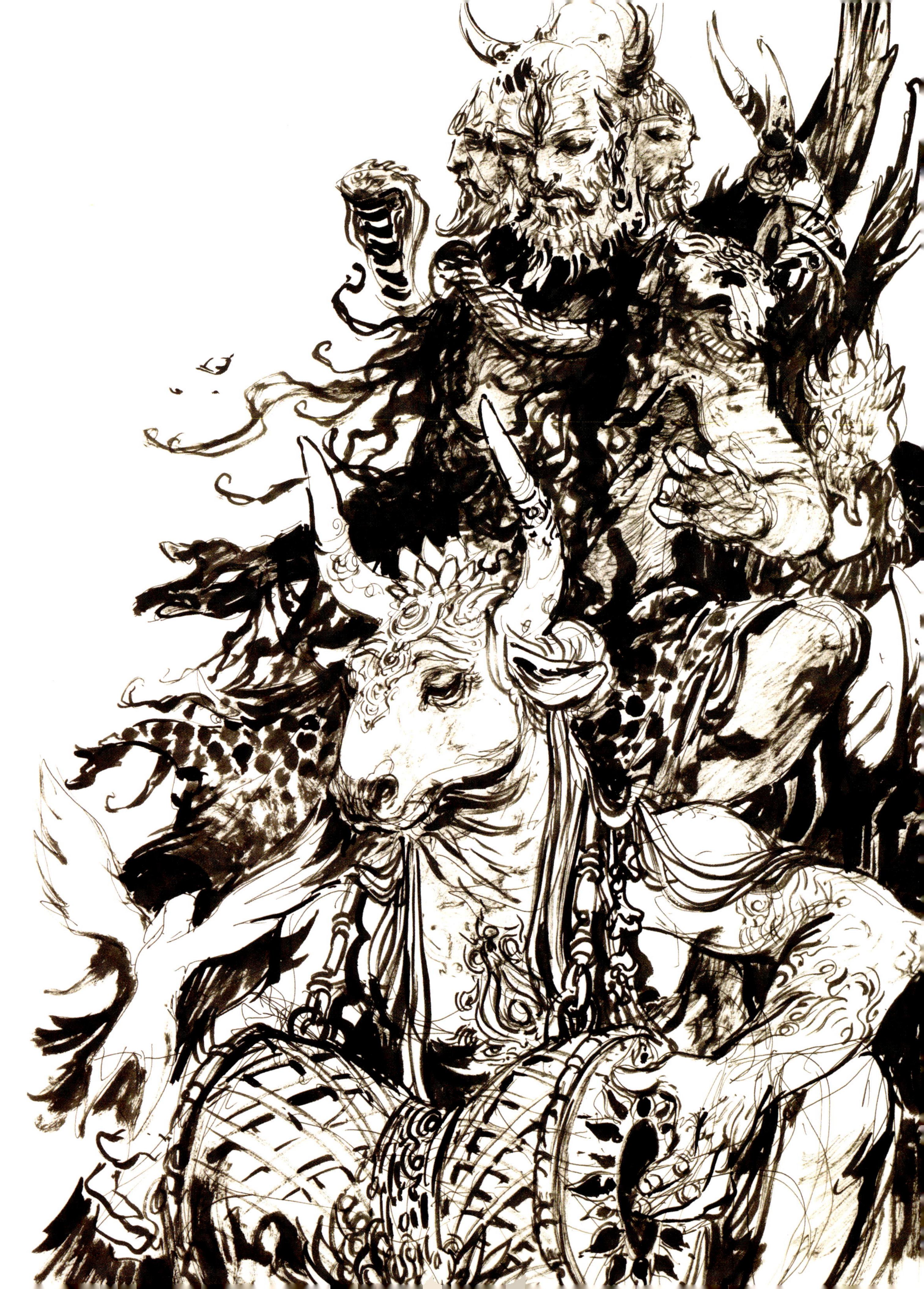

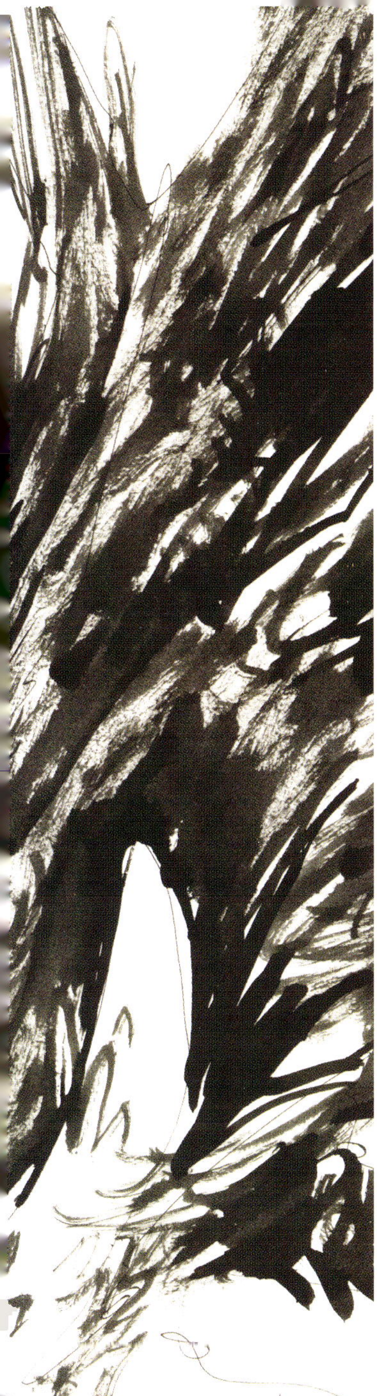

But the most important yoga is the yoga of 'kindness'."

With that, Shiva closed his eyes and light started to run from the corners of his eyes. The 'Damroo' caressed by the snowflakes started to chime. Shiva's face brimmed with the rising sun. The floating conch joined in with a sound which permeated the light flowing from his eyes. At that moment, Shiva was there, yet he was not.

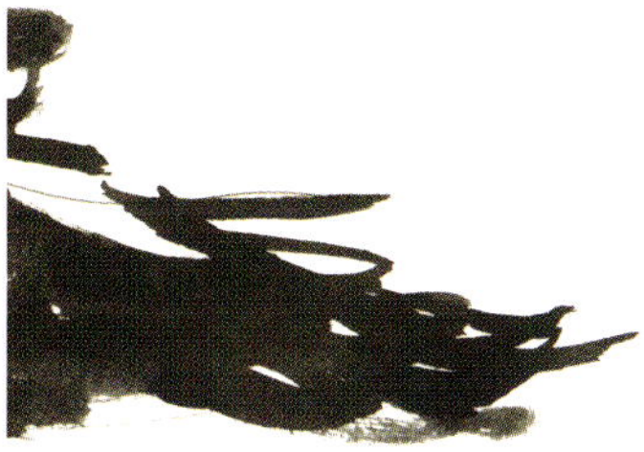

Nandi looked at this and forgot that he even existed as they both had become the music. The light remained, but Shiva was gone.

From that day, Nandi would daily feed all the animals of the forest as he continued with his practice, but somewhere for him, the real yoga was already ordained.

And it was of 'kindness'.

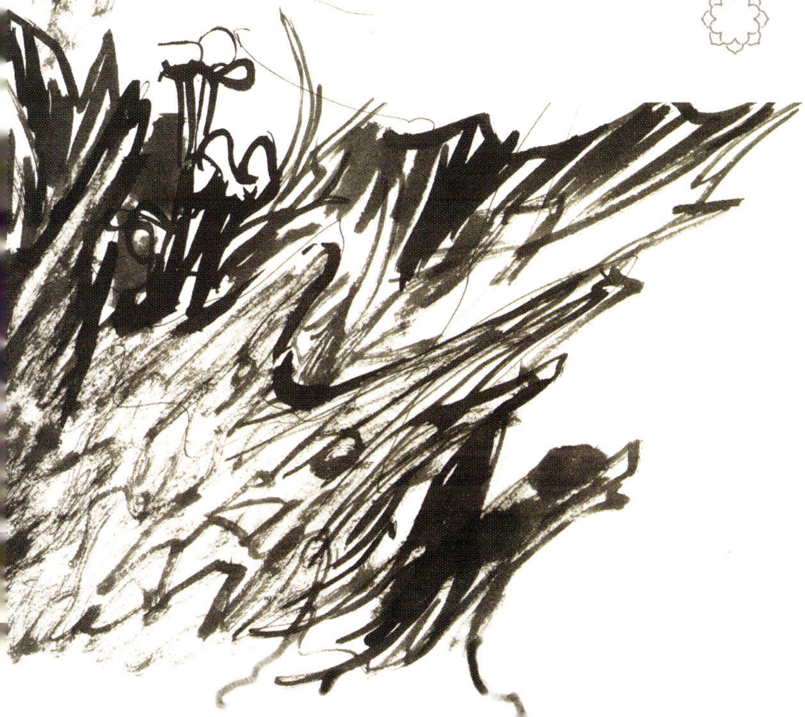

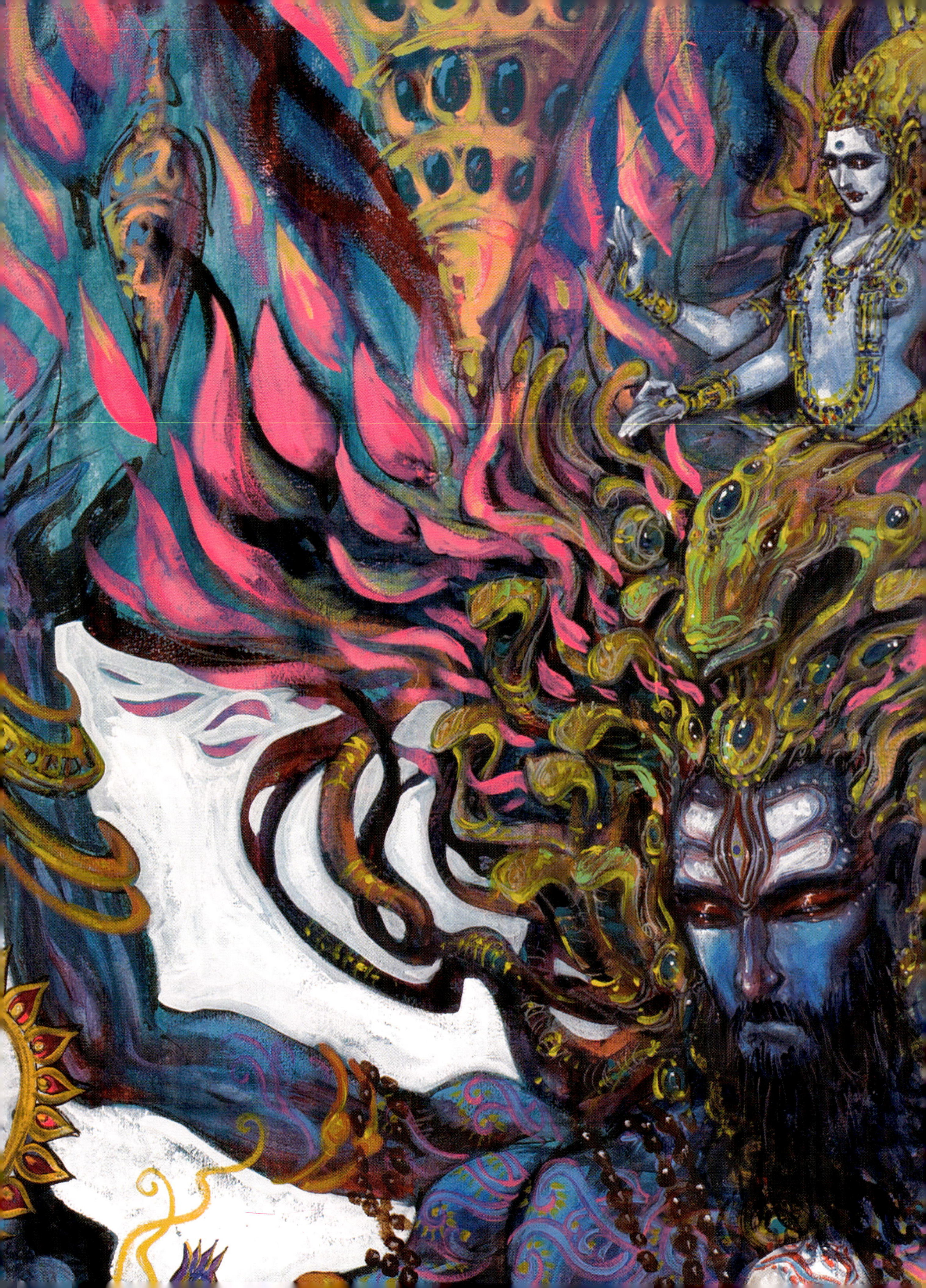

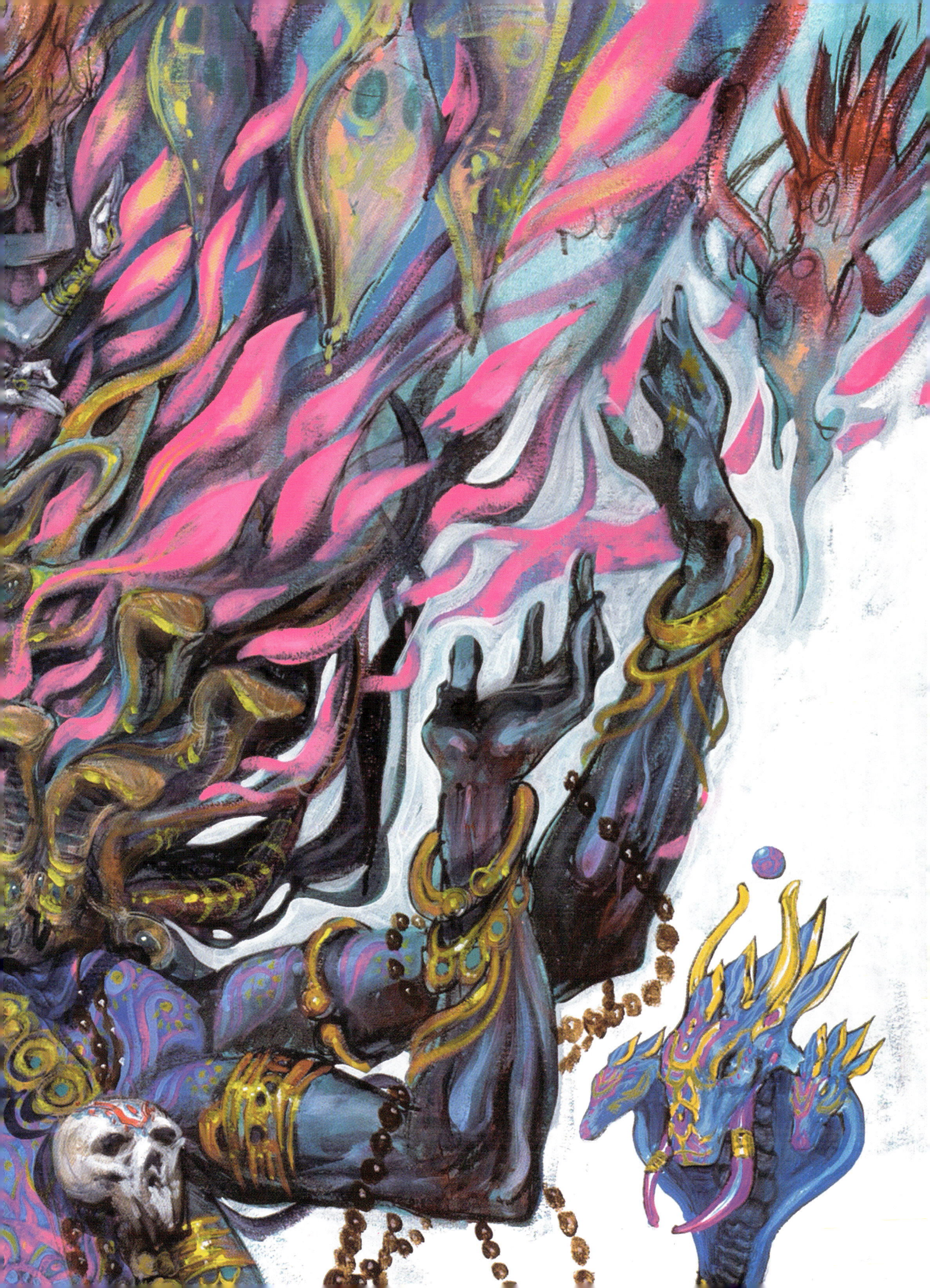

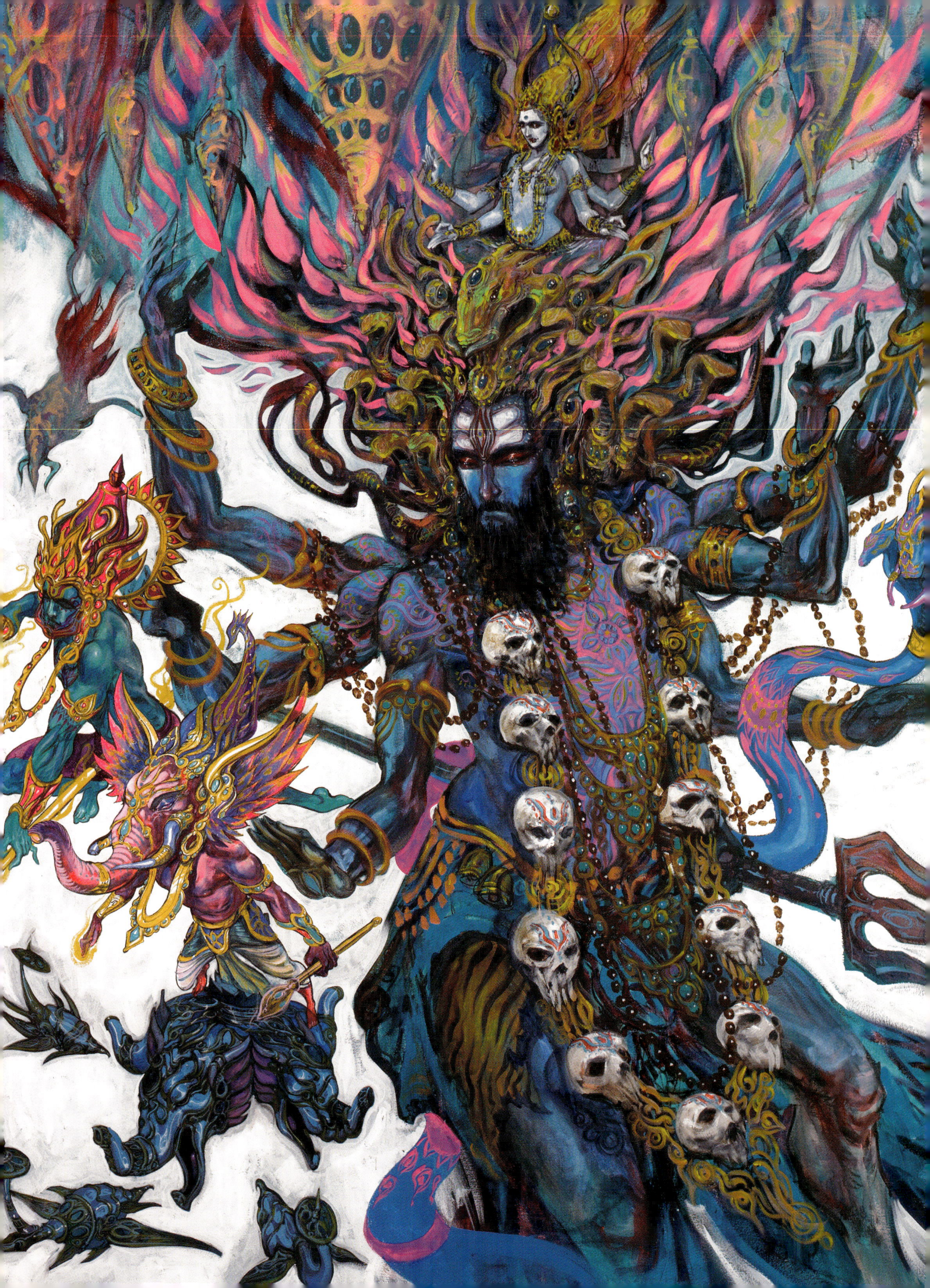

THE PILLAR OF LIGHT

Who manifested the pillar of light, the source from which Shiva appeared in the cosmic field, which baffled even the Gods?

They were new in this world compared to the ancient lotuses of creation.

The stories they had heard, of the never-ending pillar of light, from Brahma's own sons were utterly unbelievable. They could not fathom how something can neither have an end nor a beginning. Even their lives had finite confines.

A voice chanted in the ether calling all Gods.

The voice of *Sada Shiva*, the one who had witnessed the eternal pillar of light and the failed attempts to scale it by *Varah* (Vishnu) and *Hamsa* (Brahma).

The voice belonged to no man or woman. It resonated as if a thousand conchs were blown into the mahat-field of space and time, seeping into the orbits moving the planets.

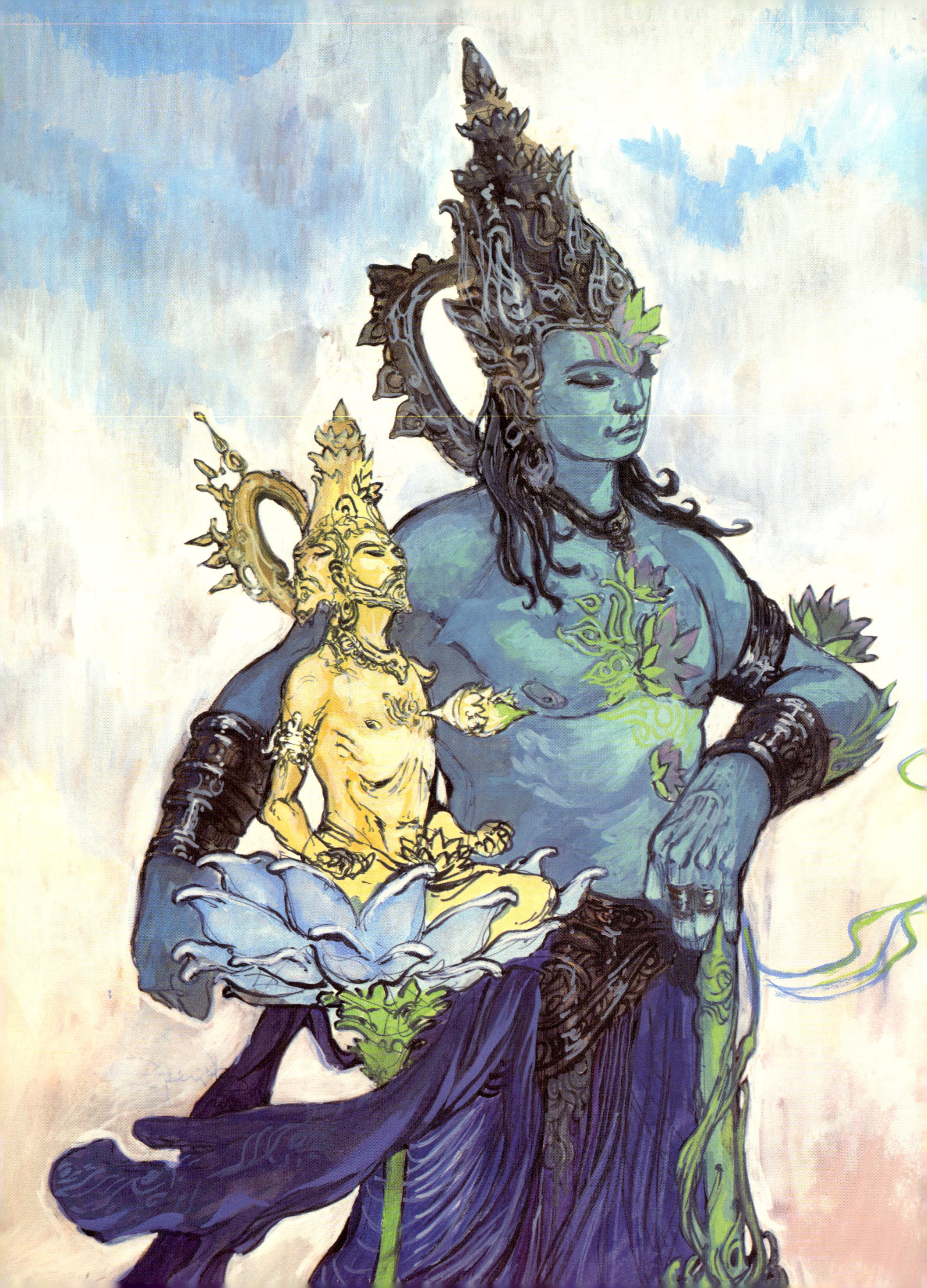

The Gods knew this voice came from a distant realm, a place which had seen the Earth and its sibling planets grow up around a draft star, which they now called *Vamana*.

This voice knew them in a way they didn't know themselves.

The voice commanded that half of the Gods become 'movement' and the other half 'stillness'. The universe started to expand and contract all at the same time.

The voice was gone. It had become a part of everything – both waves and particles.

The leader of *spandhan*, the movement, *Kartikeya* took the seekers into a circle around the cosmos, finding the star gate of the primordial mind. *Vinayaka*, the master of stillness, sat and delved deep into the synaptic rhythms to find the hidden key to open such portals.

They shall meet each other in sinusoidal oscillations and hope to witness the reappearing of the pillar of light; the source of the *Parameshwar* Shiva, their father.

The pillar may still be there, if they can go back to that moment, for which they must listen to every atom's yearning.

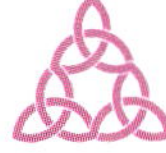

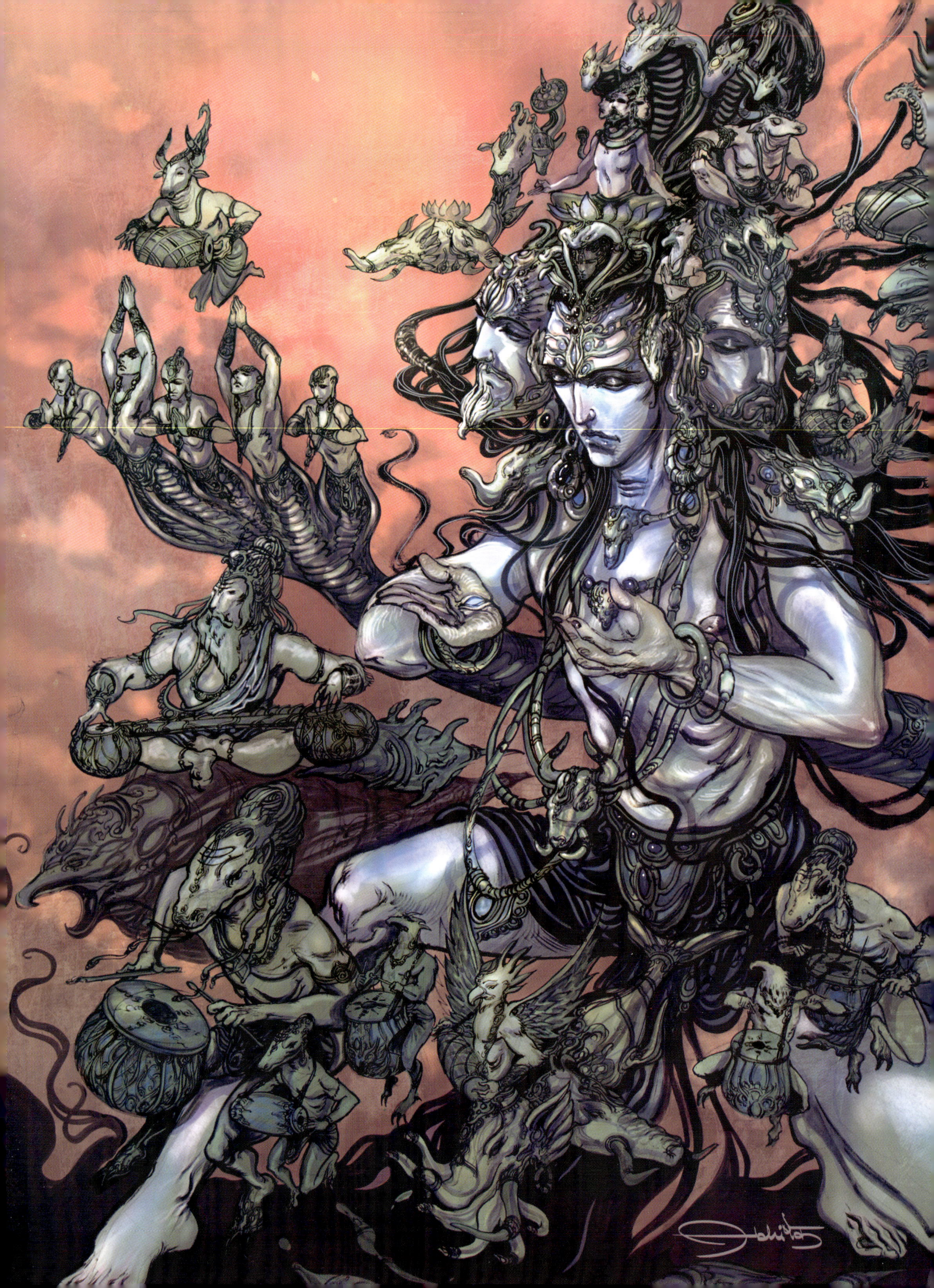

HALAHALA

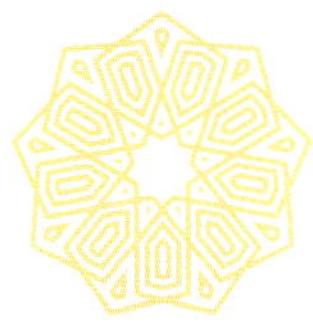

The poison "Halahala" was awakened during the churning of the ocean or some said that it ensued from the snake king Vasuki himself.
Halahala spewed unthinkable toxins into the ocean but deep down inside, he was tormented. He pleaded to the Gods that they must invoke Shiva, the Lord of stillness and pranic rhythms, as no one else could release him from his malignant nature.

The Gods and Demons were astonished by his compassionate intent, awareness of his own toxic personality and how helplessly he was clasped by it.

The Gods and Asuras were no different; they were born enemies, two opposing forces of one's mind engaged in an eternal battle. But now in the face of calamity, they had aligned their hearts to appeal to Shiva.

Shiva manifested himself in his Maha-Prana roopa, an embodiment of all the cosmic meditative powers, which started to contain the poison by inhaling the deadly fumes.

Halahala's aura was like radiation poisoning, contaminating the essence of everything it touched. Besides purging, Shiva started to revitalize the oceans and the Earth from its burns.

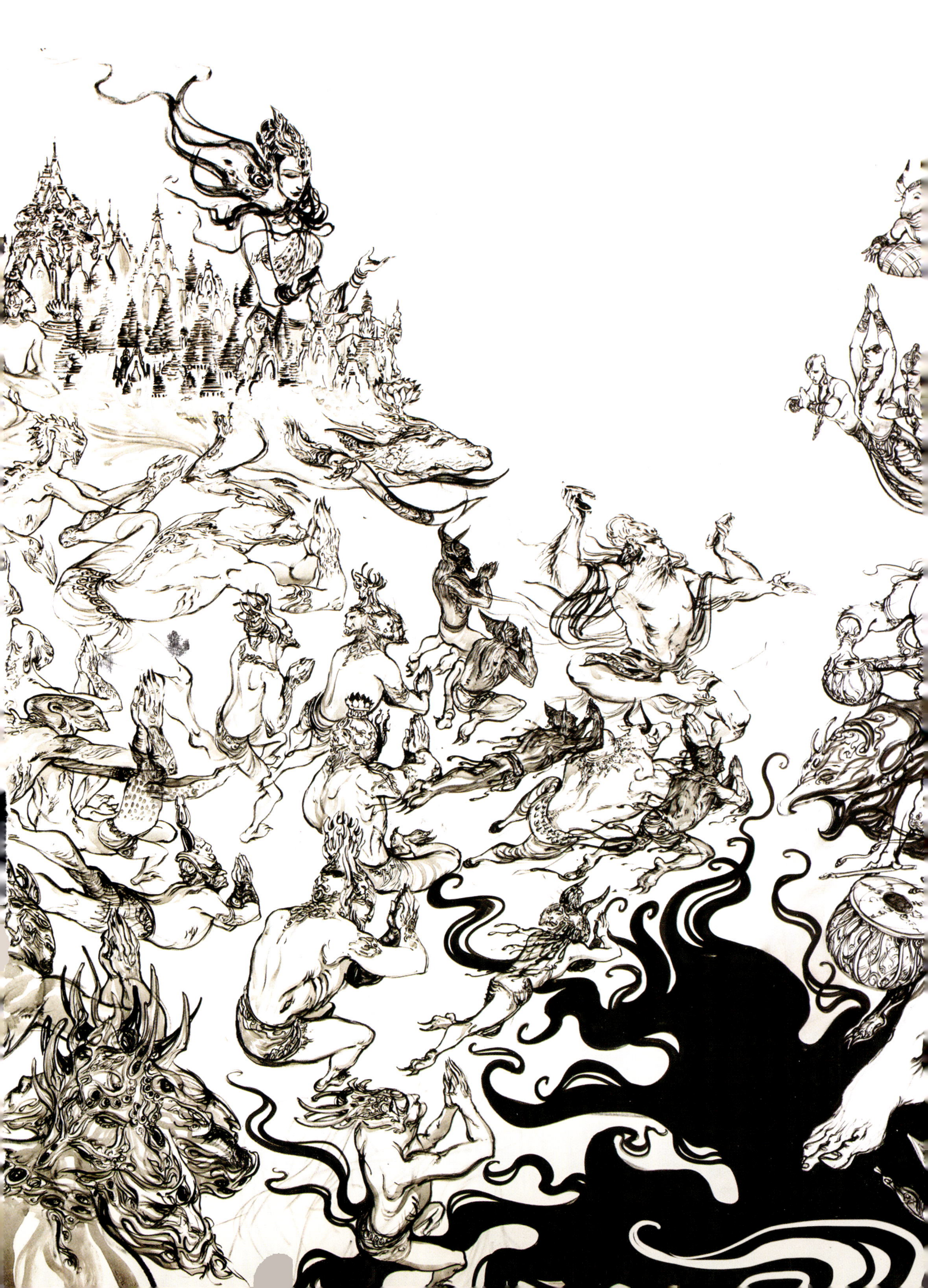

What happened afterwards?

The Gods and the Demons kept churning knowing that the 'Amritam' would follow next.

Dhanvantri, the celestial physician and the originator of Ayurveda, emerged holding the pot of nectar, healing the Devas and Asuras from their long labor, their bloodied hands cured and their burns sealed.

The togetherness they felt was now gone and the greed returned into their hearts. Soon after, a combat began between them to claim the coveted prize.

The celestial bird Garuda, descended and snatched the pot away. He took the pot to Vishnu, who morphed into a maiden, Mohini, and strategically distributed the nectar only to the Gods.

However, a few drops were ingested by a demon disguised as a deva called Rahuketu. The Moon and the Sun informed Mohini and before the nectar could pass from their mouths into their body, Vishnu cut off their heads with his celestial disc, 'Sudarshan Chakra'.

The head became 'Rahu' and the body 'Ketu'. It is said that till this day they eclipse the sun and the moon.

The Devas became very strong after receiving the nectar and defeated the demons, reclaiming the heavens.

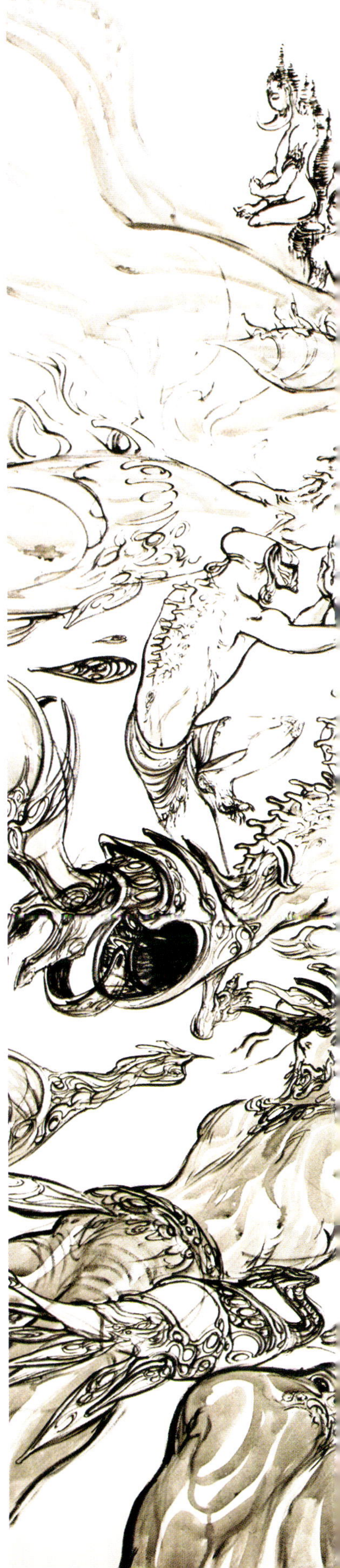

"If we revere Shiva, then like him, we must clean the oceans and the rivers too."

Created live at the ghats of Varanasi, over five days, as part of Shiva in Varanasi : An ode to the Ganges, Ojas Art.

The magnitude of the task was unfathomable but Shiva kept his being in utmost focus. For Shiva, the oceans were his home. He had meditated in them for eons, so without thinking about himself he kept drinking and channeling the poison.

Shiva's pranic forces summoned other yogic beings who started forming a vibrational bridge to carry the poison towards him.
Prachetaas - Brahma's son who chose the oceans over ruling the Earth;
Dadeechees - The selfless sage, one from each Manavantra;
Hanuman - Son of Vayu and master of Maha-Prana; and
Nandi - Shiva's disciple, he drank the last drop of poison.

The river Ganga, riding her *Makara* with the city of lights upon its back, further calmed the vibrational beings.

They all created this healing celestial vibration for Shiva as he culled the ocean from the vehement substance and held the poison in his throat with immense pranic force.

Upon seeing this unparalleled act of self-sacrifice, his consort Parvati, the daughter of the mountains, fused her energies around his throat chakra and channeled the poison to slowly morph into an etheric pranic substance.

He was called 'Neelkanth', the one with the blue throat, shimmering with expansive energy fields that replenished the fatigued ocean.

Soon after, Shiva vanished into the trance he had emanated from.

Halahala's true intent had found a place in Shiva's selfless being.

The 'Ratnas' are the gems which emerged from the churning.

(All these ratnas/treasures have their own stories and symbology)

Lakshmi - the goddess of light, chose to be with Vishnu, the god of preservation and harmony;

Apsaras - the frequencies of light went to the devas;

Varuni and Sura came out with the wine (*soma*);

Kamadhenu or Surabhi, the wish-granting cow, represented the regenerative nature of Earth;

Airavata - the eight elephants made from Garuda's eggshells, represented the eight cardinal directions;

Ucchaishravas - the divine seven-headed horse was given to the Demon King Bali;

Kaustauba - the elusive gem, represented the mineral wealth of the Earth's core;

Parijaat represented the pineal gland, as it is associated with the heavens, the etheric field inside the human skull;

Sharanga, the bow, represented the knowledge of the spine;

Chandra, the moon, represented the ebb and flow of the mind;

Dhanavantri, the god of medicine and the physician to the Gods, also the creator of Ayurveda, came out with the Vidyas and the 'Amritam';

Origin

Shukracharya, the guru to the Demons, brought them back to life each time they were slayed in the war. The Gods did not have the power to combat something like that. Brahma guided the demons to make a pact with them, and propose to churn off the ocean to obtain the nectar of immortality, 'Amritam'.

Another version of the story says that it was a curse by Sage Durvasa to Indra, the King of the Gods, which resulted in his collapse from the throne and eventually Indra got it back by procuring the nectar of immortality.

Symbology of the Samudra Manthan.

Mount Mandara: The spine

The tortoise 'Kurma': The five senses

The snake 'Vasuki': The oscillations of the mind between the two opposing forces, 'Asuras' and 'Devas'

Asura, the opposite of sura, means 'out of sync'.

Deva is the 'shinning one'.

Both tendencies reside inside our mind and their tussle produces good and poisonous things. The ocean is the etheric field of creation. The juices produced inside the cranium and the brain.

Throat chakra represents the thyroid gland, which controls metabolism and body heat. Parvati symbolizes the healing force which stabilized the incremental heat and pressure.

The 'Ratnas' are the gems which emerged from the churning.

(All these ratnas/treasures have their own stories and symbology)

Lakshmi - the goddess of light, chose to be with Vishnu, the god of preservation and harmony;

Apsaras - the frequencies of light went to the devas;

Varuni and Sura came out with the wine (*soma*);

Kamadhenu or Surabhi, the wish-granting cow, represented the regenerative nature of Earth;

Airavata - the eight elephants made from Garuda's eggshells, represented the eight cardinal directions;

Ucchaishravas - the divine seven-headed horse was given to the Demon King Bali;

Kaustauba - the elusive gem, represented the mineral wealth of the Earth's core;

Parijaat represented the pineal gland, as it is associated with the heavens, the etheric field inside the human skull;

Sharanga, the bow, represented the knowledge of the spine;

Chandra, the moon, represented the ebb and flow of the mind;

Dhanavantri, the god of medicine and the physician to the Gods, also the creator of Ayurveda, came out with the Vidyas and the 'Amritam';

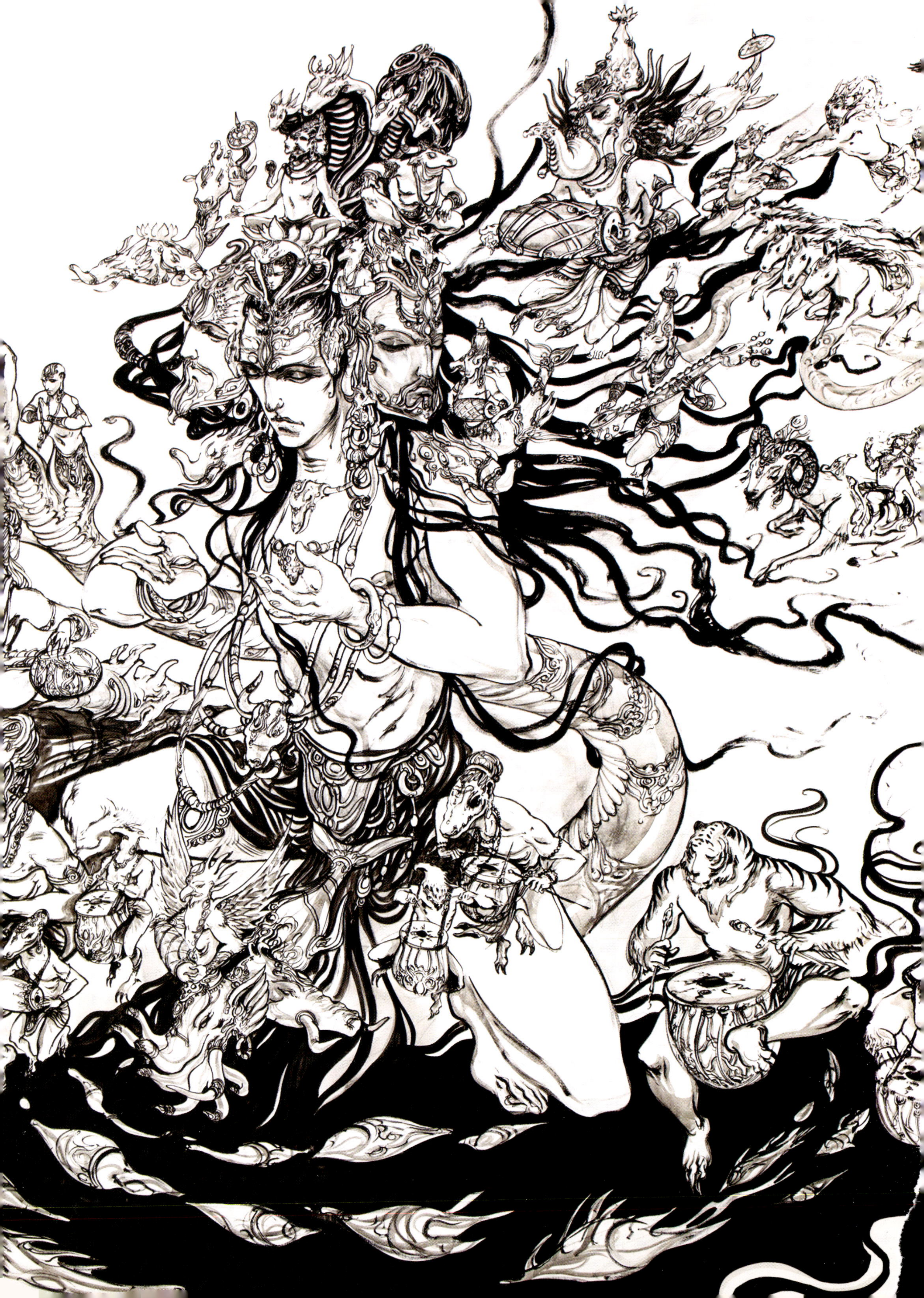

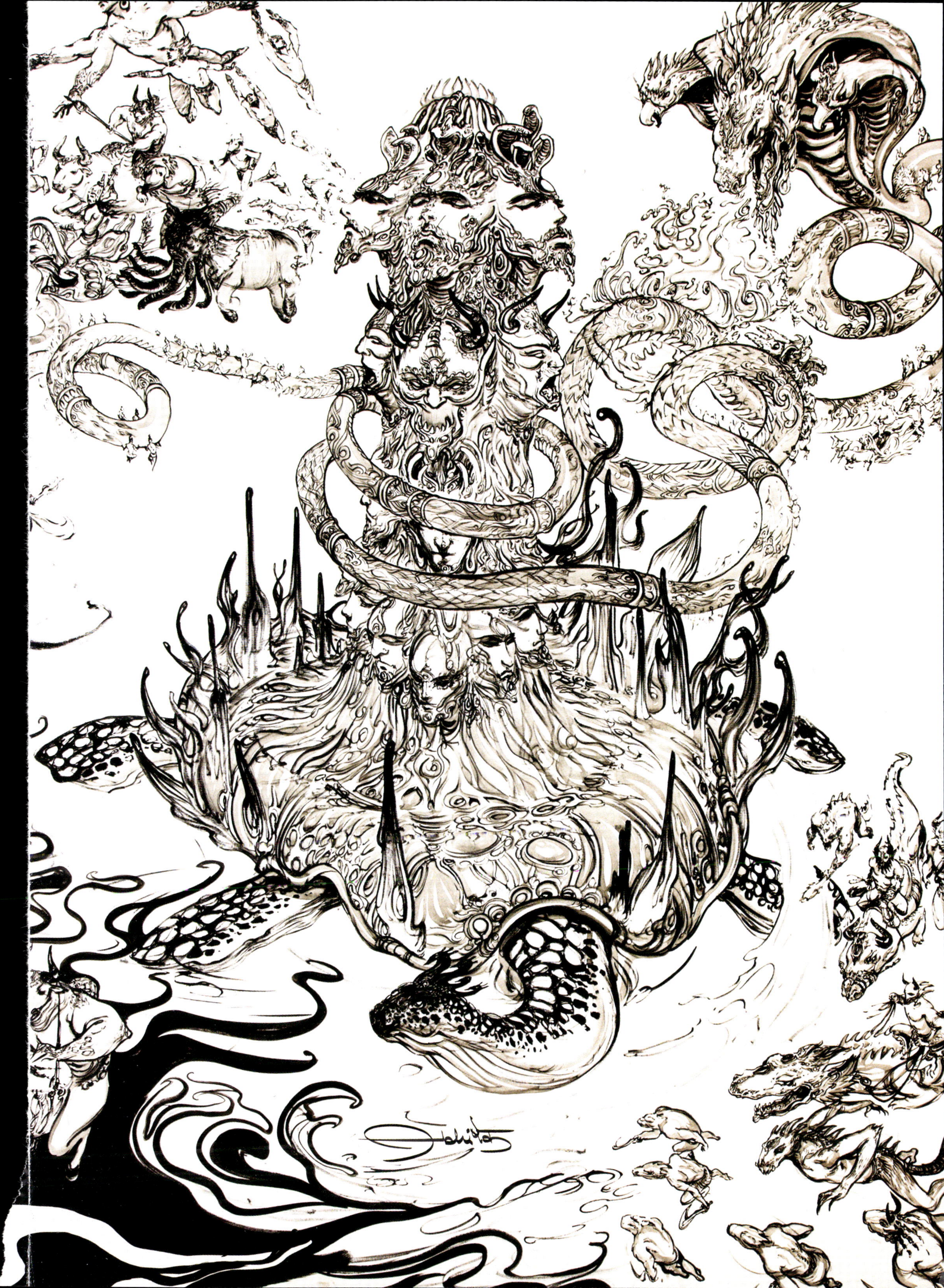

Origin

Shukracharya, the guru to the Demons, brought them back to life each time they were slayed in the war. The Gods did not have the power to combat something like that. Brahma guided the demons to make a pact with them, and propose to churn off the ocean to obtain the nectar of immortality, 'Amritam'.

Another version of the story says that it was a curse by Sage Durvasa to Indra, the King of the Gods, which resulted in his collapse from the throne and eventually Indra got it back by procuring the nectar of immortality.

Symbology of the Samudra Manthan.

Mount Mandara: The spine

The tortoise 'Kurma': The five senses

The snake 'Vasuki': The oscillations of the mind between the two opposing forces, 'Asuras' and 'Devas'

Asura, the opposite of sura, means 'out of sync'.

Deva is the 'shinning one'.

Both tendencies reside inside our mind and their tussle produces good and poisonous things. The ocean is the etheric field of creation. The juices produced inside the cranium and the brain.

Throat chakra represents the thyroid gland, which controls metabolism and body heat. Parvati symbolizes the healing force which stabilized the incremental heat and pressure.

Halahala, the poison, represented the physical and psychological toxins;

Conch represented the cosmic sounds;

Jayeshtha, goddess of misfortunes or Alakshmi (opposite of Lakshmi), represented dissonance of light frequencies.

Umbrella taken by Varuna.

Earrings given to Aditi by her son Indra.

Kalpavriksha or divine tree.

Nidra or sloth.

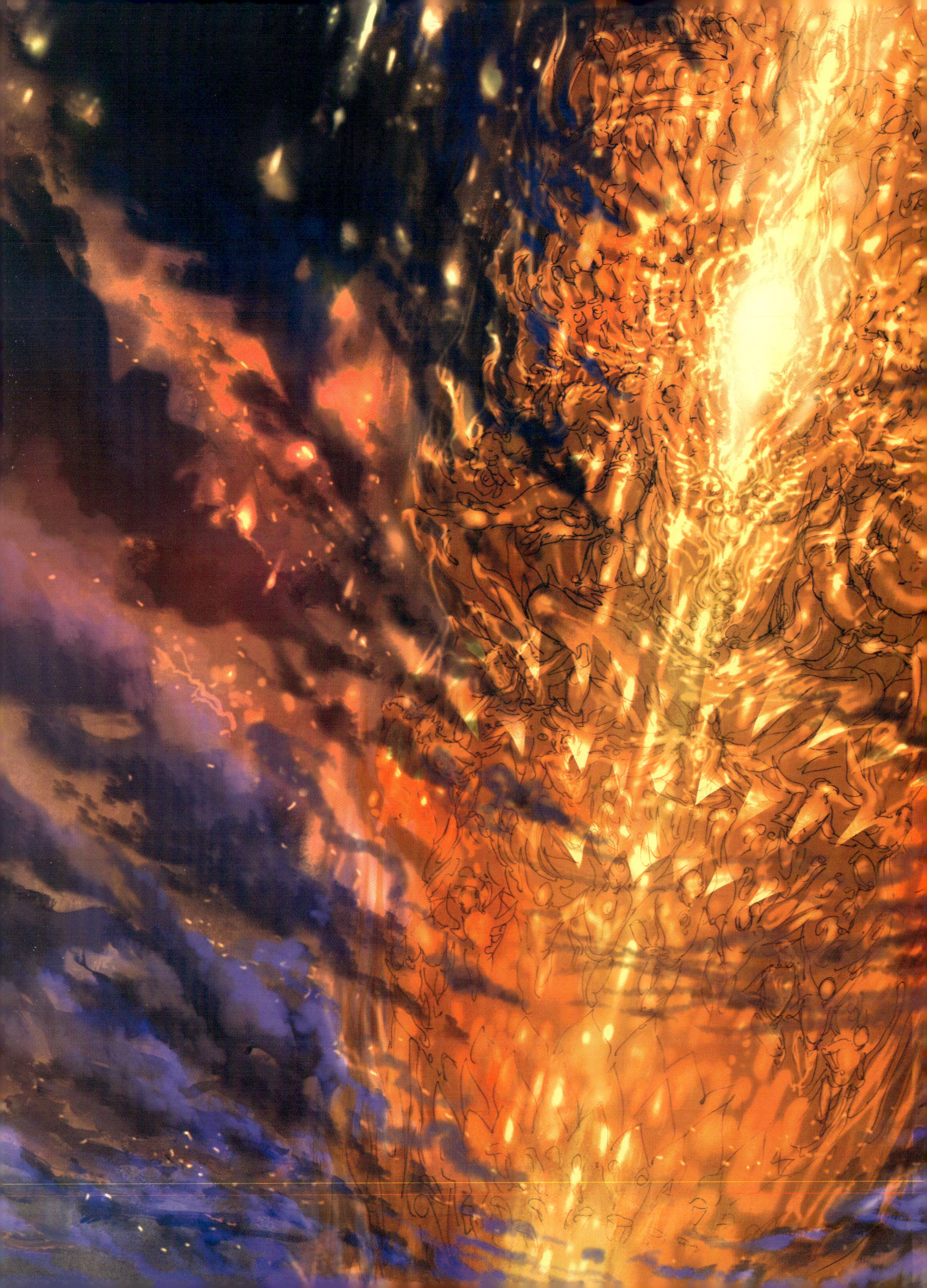

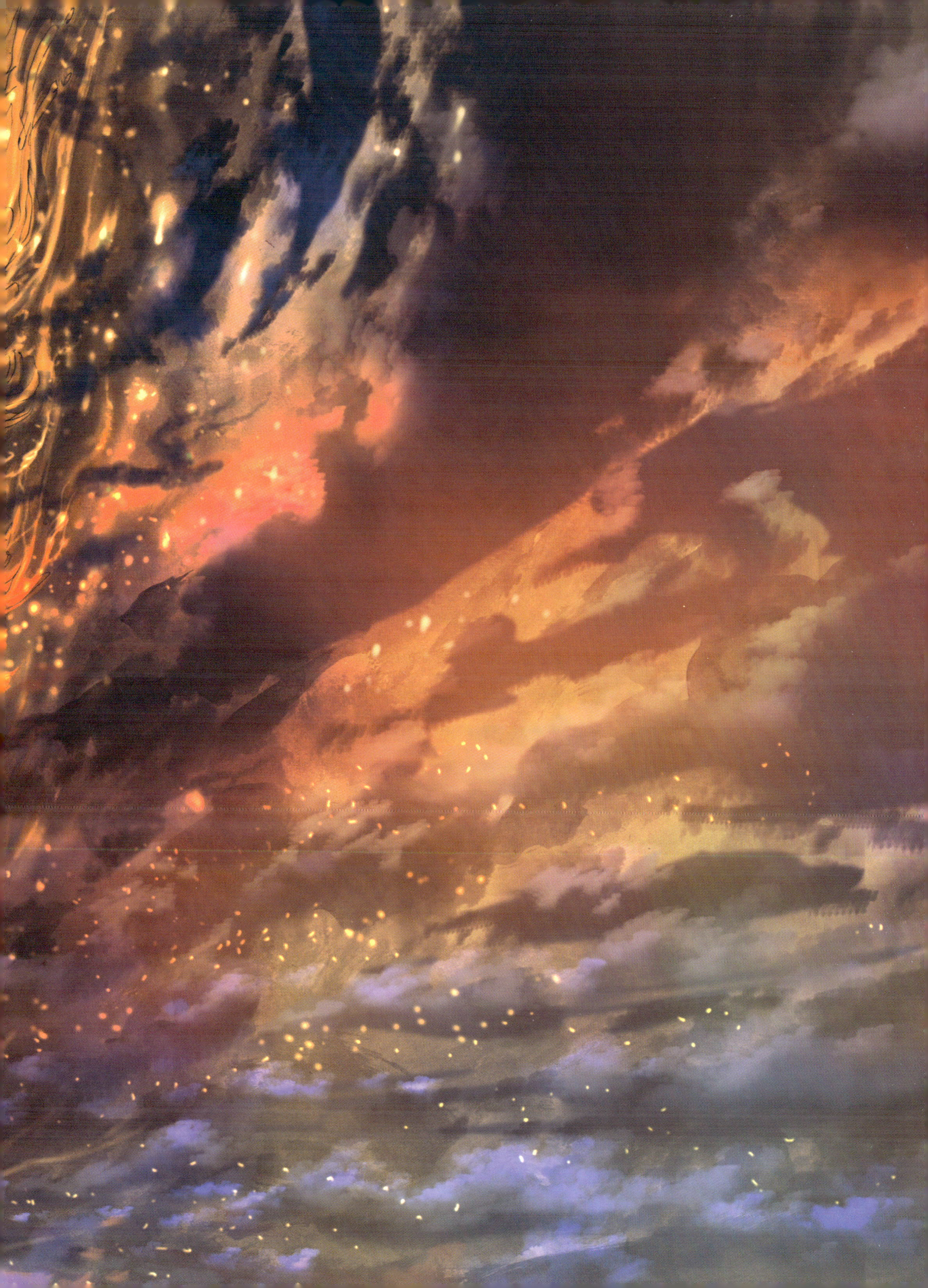

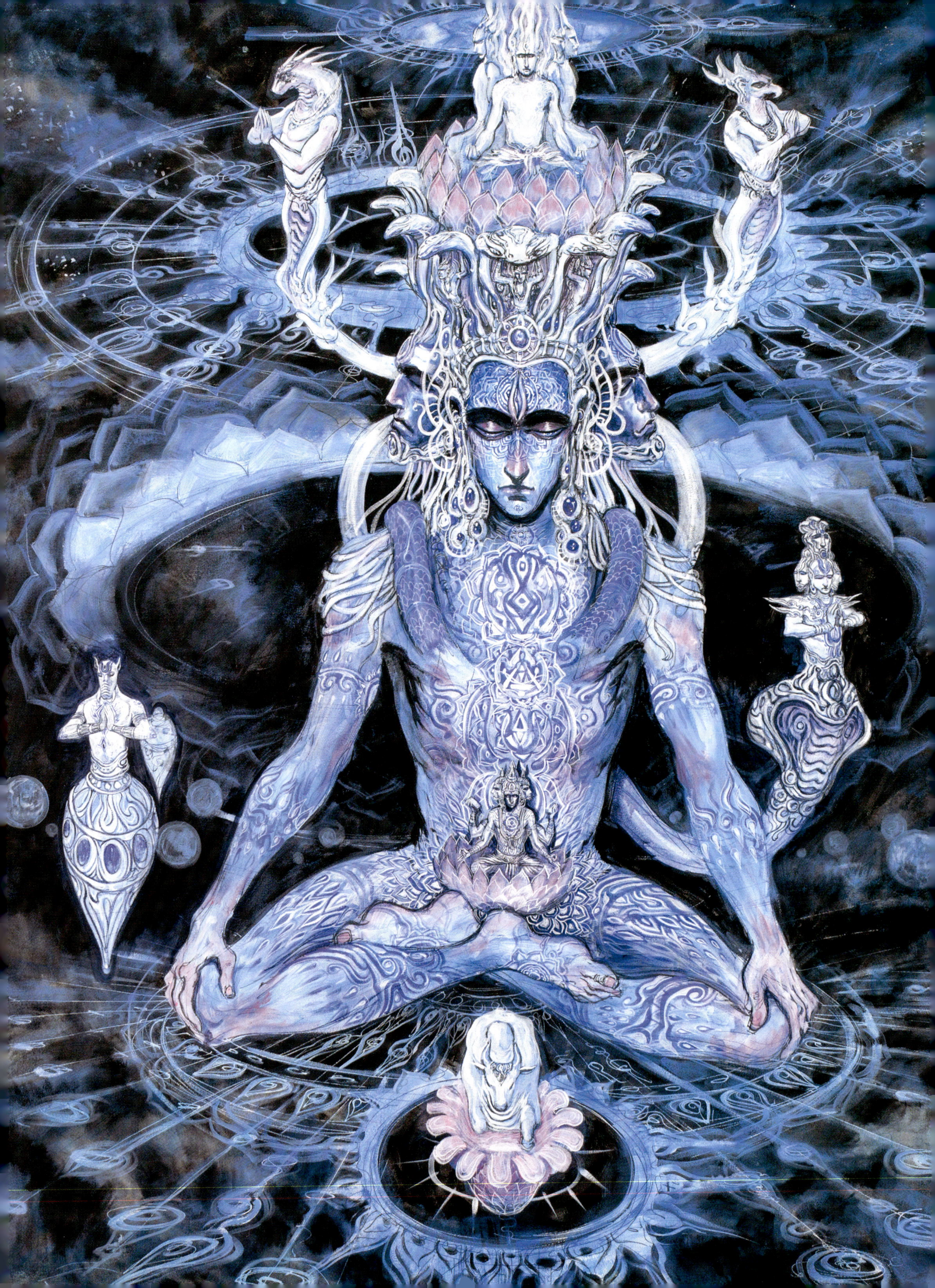

THE CREATION OF THE SUN

Shiva took to the depths of the ocean to meditate with his intent to create the perfect Earth, while Vishnu and Brahma waited observing the Nakshatras.

Eons passed but Shiva did not return.

Anxious, Brahma said to Vishnu, "Maybe Shiva will never return for another Yuga, and Brahma will be dead by then, so we must create the Earth."

Hence, without Shiva, they manifested the Earth. At that moment, Shiva appeared magically! Looking at the imperfect world, he became angry and started burning it with his fire, slowly turning the Earth into ashes.

A melancholic Vishnu asked Shiva to stop the destruction, to which Shiva said that he cannot put out the fire, but he will cease to unleash it. Vishnu was humbled. He said, "This fire which emanated from your tapa shall become the very source of life. It will become the Sun."

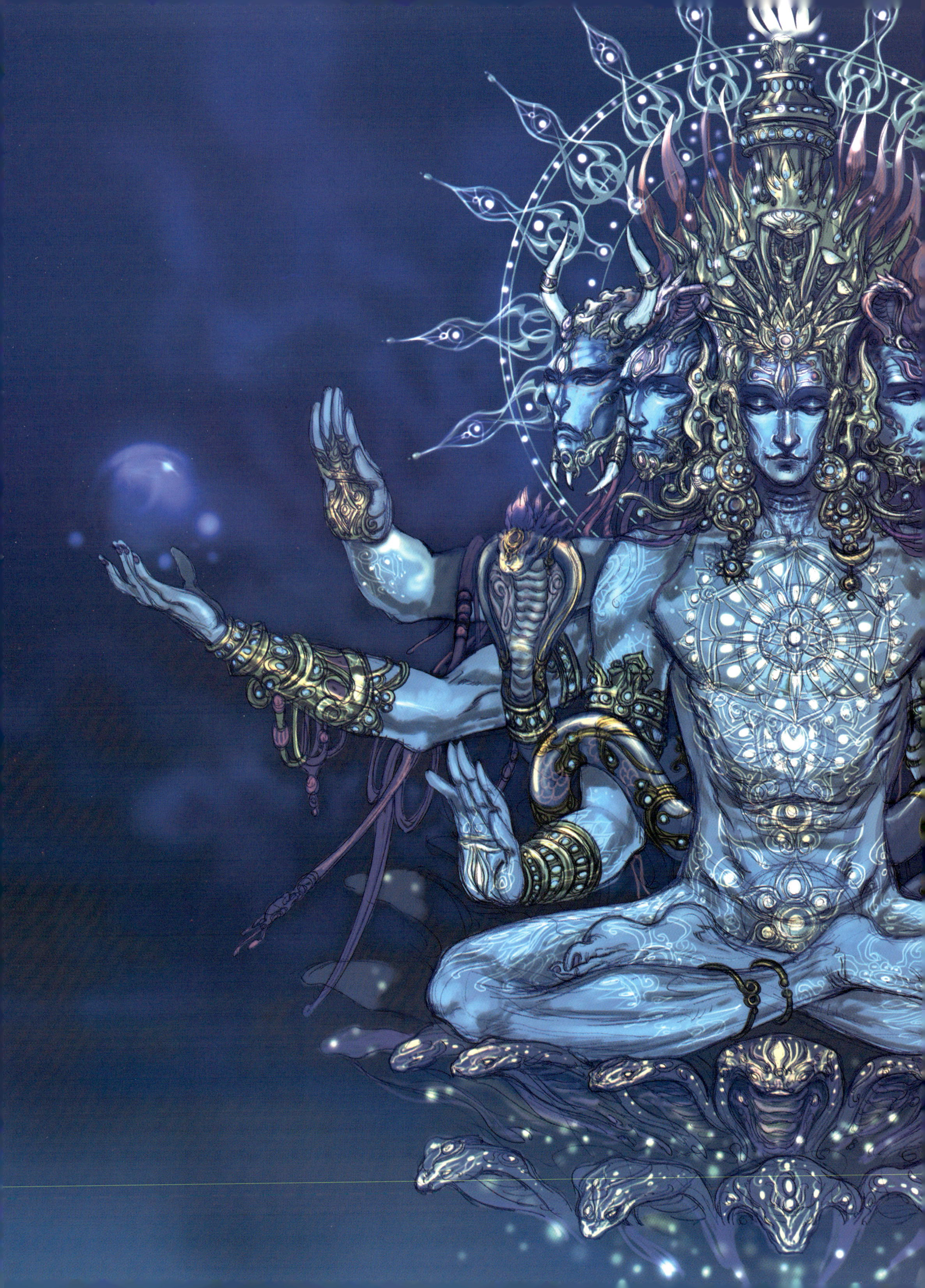

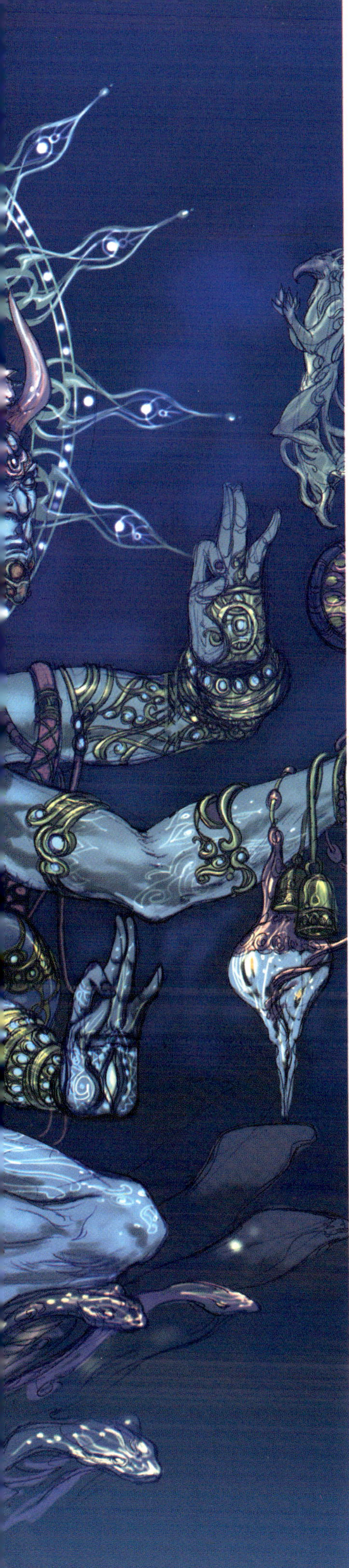

ISANA

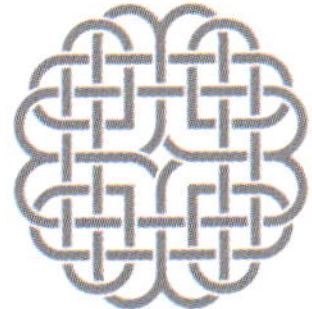

Shiva's breathing was aligned with the expanding and contracting of the universe, each a long eon. He was everything beyond and within time and all that wasn't.
Yet he was present in the space away from the beings of matter.

Water: “Oh Trilochana, the three-eyed one. What are the five faces you adorn?”
A silent hum rippled inside the water and stirred the ancient elements.

"Sadyojita", the west, manifesting Brahma; representing the Earth.
"Vamadeva", the northern aspect, is Vishnu's energy; representing water.
"Aghora", the southern aspect, associated with Rudra; representing fire.
"Tatpurusha", east-looking, embodies the sages and yogis and is the air element.
"Isana", the one which looks within, connected with all that exists; representing space.

The water now rested in Shiva's third eye, calming the fires of creation.
He understood the harmony between the five elements and their purpose.

To explore all directions, but ultimately let it all coalesce, and look within.

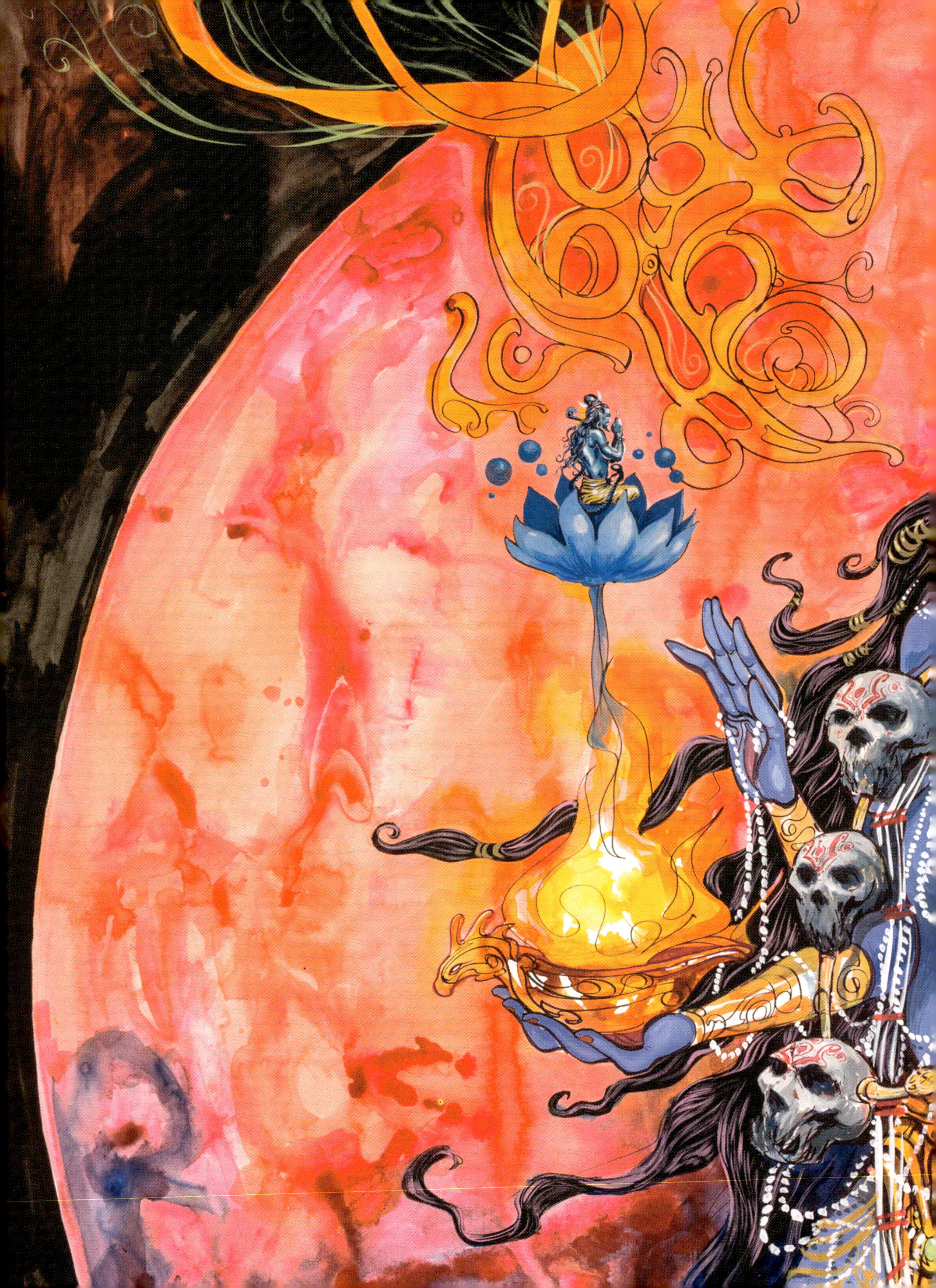

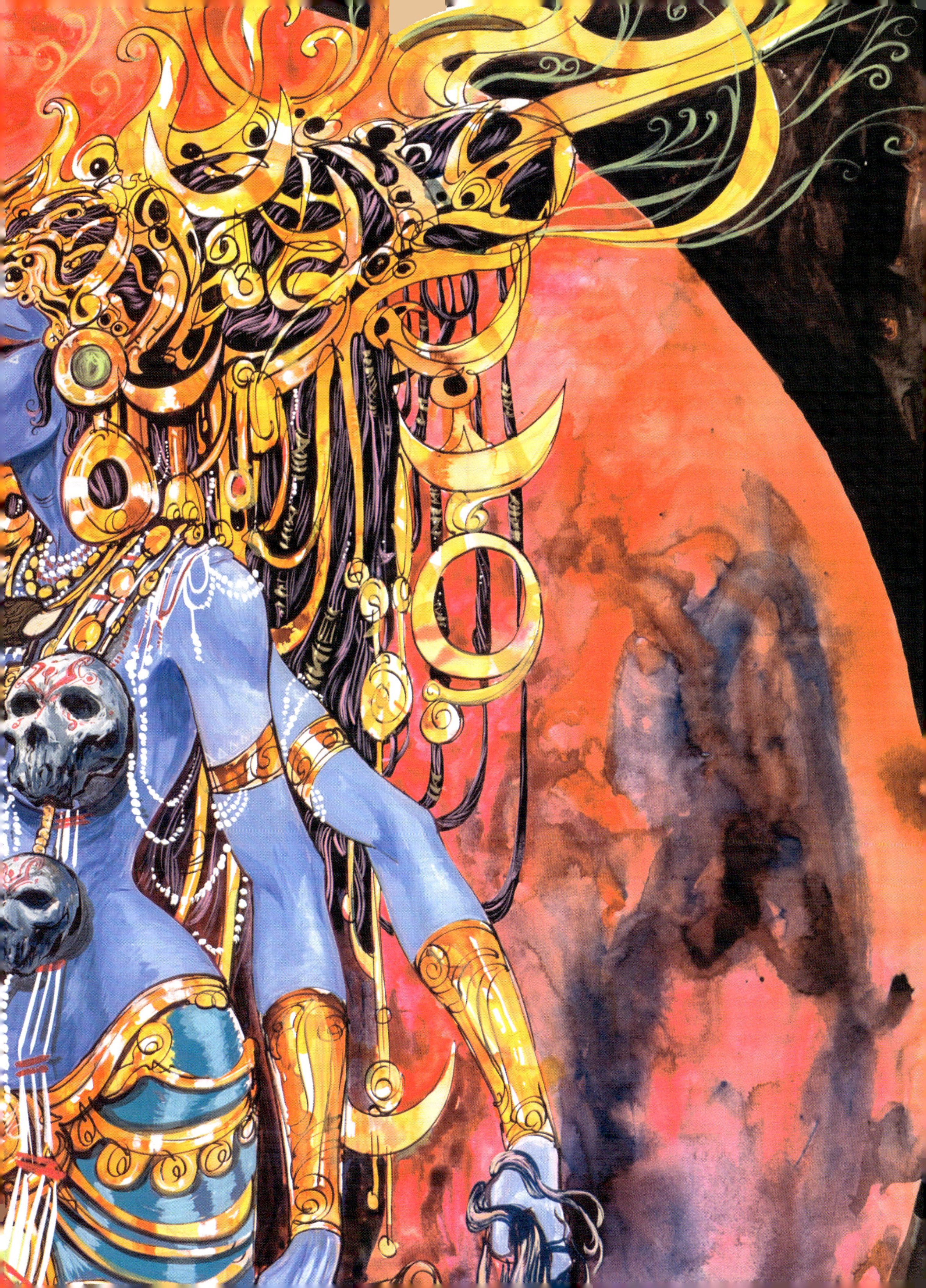

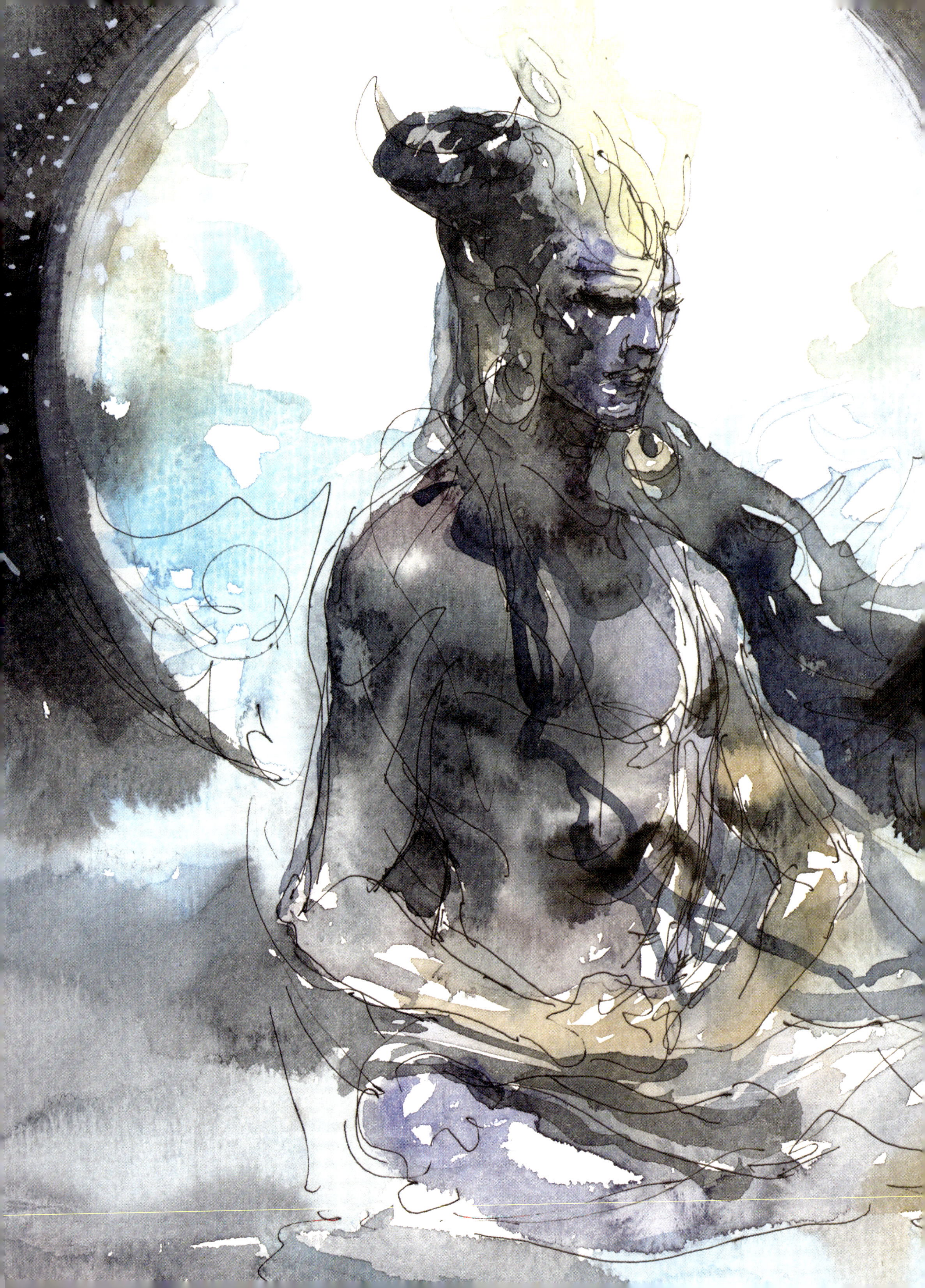

GRI-INVOKED

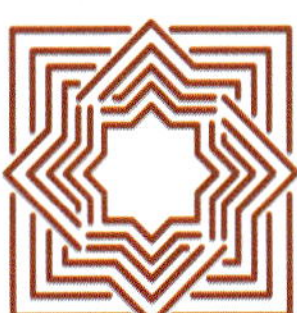

The mind is a labyrinth of concepts and constructs, where we live most of our lives, confused.

The elusive clarity is only momentarily apprehended.

Often, it's someone out there who reminds us of its presence.

When we are incapacitated, stripped of our mental solitude and social balances. Who invokes in us this clarity and the strength to confront our worst fears?

The wise say someone is always listening if you are truly yearning.

Who helps you see through the skins of life. It's sinew, bone and ash.

To become like a photon, a wayfaring traveler in space and time.

The alchemist stone, which makes all iron into gold but chooses to remain a stone.

The ocean which doesn't want its own pearls.

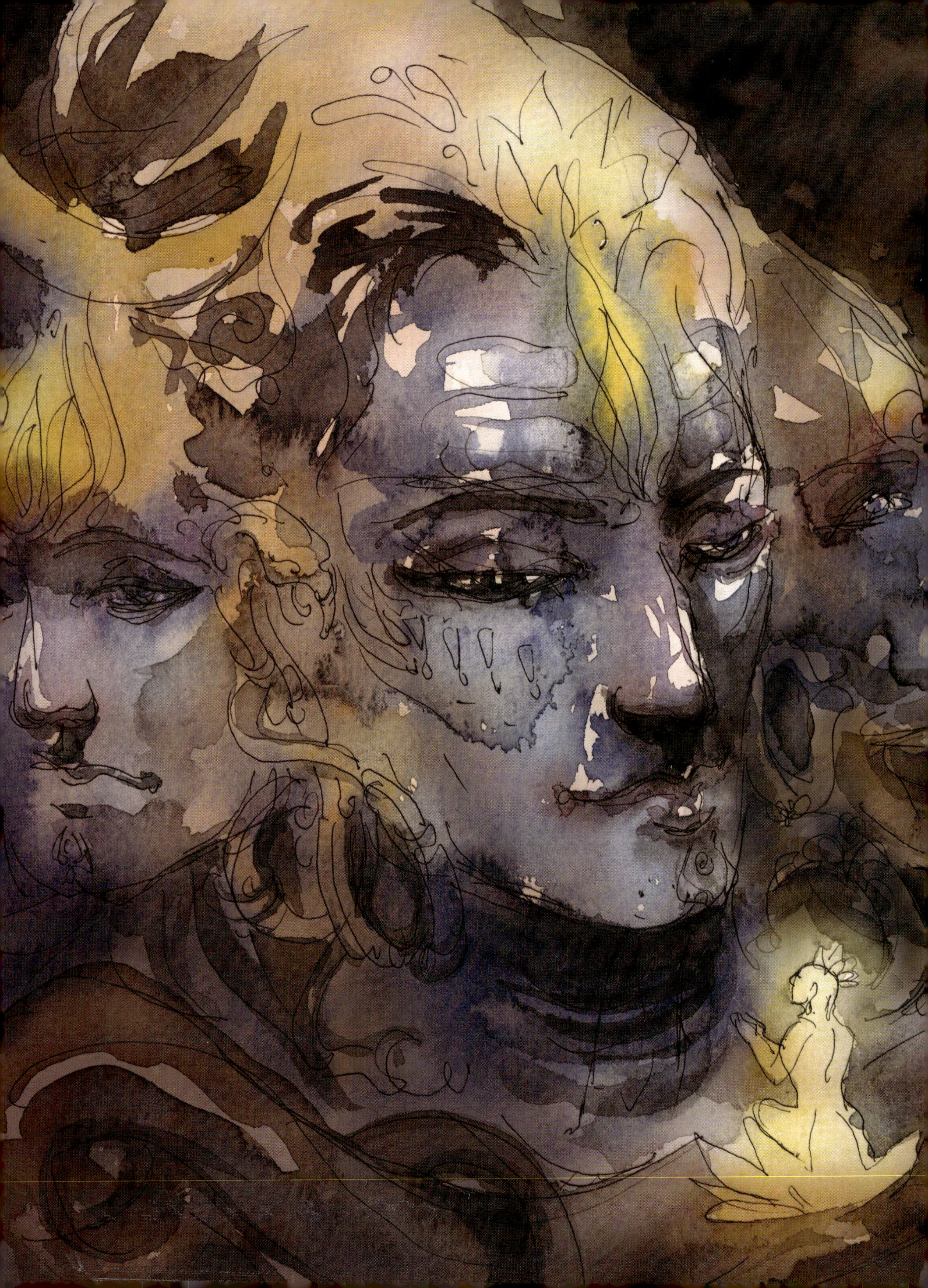

Who is Gri, the one who invokes?
Gur, the one who lifts up.
The one who helps you rise up is the 'Guru'.

To the Guru which is the 'Nothingness'.

The 'Womb', the amniotic fluids of creation.

The Mother and the Father,

The mountains and the rivers,

Every tree and root and the helping hand that plants it.

To the Guru which is Life, I bow down in reverence.

Thank you for teaching me, that sometimes it is okay to lose one's way, and that is how a 'way' becomes a 'path'.

For teaching how to embrace long phases of obscurity and anonymity courageously. That even at our worst, we can always give and share.

For ingraining the power of simplicity and common sense.

Thank you for sending people, creatures and beings who love.

Without them, I would not have understood your presence.

I bow to you, with love.

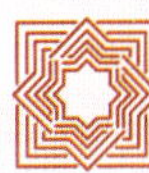

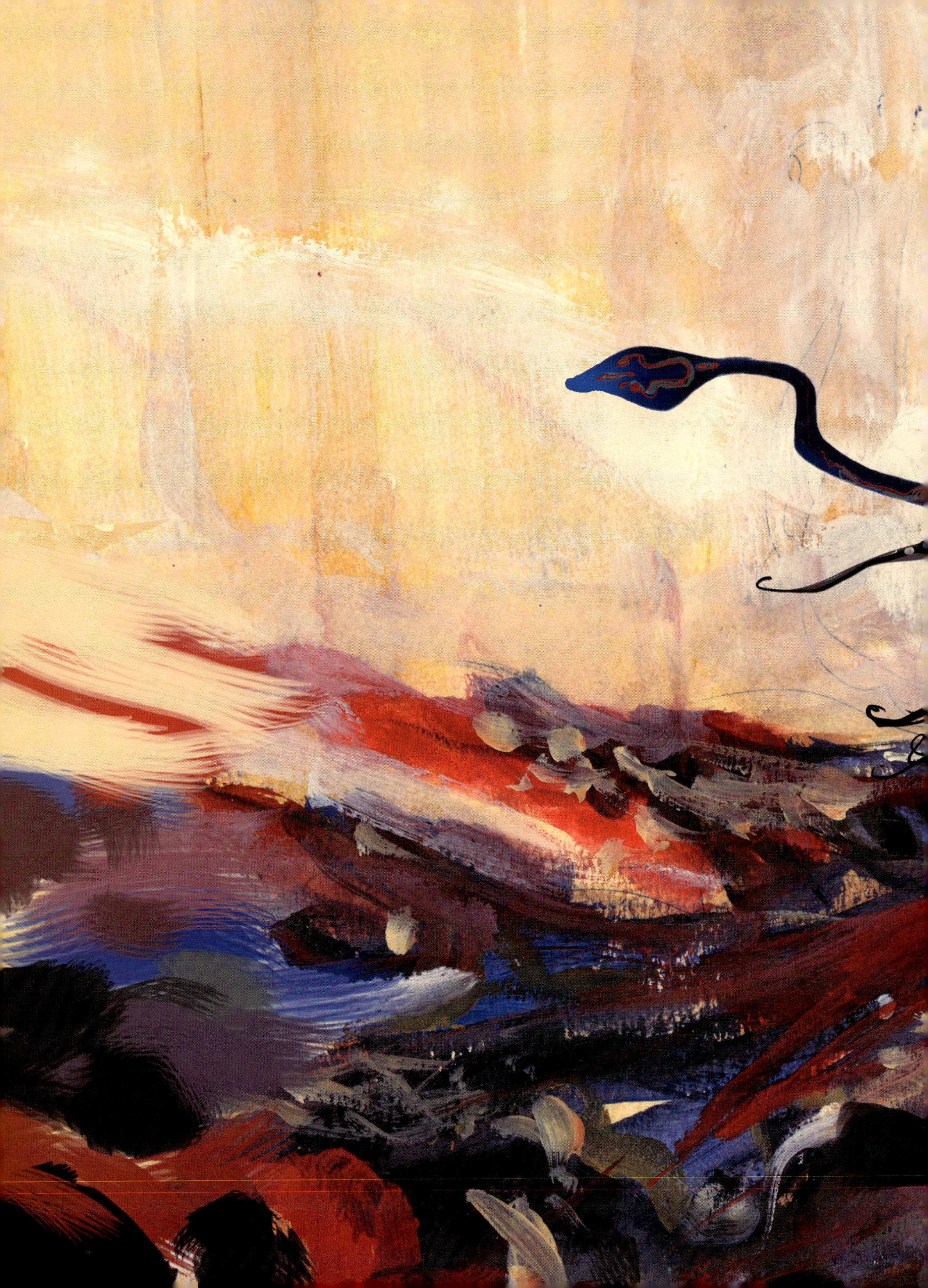

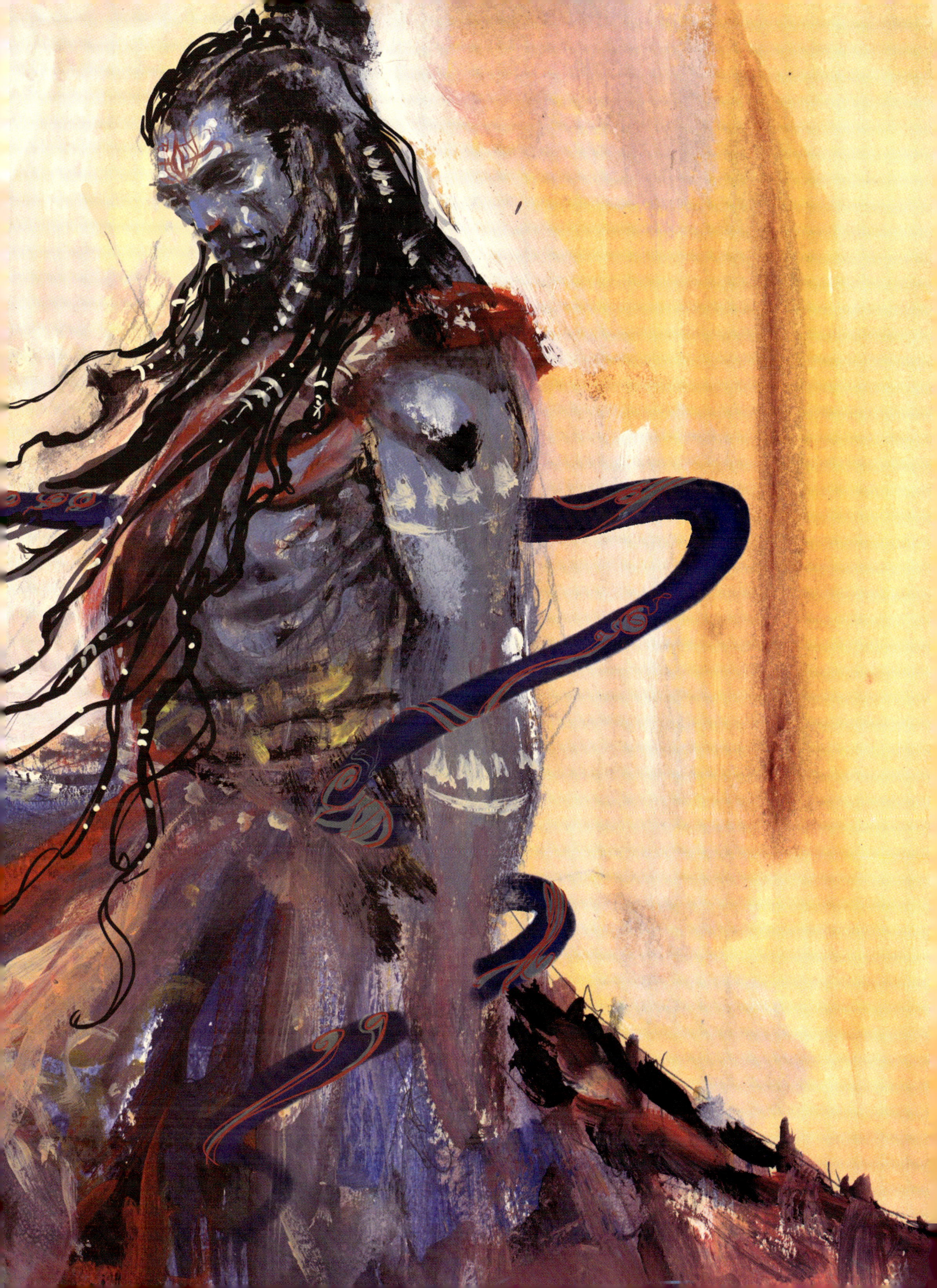

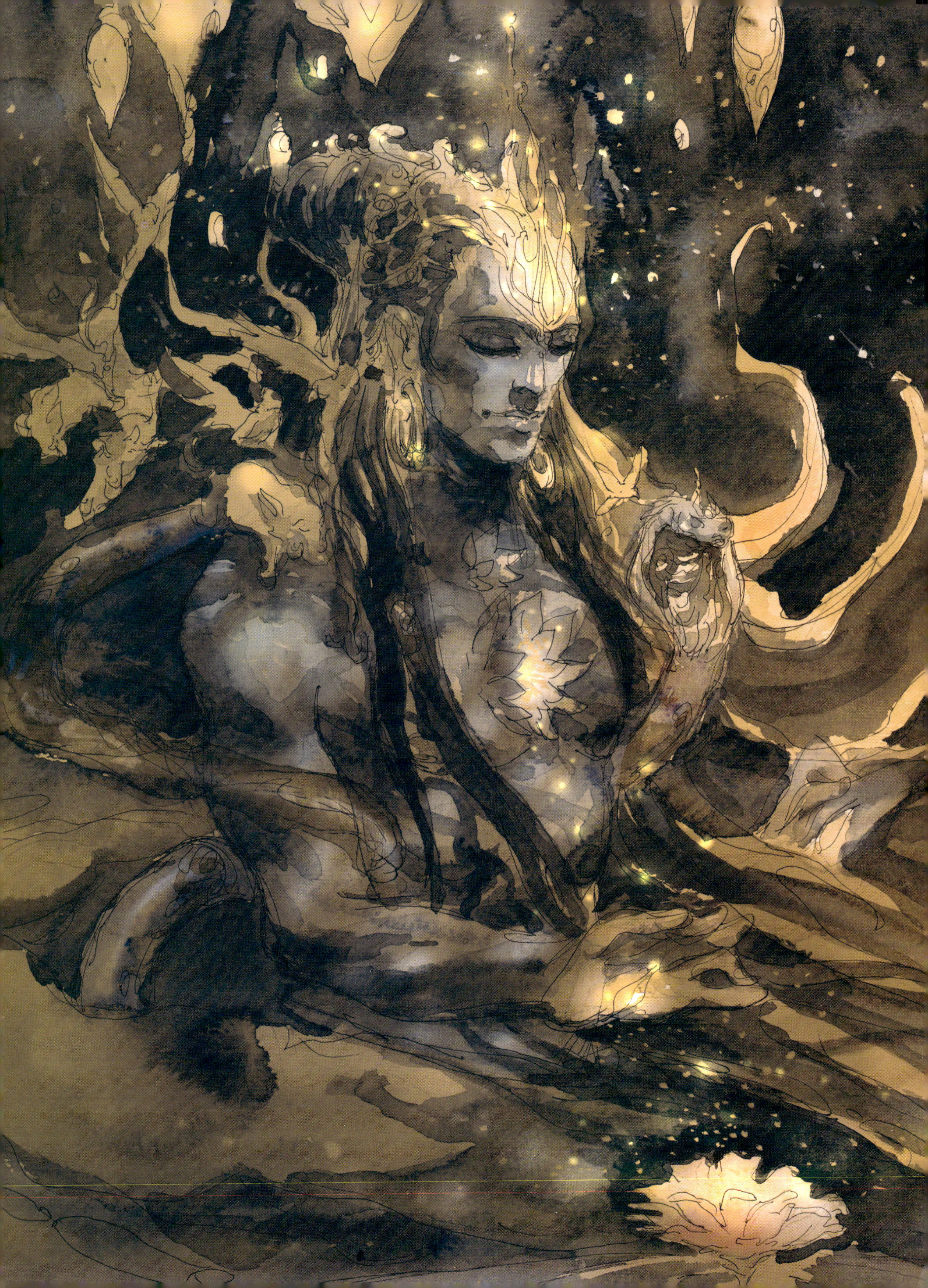

BLOOM

Flower: "What holds the world together, *Shankara*?"

Shiva: "A vibrational rivet holds its transient presence. Just like you, the world sprouts, blooms, decays and gets consumed by time for many cycles, till it's liberated."

Flower: "And how can one be liberated, *Shankara*?"

Shiva: "Just bloom inwards this time."

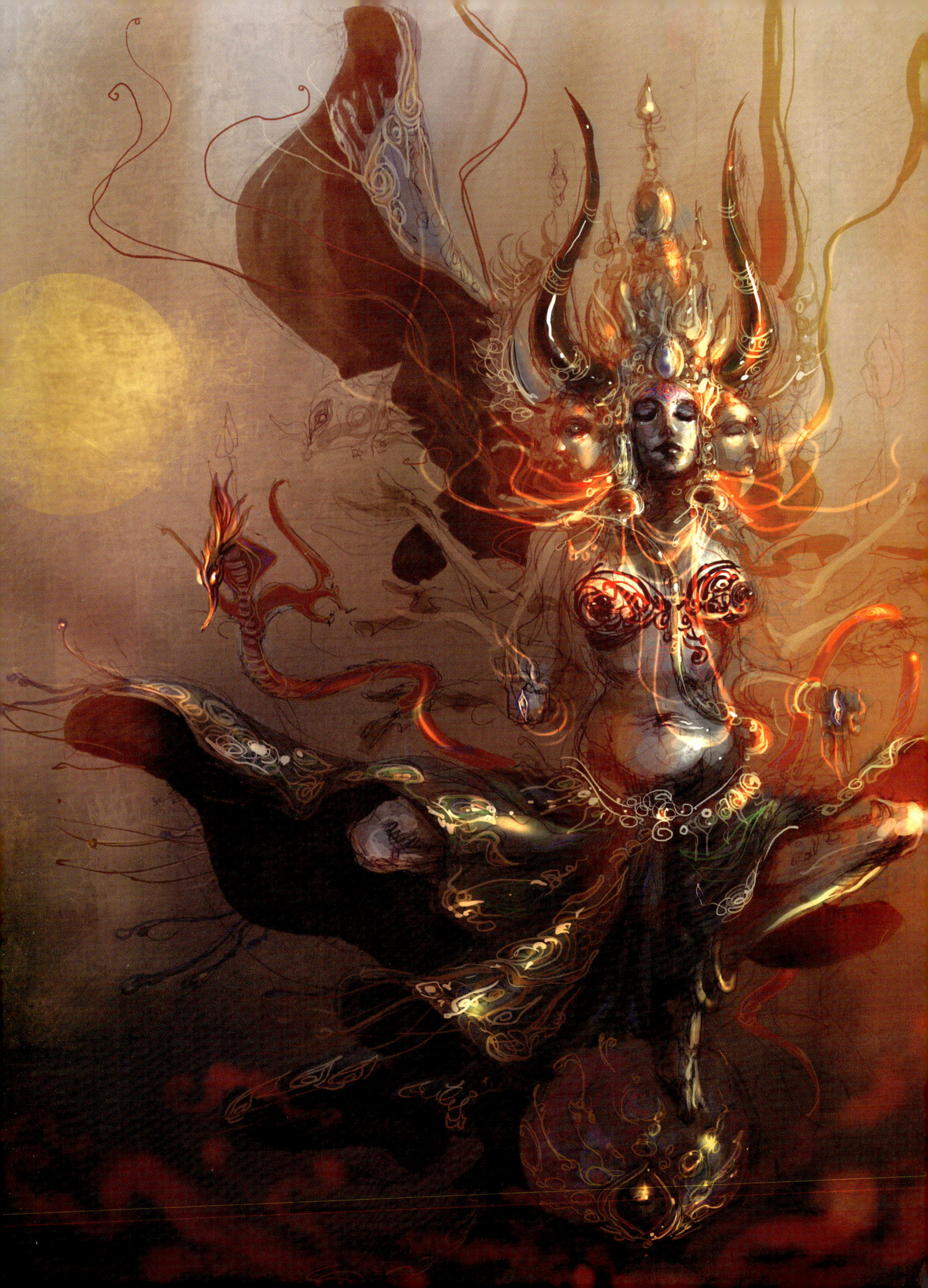

PASHYANTI –
THAT WHICH IS WITNESSED

"Oh Bhadrani! What do you guard day in and night out?"

"All thirteen fires. They run from head to toe; from one pole to the other; and across the fabric of the orbits.

Adi-Agni, the primordial fire of creation;
Jataragni, the essence of fire which breaks down the most complex matter;
Bhutagni, the elemental fire;
Akash Agni, sky fire: atmosphere;
Dhara-Agni, the earth fire: mantle;
Varuna-Agni, the ocean fire: fossil and core;
Mandar-Agni, the mountain fire: fossils and lava;
Manas-Agni, the fire in the mind;
Antaragni, the fire in the soul;
Mahat-Agni, the fire as the messenger to beginnings, as nothingness;
Suragni, the fire in sound;
Dhatu Agni, the fire inside all minerals and enzymes;
Jivaagni, the fire which animates the sentinel being.

Yet, the fire of greed encompasses all of the ethereal fires. The fire of greed is one fire I chose to not obliterate.

I simply manifest into the hearts of those who endeavor to end it themselves."

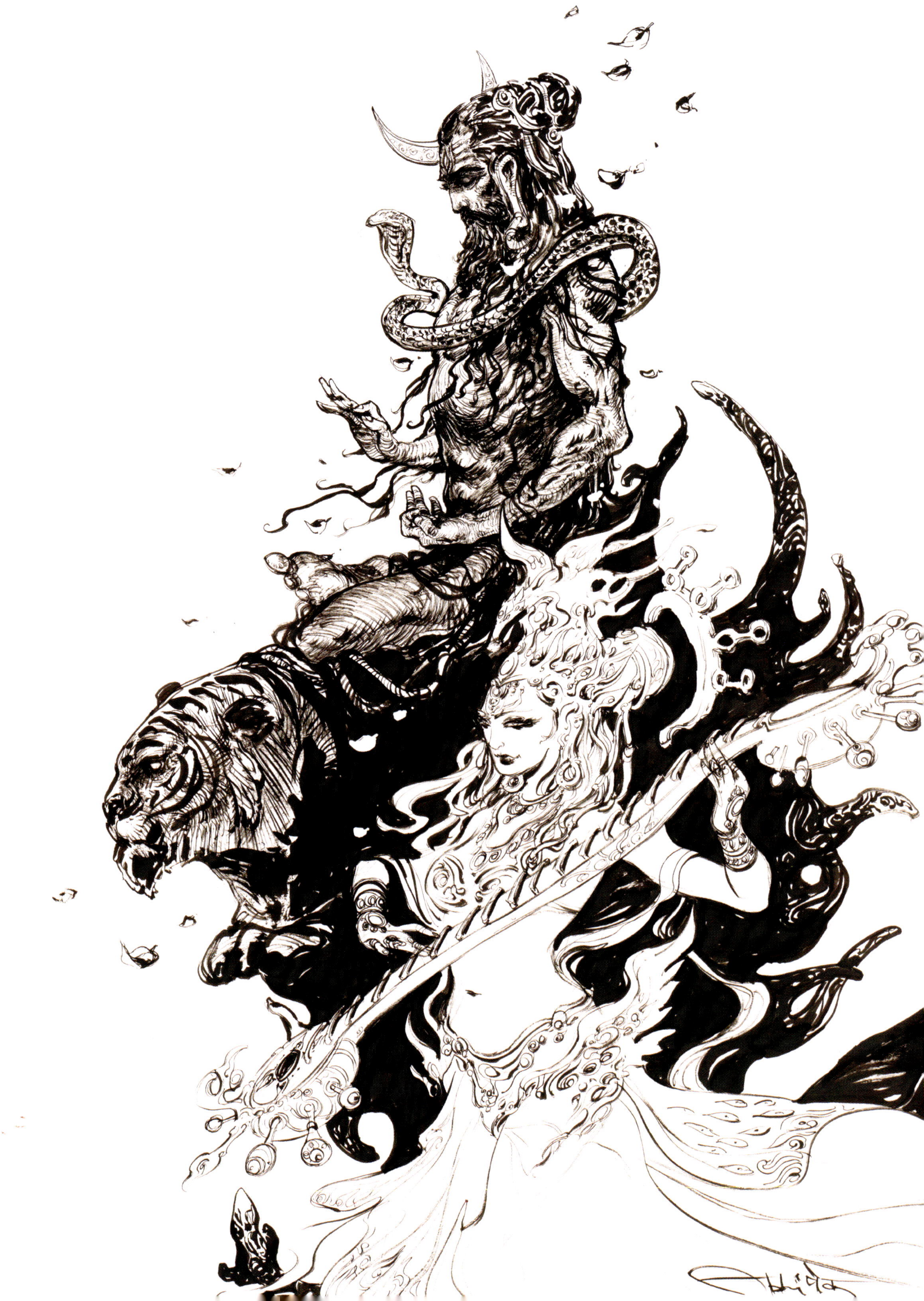

ADI-YOGI

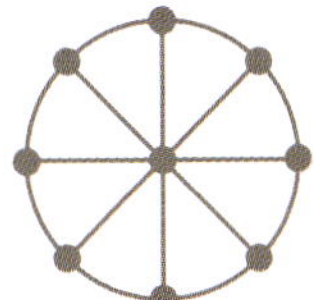

Parvati: "Shiva, who is the biggest yogi of all?"

Shiva: "Kala (time) as it aligns existence itself."

Parvati: "And who is greater than Kala?"

Shiva: "Yama (death) as every universe dies and is reborn."

Parvati: "No one is greater than Yama?"

Shiva: "The Mind (manas) as that is where it all exists."
So the one who can transform the mind, is the greatest yogi of all.

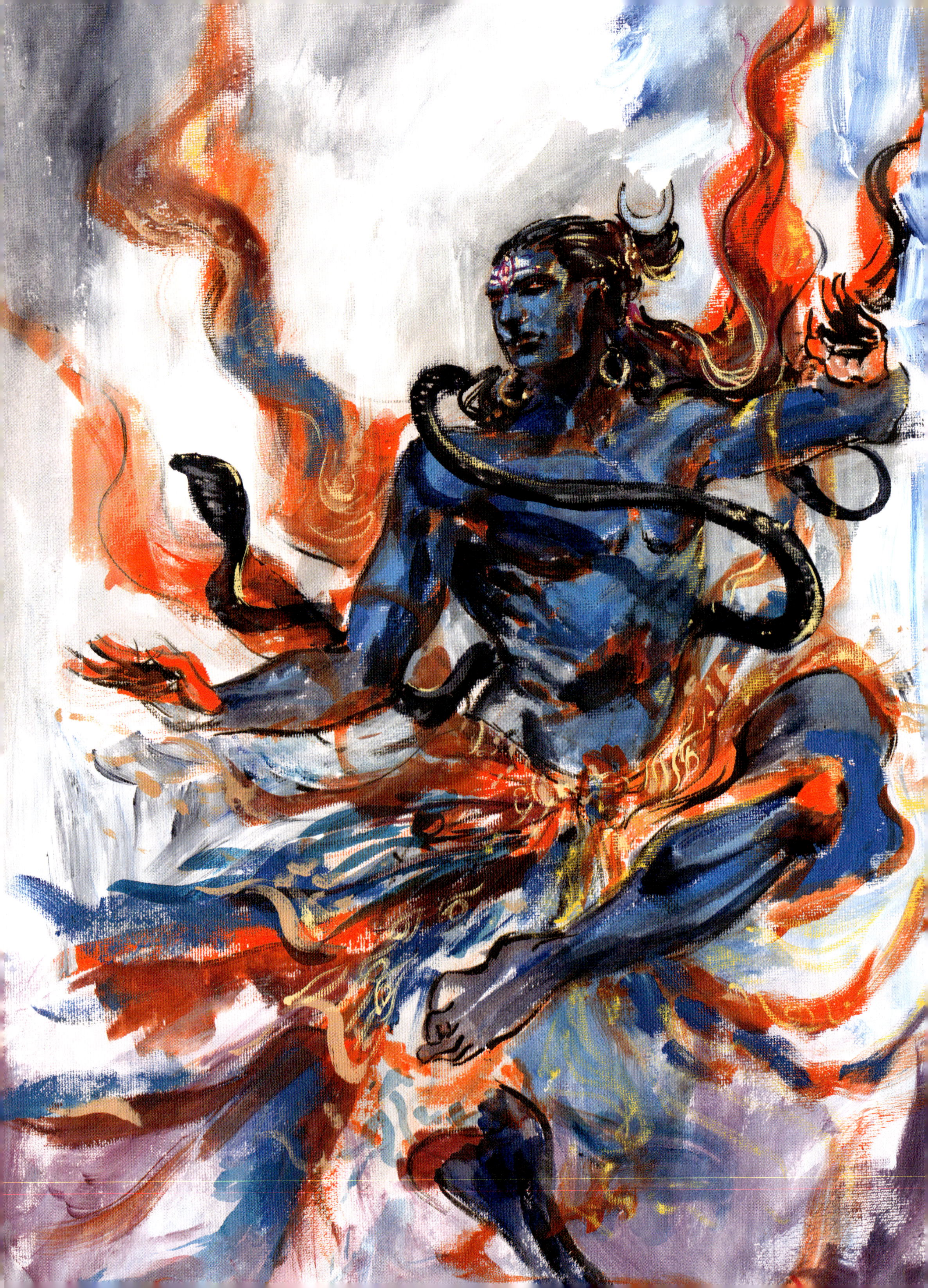

FOURTEEN SOUNDS, ONE OUTCAST

Shiva's dance emanated such aura that not just *kailasa* but also the heavenly abode of Swarga shimmered like the sun.

Sage Brahaspati, who was a prolific percussionist, endeavored to keep the rhythm to Shiva's dance of bliss. This was not *tandava* but simply a manifestation of Shiva's love for nature, his ecstasy and tapa churning out a mesmerizing display of cosmic movements.

Laced in a trance which perhaps came from the *Mahat* fields of creation, Shiva danced and picked up a flaring speed.

The energy was so immense, that everything around started collapsing. Even the stars which were dying and glinting with extreme light, looked feeble in their glow.

Only the elemental Gods who closed their eyes and meditated, could see this majestic display by Shiva.

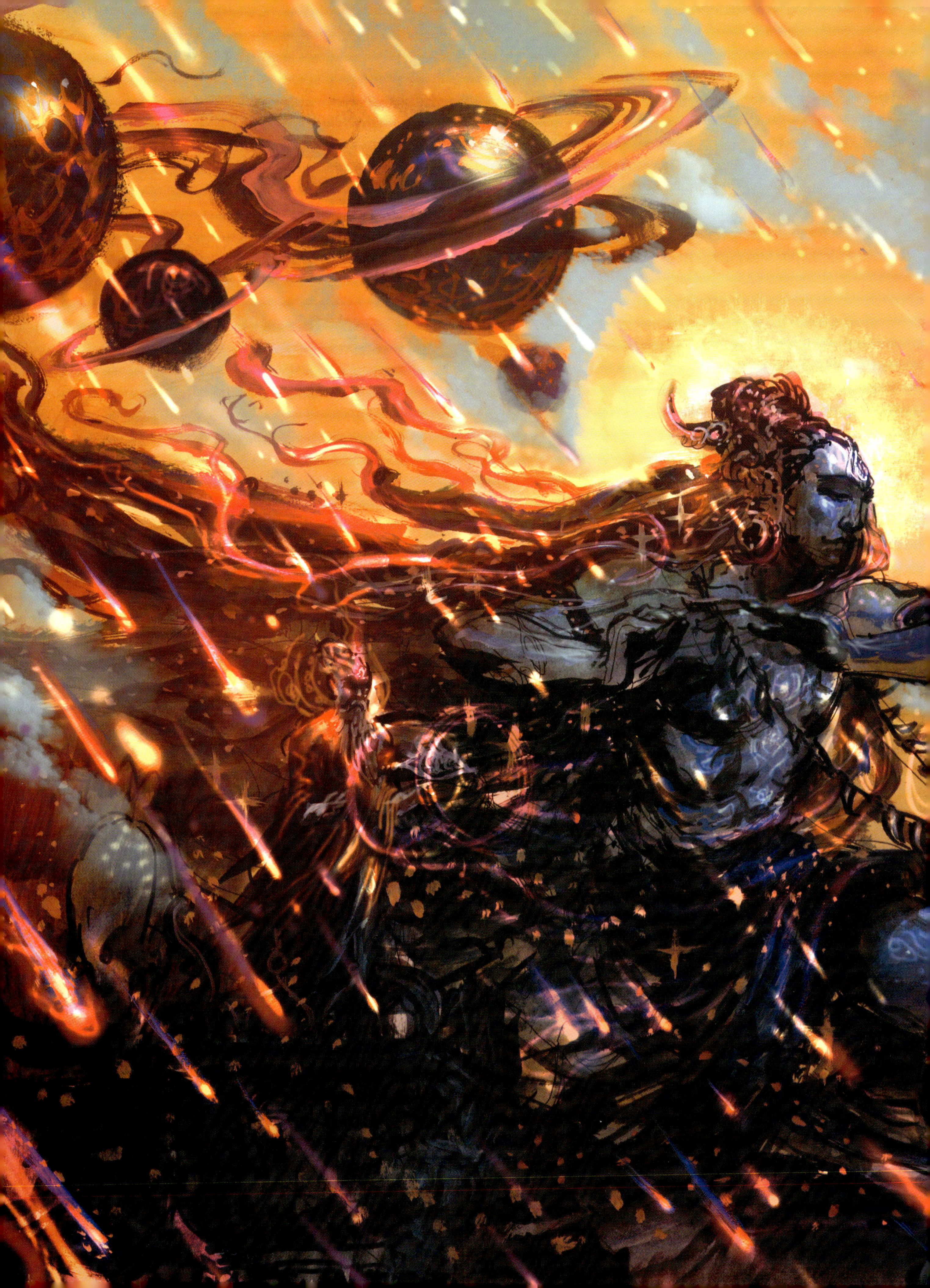

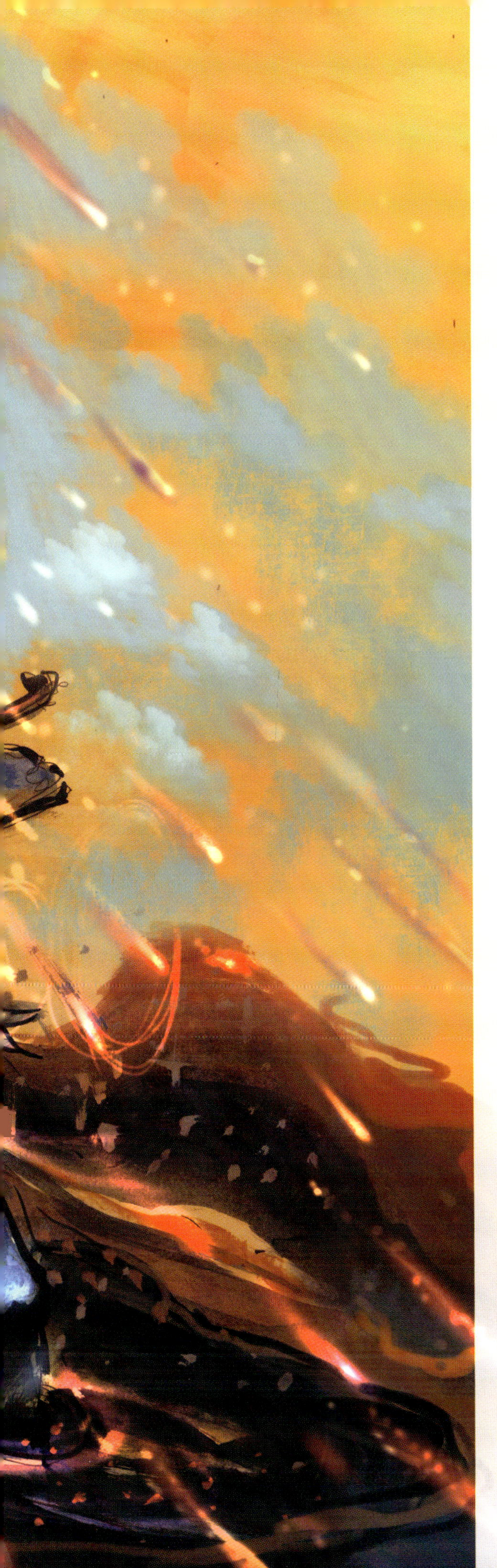

Brahaspati struggled to keep up with the rhythm. His hands wavering from the meter; fatigued and exhausted, he gave up.

He thought that now when there is no beat to keep, it will slow Shiva down slightly. But this was soon laid to rest.

Shiva's dance had only become more fierce and splendid. The stars were now swirling around him, producing colors only Uma, the Earth could see.

This surprised the sage. "How is he still dancing without any rhythm?" he wondered.

He asked, "Shiva, the Lord of Lords, what rhythm of music are you dancing to? There is no beat, I can't even hear a faint pulse."

The sage was extremely curious.

Shiva's voice echoed inside Brahaspati's heart and he spoke, "I am still dancing to a rhythm which is coming from afar. I hear it even in my meditation; it's pure and blissful."

Brahaspati looked afar into places beyond the Swarga and then he saw him.

A tall gaunt man dressed in simple attire but with the demeanor of someone celestial, sat amidst a Shamshaan alone, playing his percussion fervently, a curious object clearly made from the bones of the most ancient beings.

Deep was his yearning, like he wanted to meet his father, who Brahaspati knew was gone.

Even Brahaspati was mesmerized by this revelation.

Shiva spoke again, "Ravana, my child, come close to me and play in the abode of the Gods."

Ravana said with his head bowed in reverence, "Oh Asureswara, I'm not welcome there, I'm a demon. Brahaspati and other Gods have prohibited me from playing there. So I make music here amongst the dead as they are closer to you, swooning over the music which resonates in leaving this material world.

Through them I always hoped my music would reach you.

Hearing this, Shiva embraced Ravana and welcomed him into the land of the Gods.

Ravana played with so much fervor that this time, Shiva danced with all the creatures of the world in his heart, becoming Pashupati, the lord of beings.

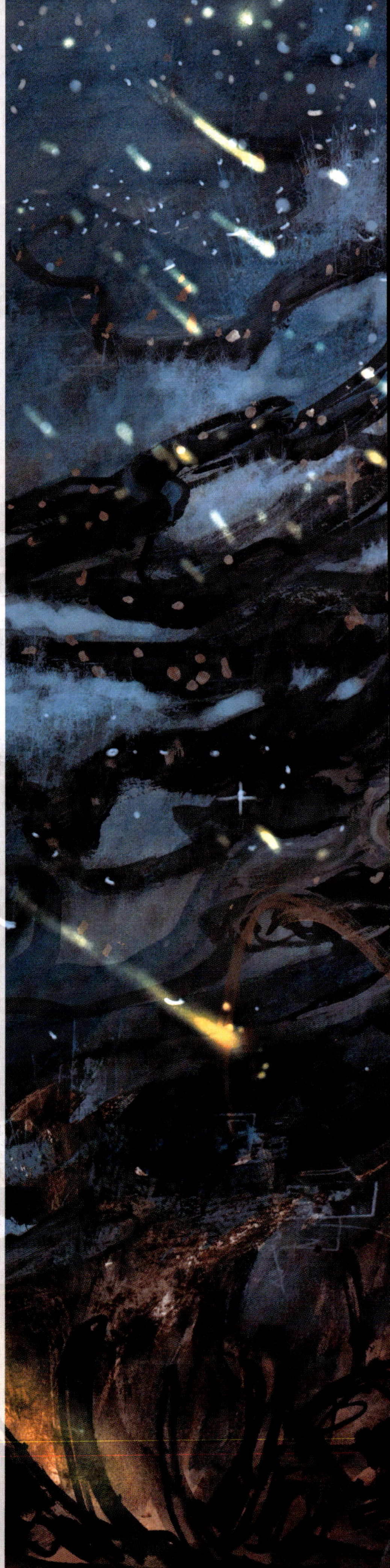

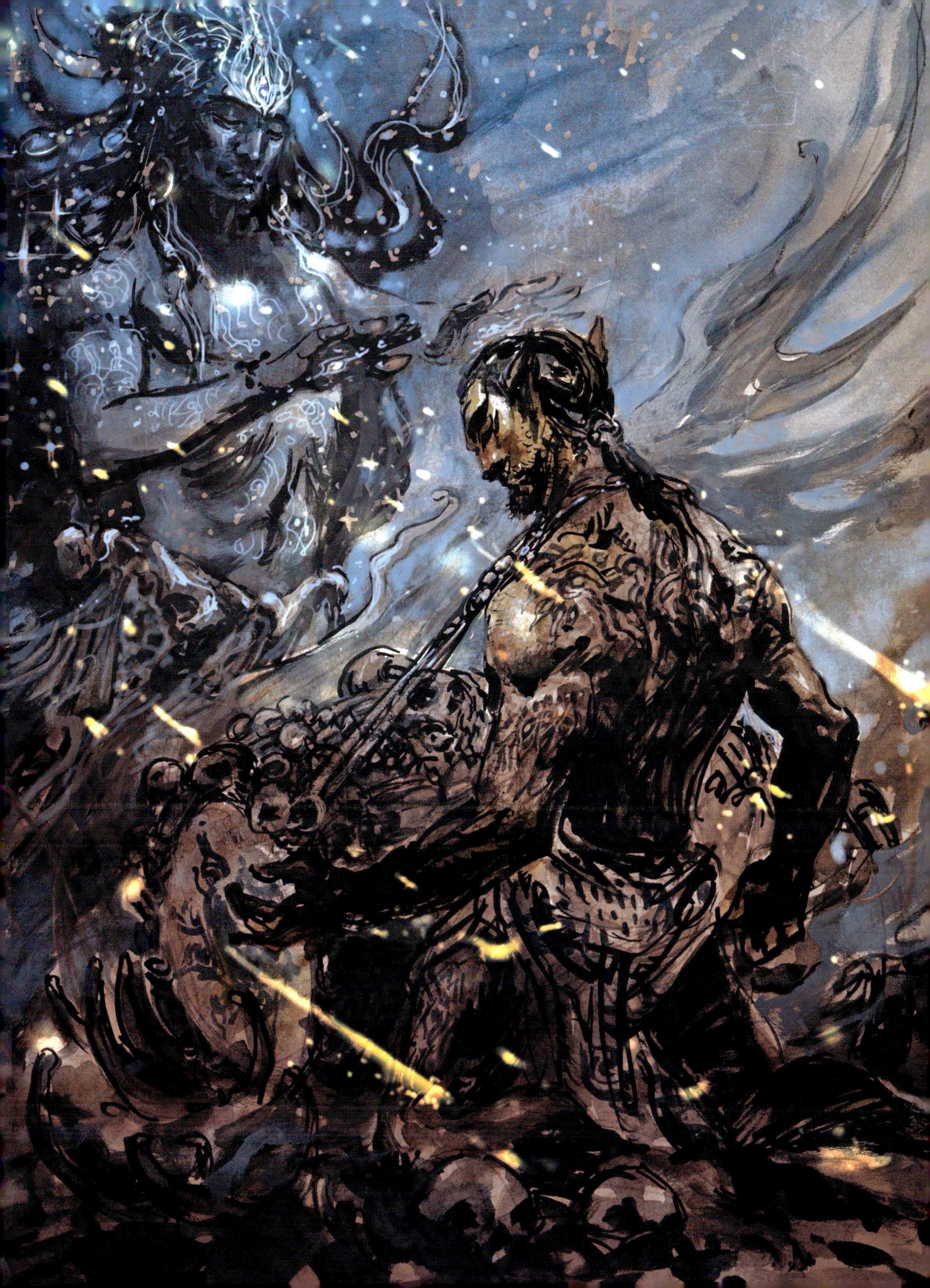

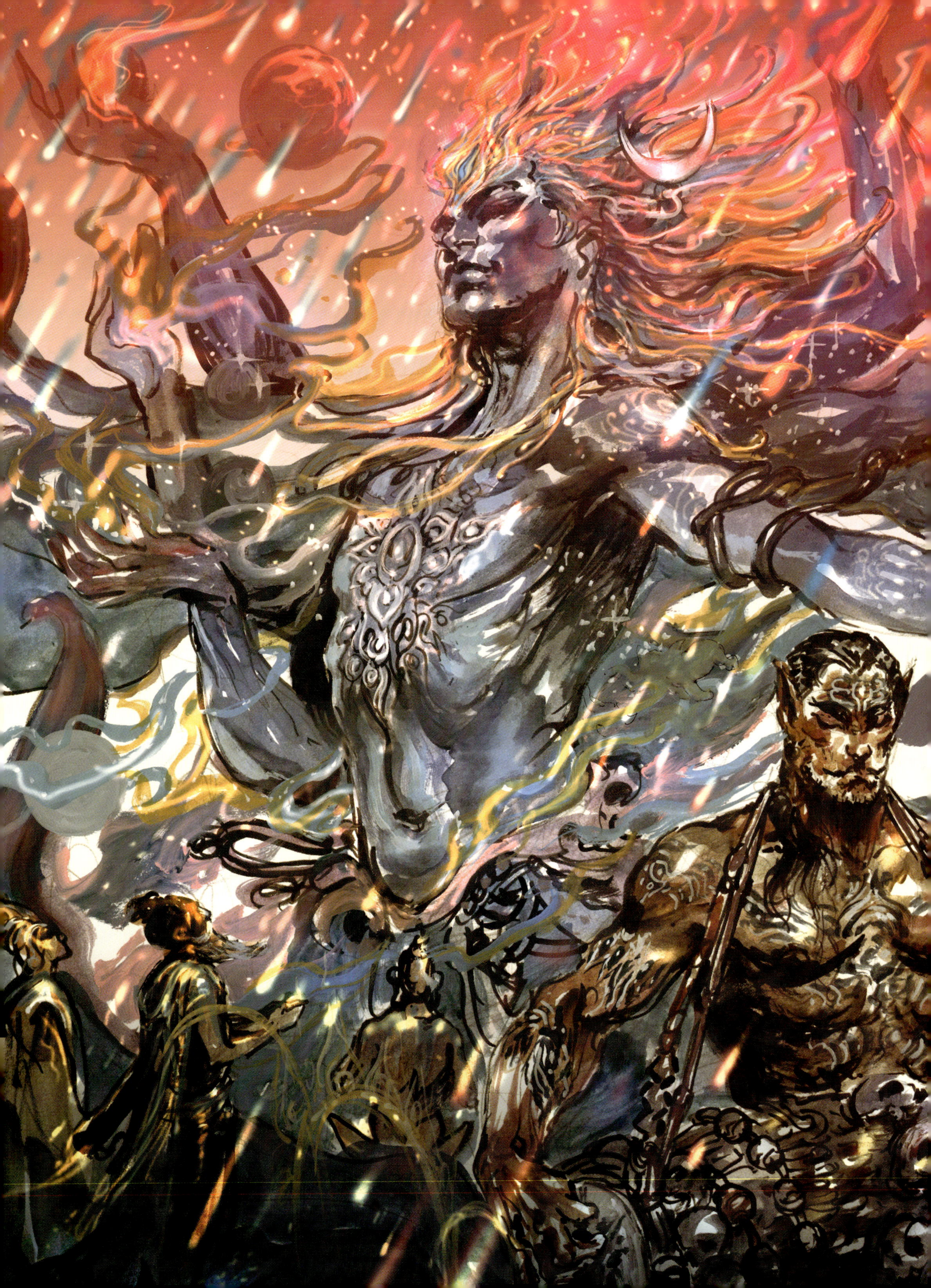

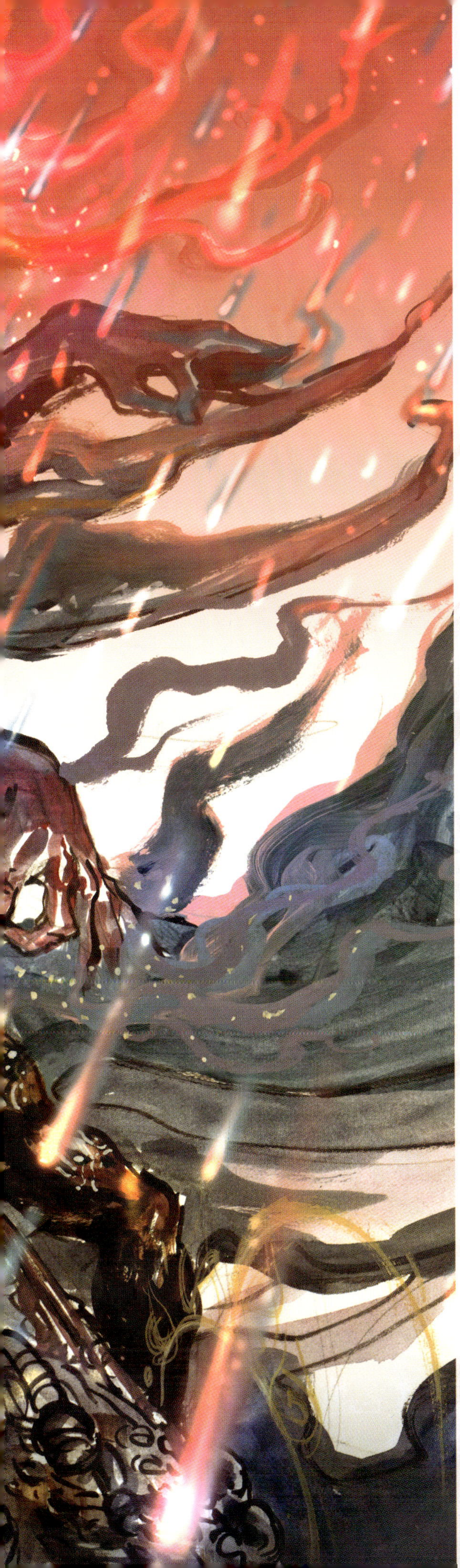

As the *taal* progressed, Shiva manifested himself in the myriad *roopas* which expanded across the belts of time, consuming *manavantras* and many *kalpas*.

He was so entrenched in the bliss, that he played his *Maha-Damroo* fourteen times, and from there, originated fourteen texts of music — the fourteen sounds.

Of these, seven were gifted to the human world and the rest could only be heard by animals and nature. Though, if one listens closely, those sounds can be experienced by even a mortal.

Ravana had found his father in the music, and by welcoming Ravana, Shiva had dissipated all bias towards who can and who cannot create music.

"When you play the music for yourself with love in your heart, it'll always reach me. I'll dance to it and the universe will be replenished."

With that, Shiva, the auspicious one, dissolved into the indigo stars which were calling him towards another dance.

Both Ravana and Brahaspati wondered who would keep rhythm to that.

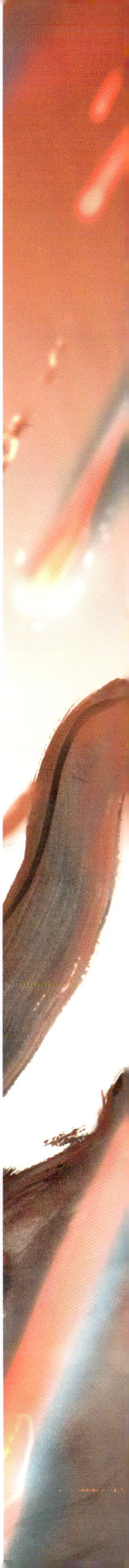

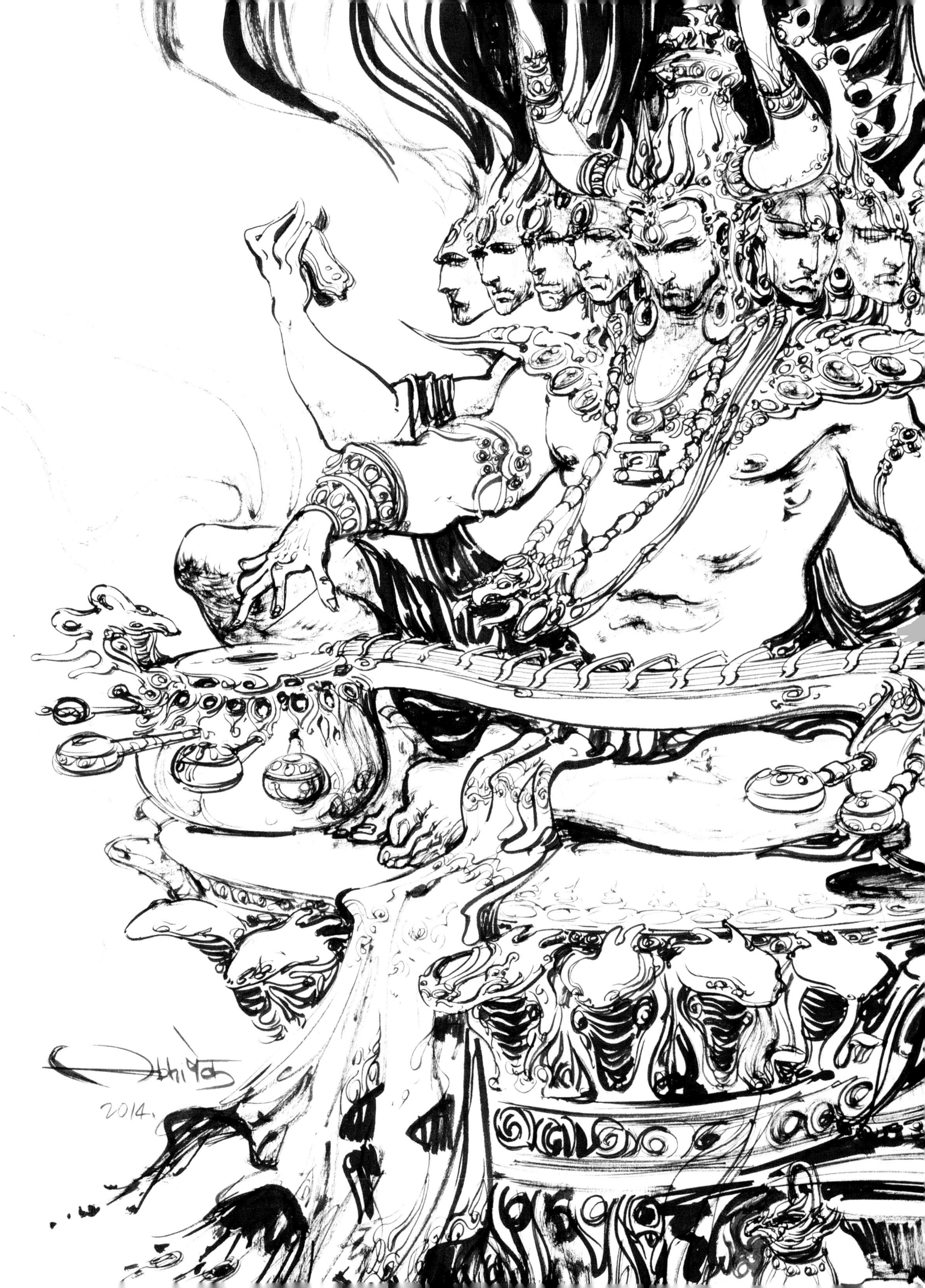
2014.

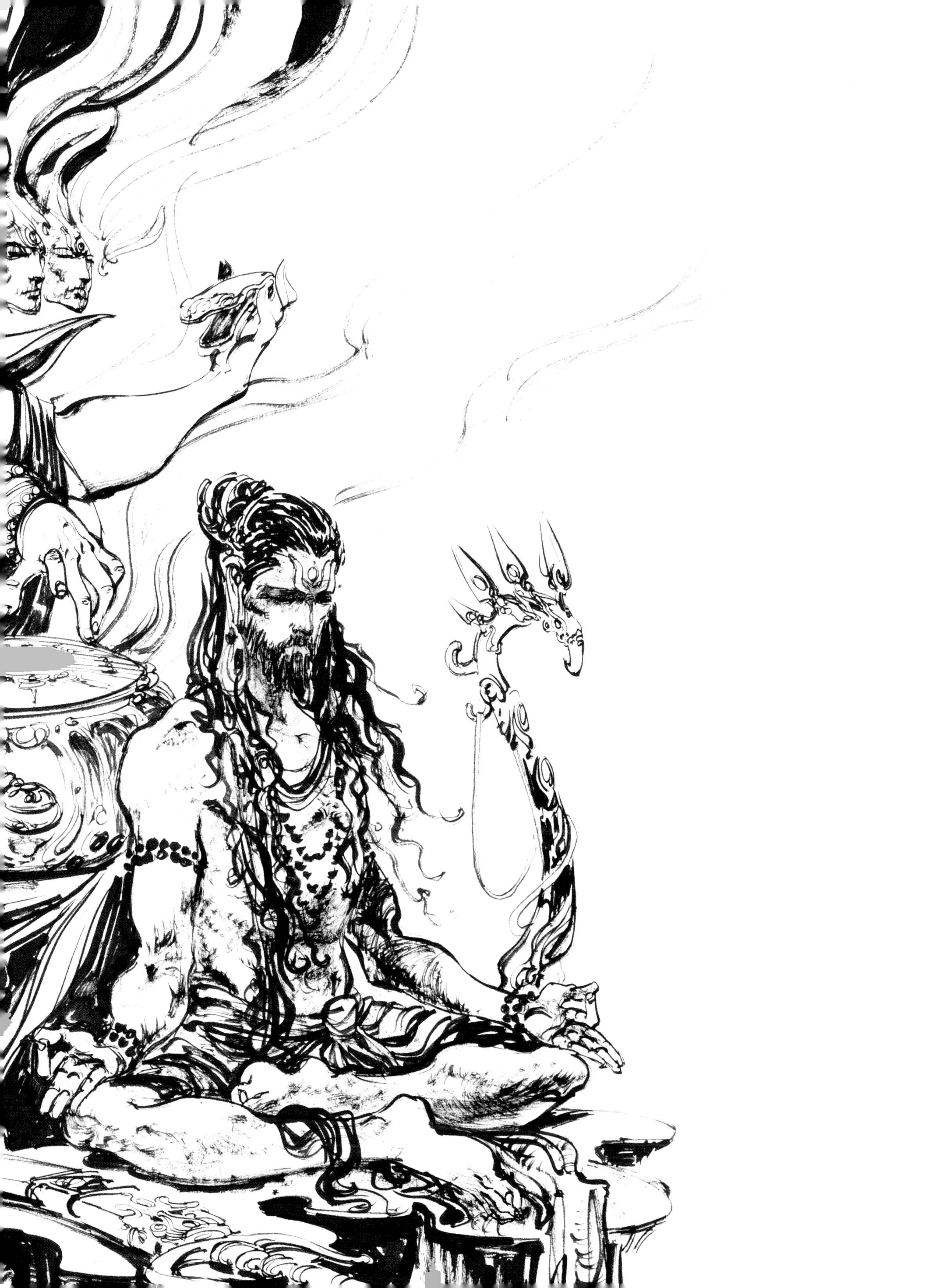

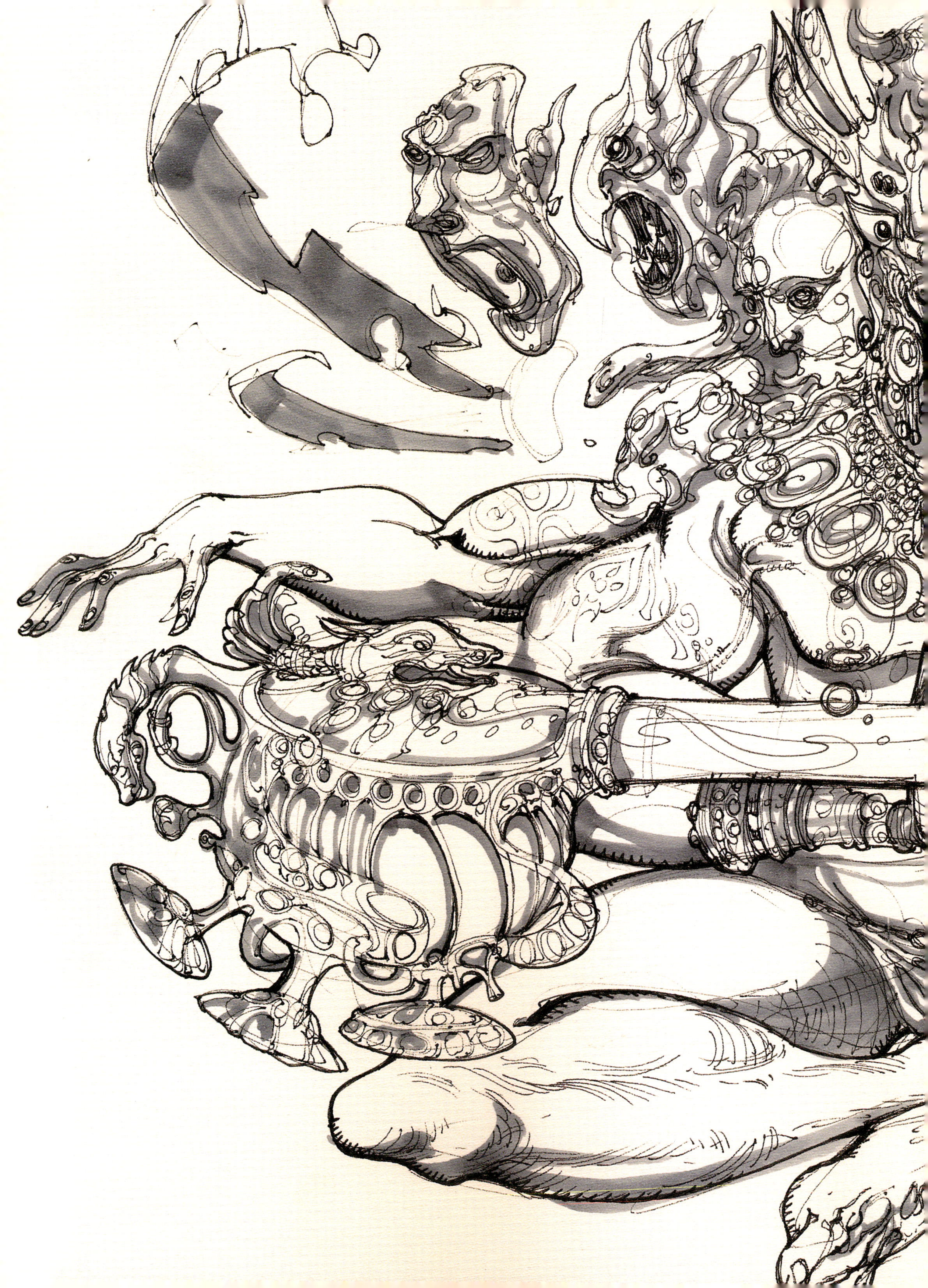

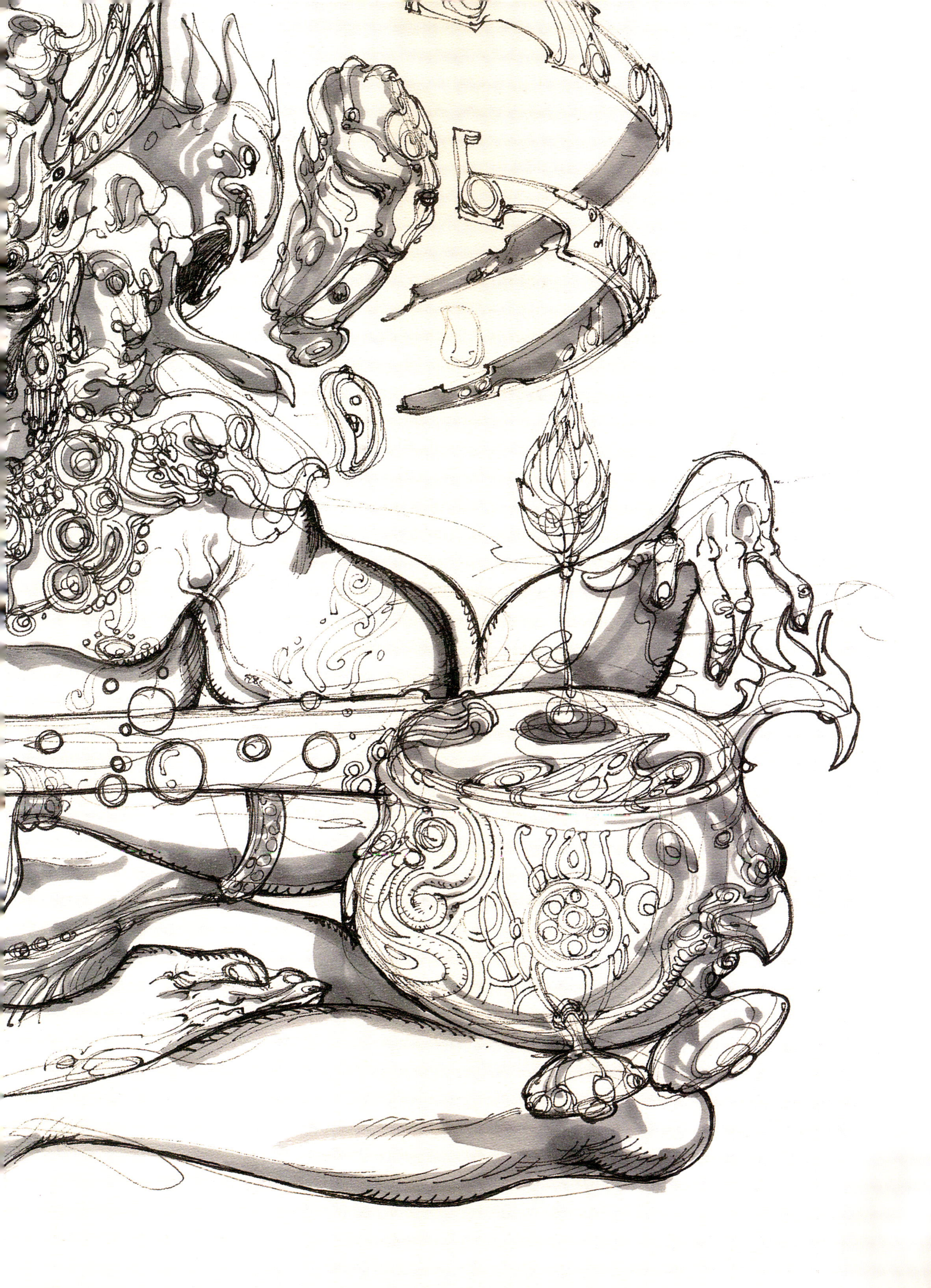

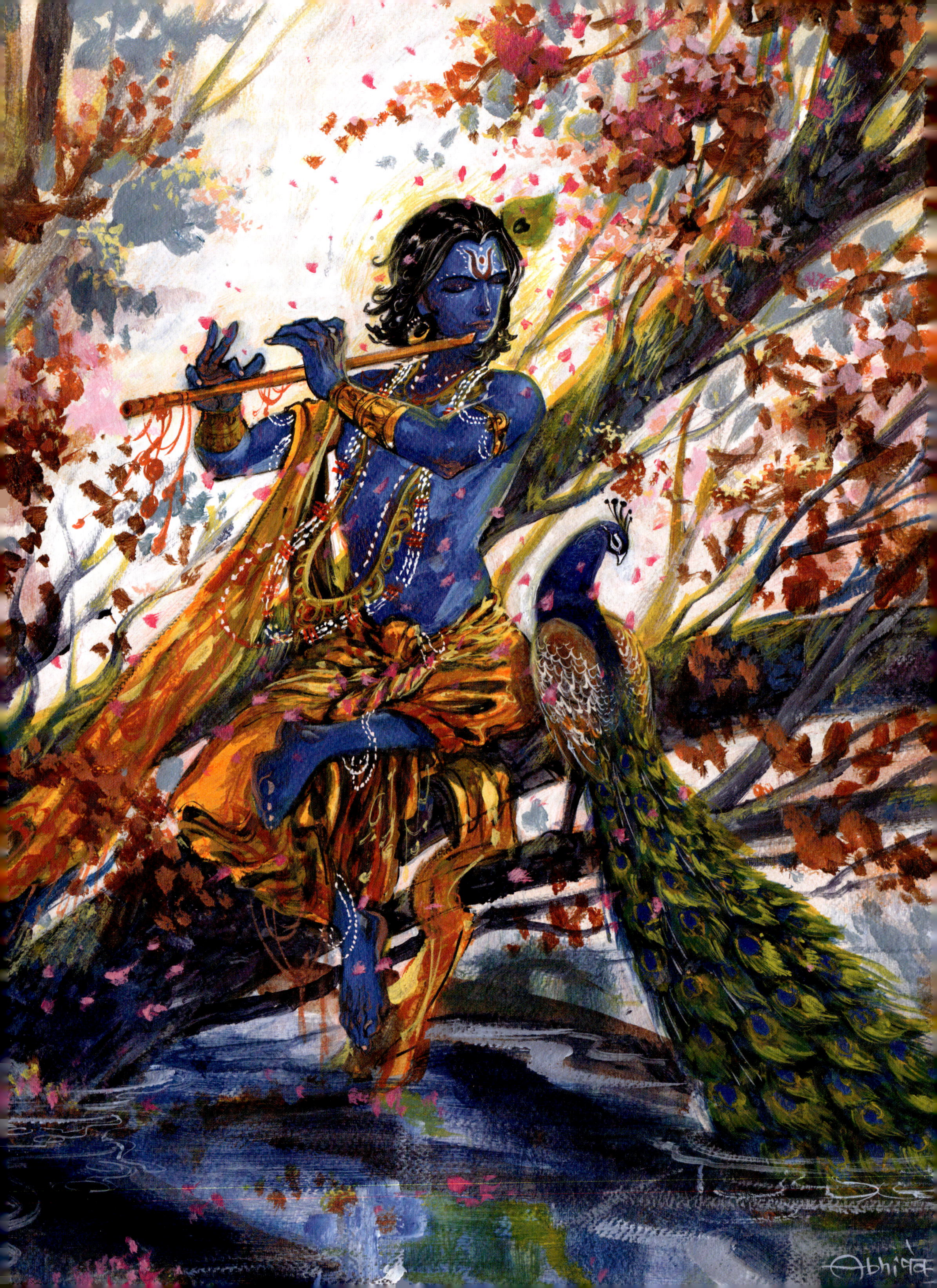

THE FLUTE

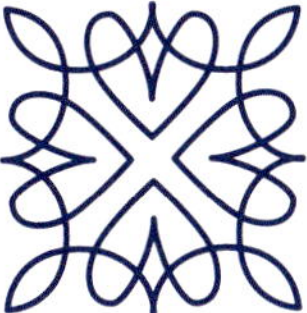

"Why do you play the flute, Krishna?" asked the banyan trees and marigold flowers.

Krishna: "Because it's a 'wind' instrument, played by one's breath. But then, whose breath is it that we are breathing into this reed? Is it the trees, is it the air they take and give back?
Or is it of *vayu* which permeates all beings? Is it of lovers who exist in each other's breath? Or is it of yogis who exist to observe breathing? Is this breath made of air? Or does it have sunlight in it too? Maybe even rain and the fragrance of Earth.

Oh majestic tree, my friend, it is our breath, passing through me and you. I'm nothing but a flute myself. "

The banyan tree and marigold flowers smiled brightly. They knew Krishna could hold his breath for hours like a tortoise. Imagine a man who can play music without any pauses. Eternity, if it ever gleaned into our mortal world, could do so through Krishna's flute.

Everything was immersed in music now. All the trees, birds and flowers swayed with it. The forest had become a flute itself. In its music, the Earth was listening to its own children loving her back.

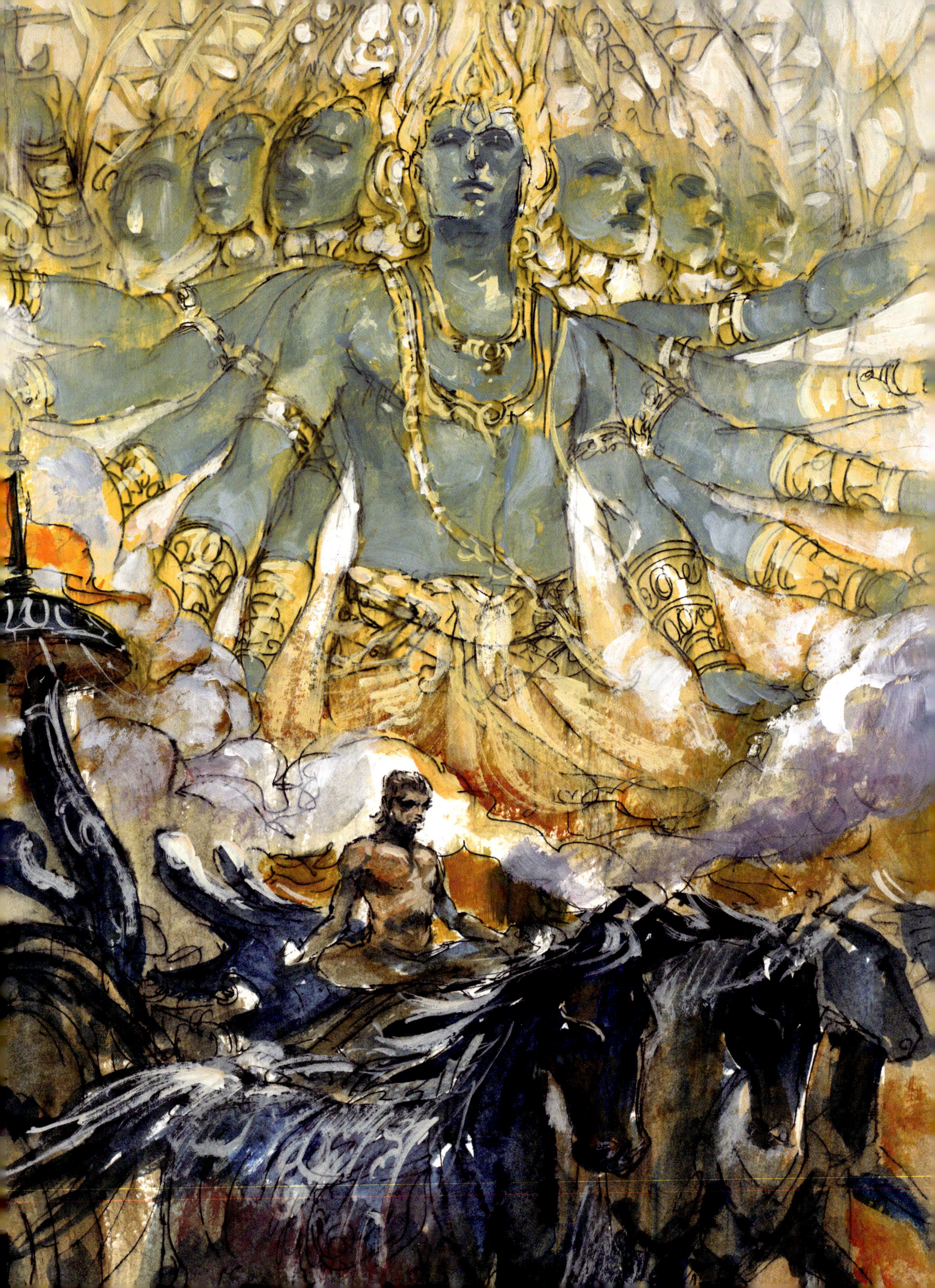

UNMANI

What is this world? The permanence of which is but an illusion. Is there any peace in this *samsara*?

Arjuna, hovered in the air, his skin cells still quivering and absorbing the *maha prana* emanating from the *Aseemroopa*.

He was being assaulted by the incremental heat, the *vishvaroopa* hadn't even fully bloomed.

Did he have the energy to take what he had summoned upon himself?

Still as he was, his mind was harrowed by thoughts which ate at his determination.

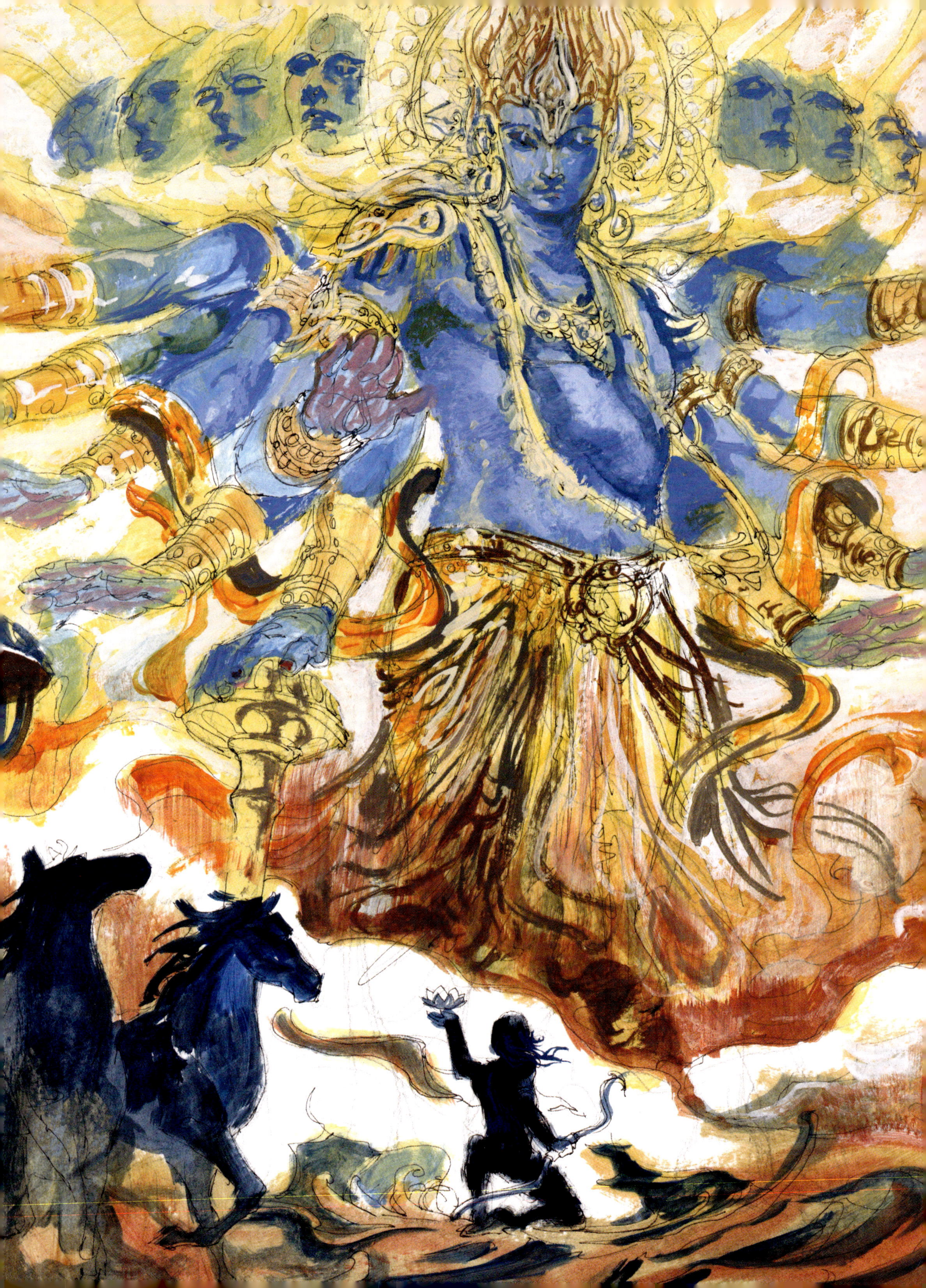

The inner being was suffering.

Nothing in the expanse of his mind came forth to rescue. Instead it hurled more despair at him.

“You are not this strong Arjuna. You never were. You should be ruthless in a world full of malice. But no, you want to be kind, thinking that you're better than everyone else.

You’re just another prince born with privilege whose merit comes from the biased love of his teachers and from a father who is the God of Gods. Without them you are nothing. NOTHING!” shouted the myriad voices, filling him with inferior emotions.

Arjuna knew the voices were right. He was not special, yet he had withstood the blazing heat so far. Only the most astute of yogis could do that.

He had never wanted the war. He loved his ascetic life in the Kamakhya forest. He was content with being a seeker alone.

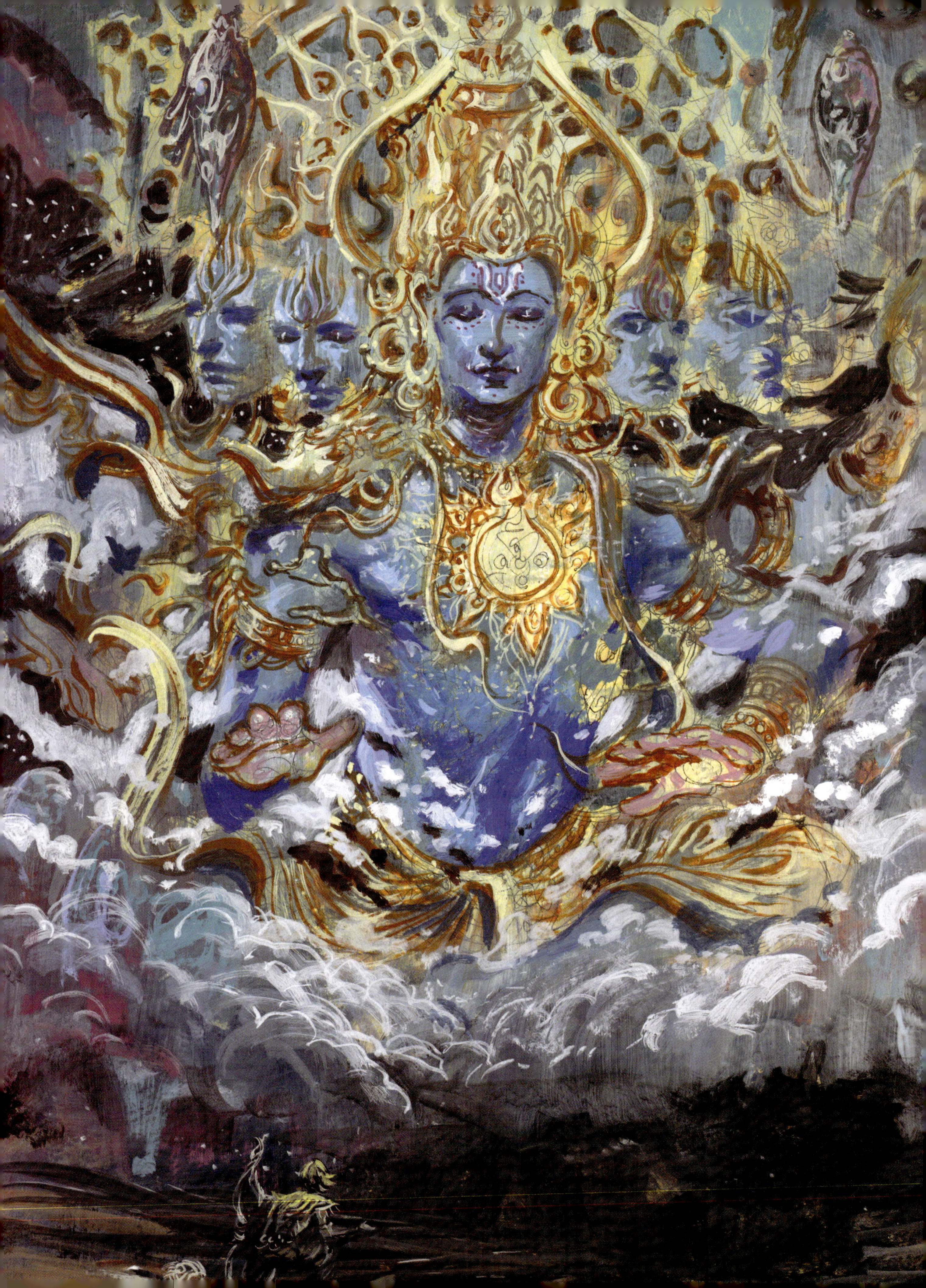

He remembered his resolve was brought back by Madana, besides safeguarding his brothers, to protect the forests he loved so much, his family, the trees.

And he knew that in that moment, the voices had given him an answer.

He must become *Unmani*.

Thoughtless.

So he did. A yellow flower fell on him.
He could see the gigantic Vasudev taking up an entire sky. The magnificence eased his burning body.

He had emptied himself out, so the nectar of wisdom could pour in.

The Divine Song had begun.

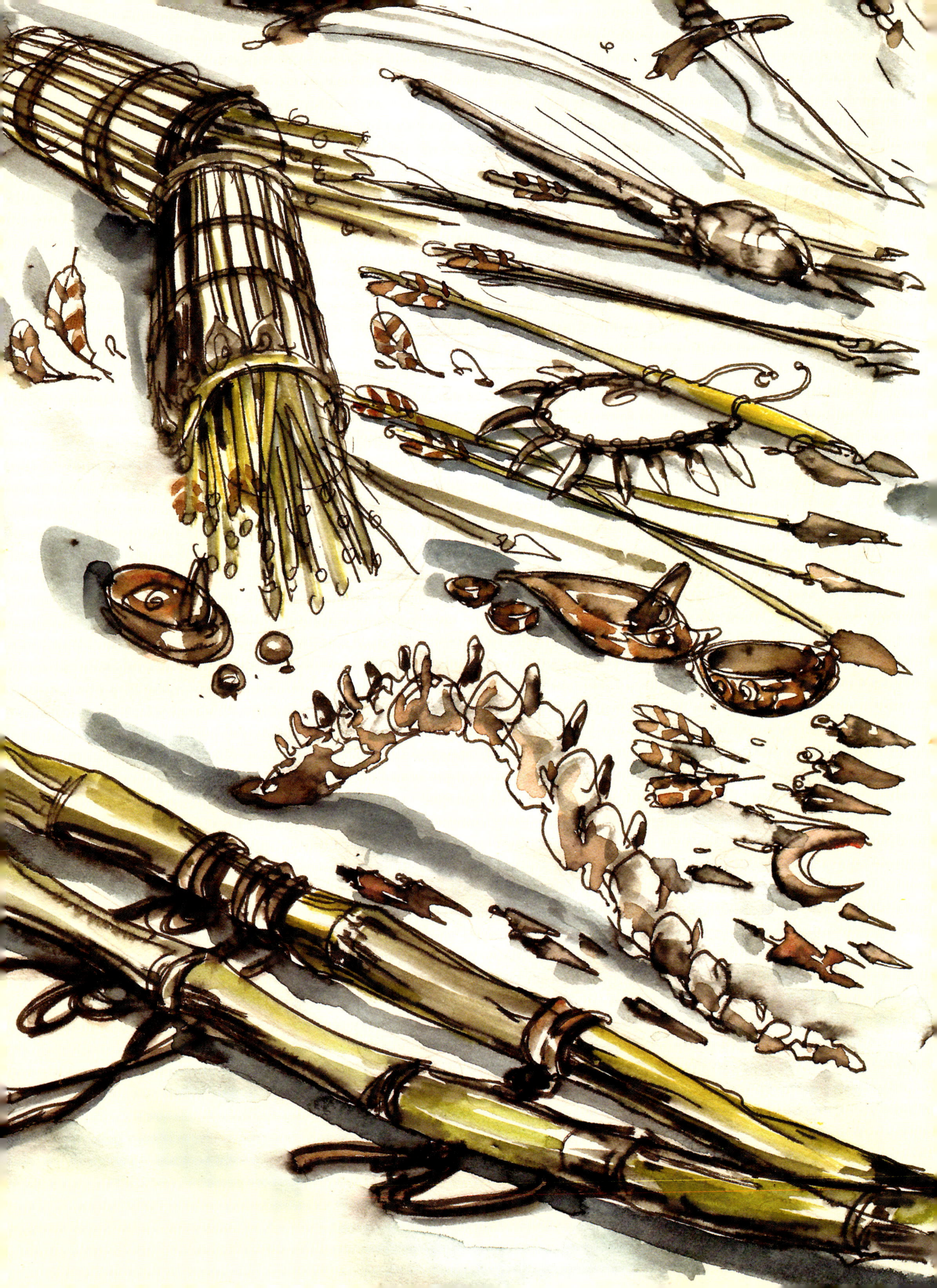

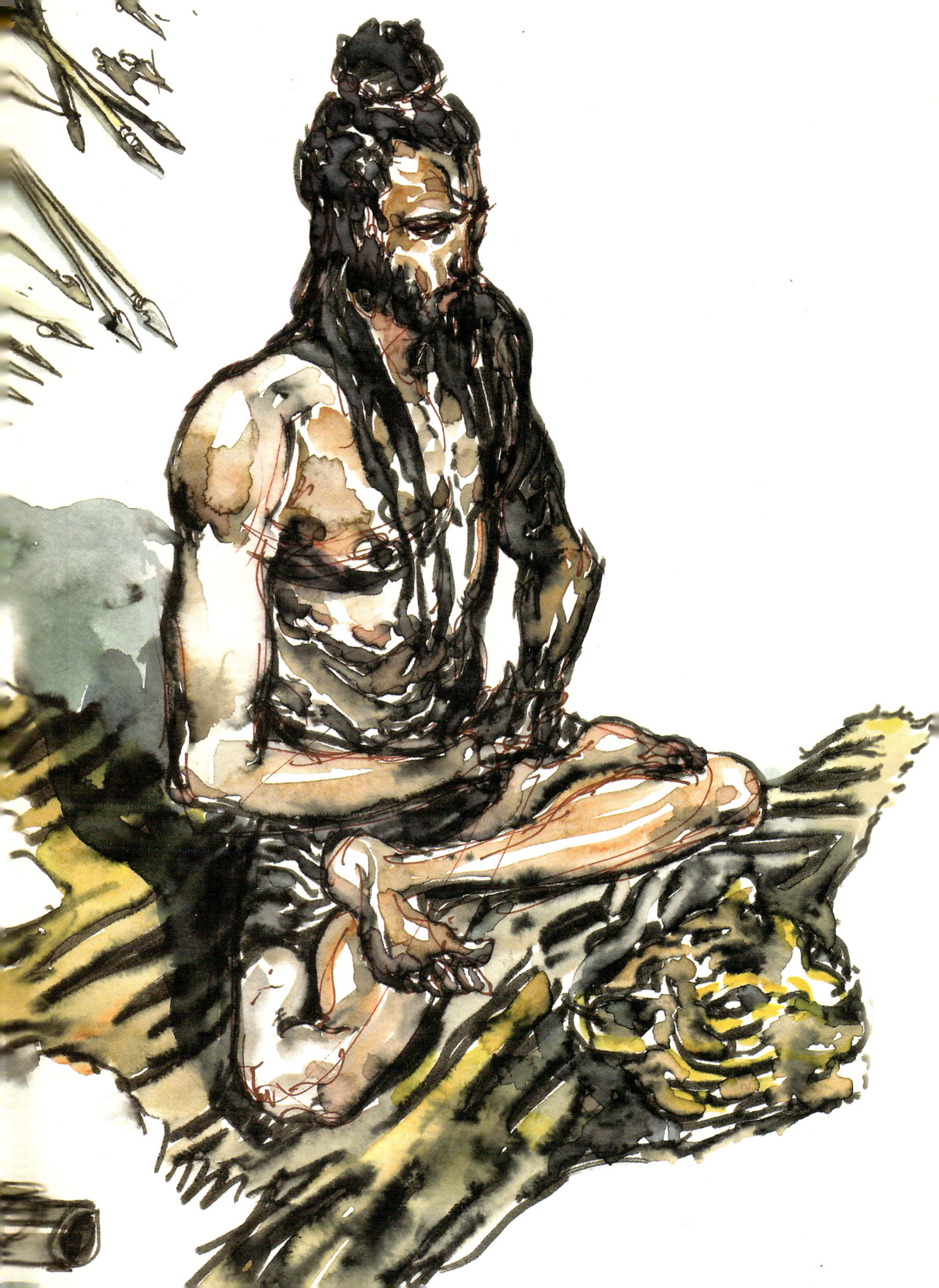

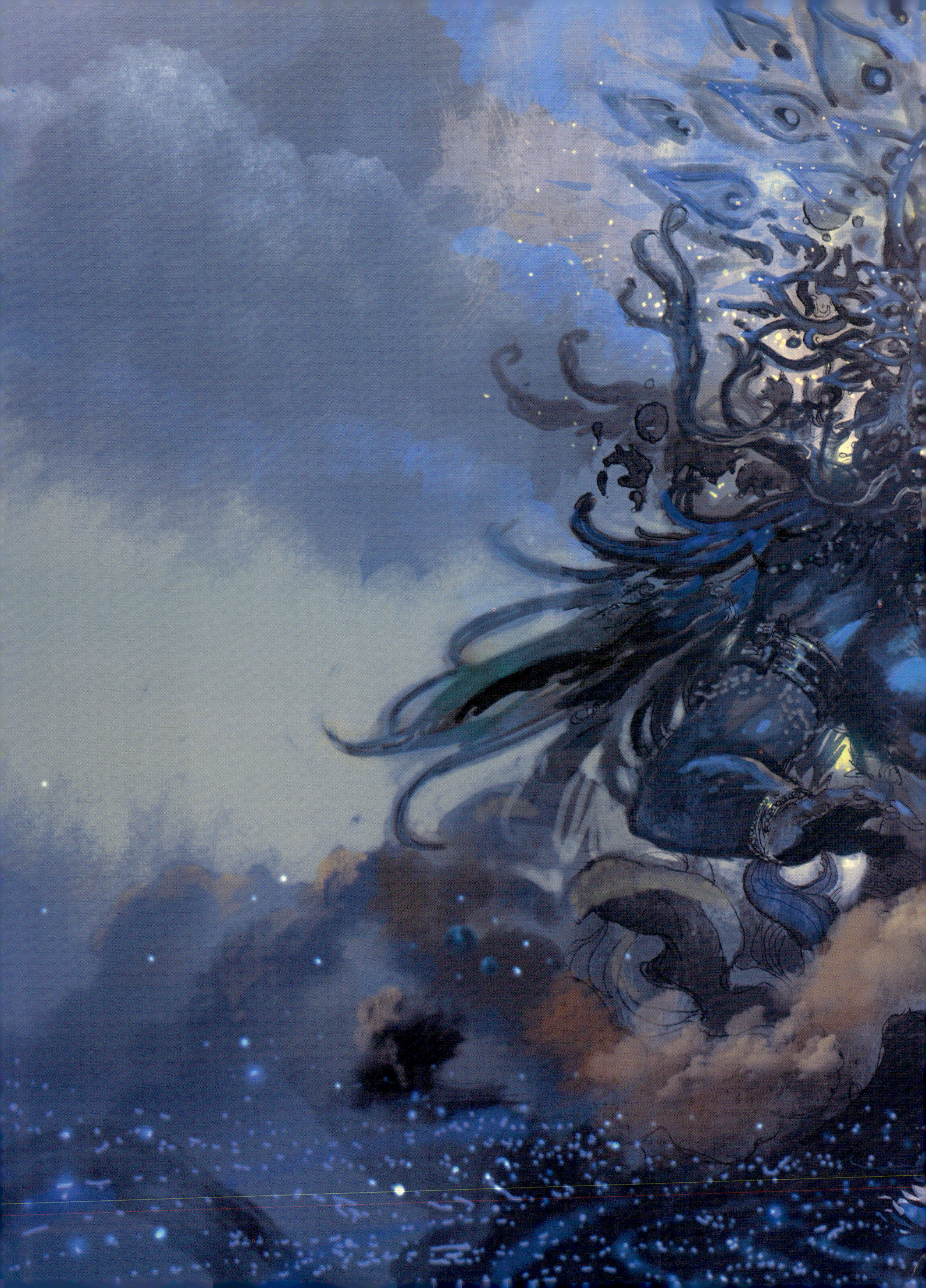

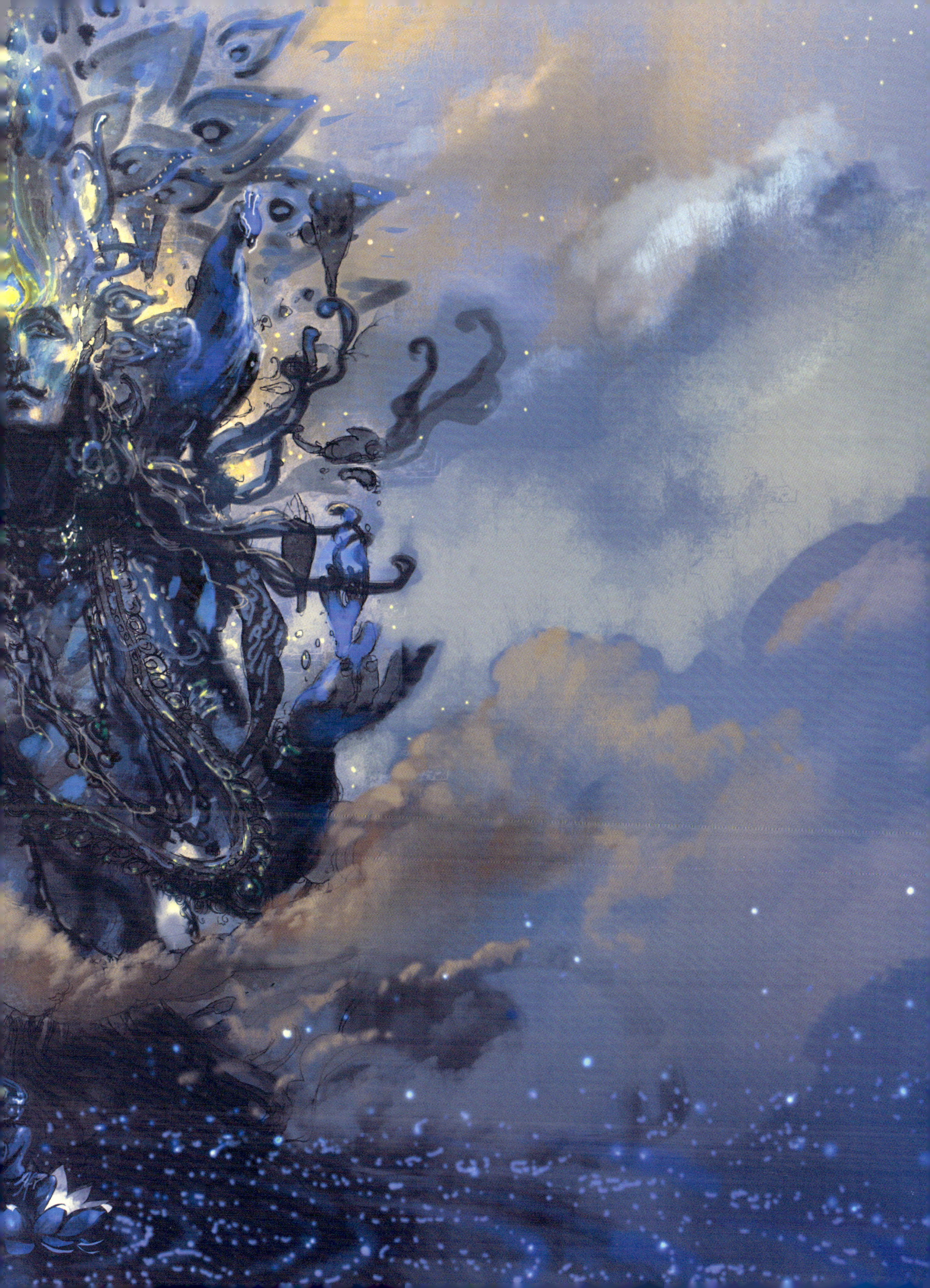

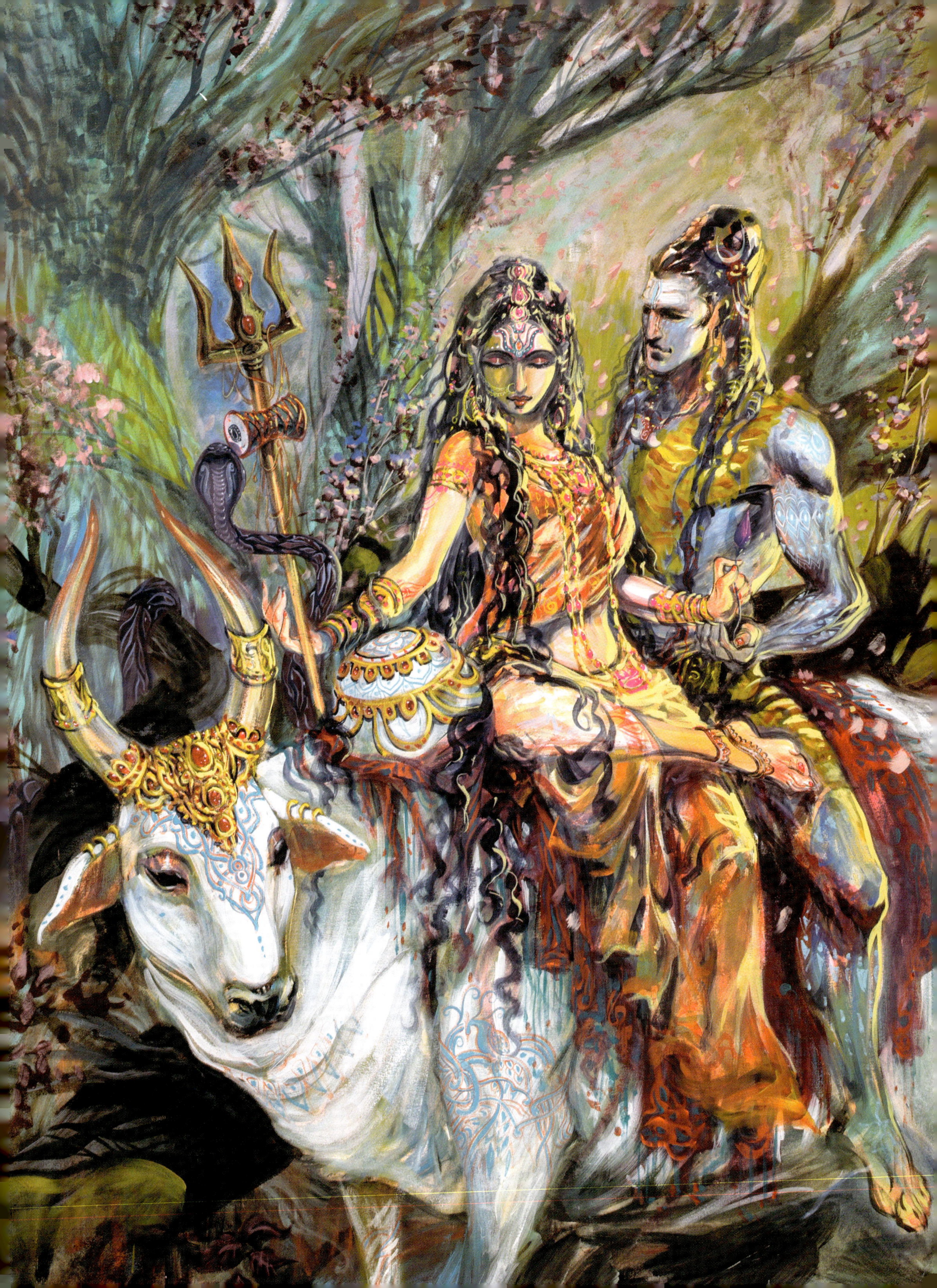

"The one who is shimmering golden with the kindness of the Moon, invoke in me the knowledge of light."

"To hear what is subtle, to see what is kind, to pray from an unbiased mind, is to truly become part of the forest of Shakti."

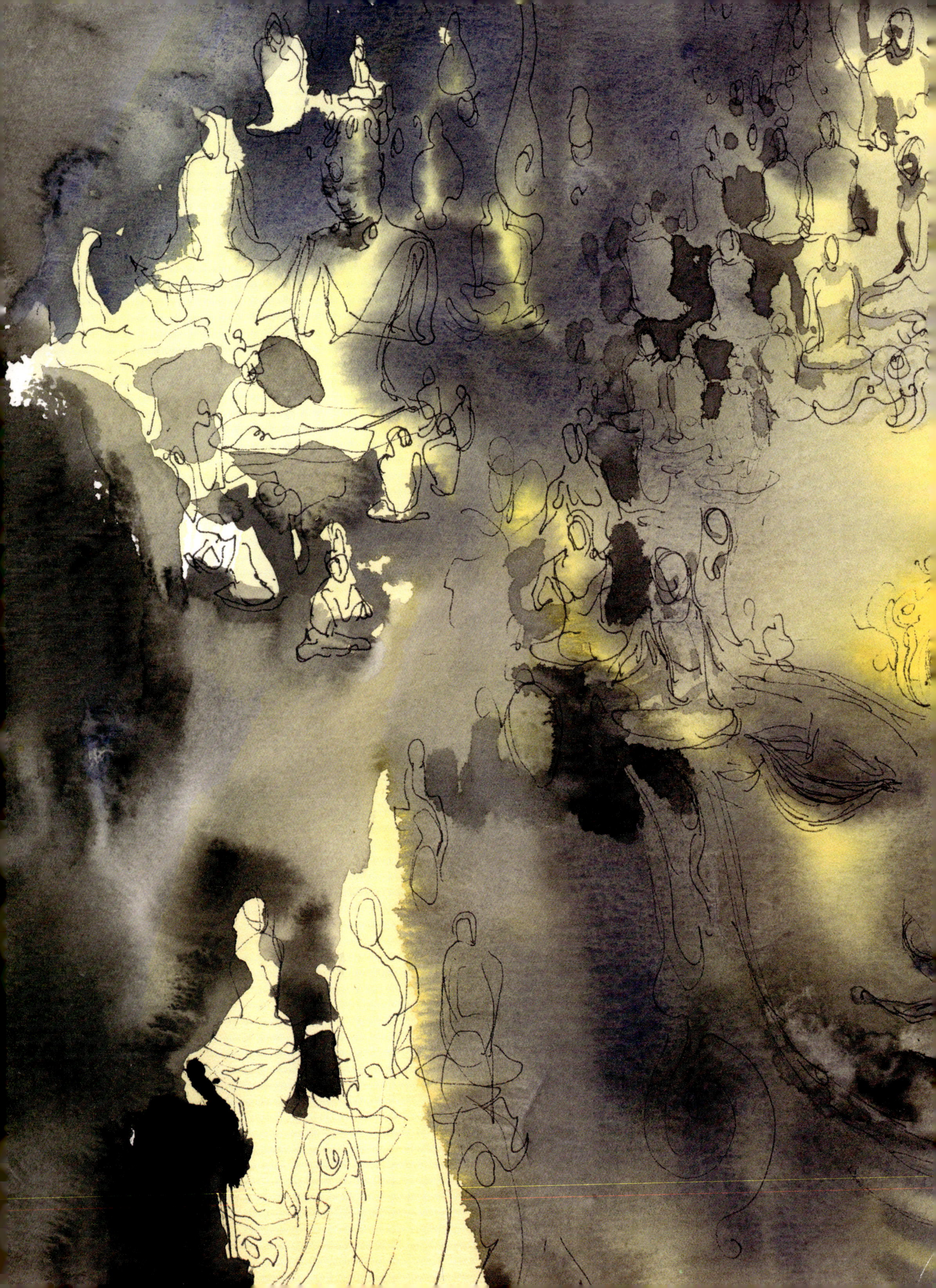

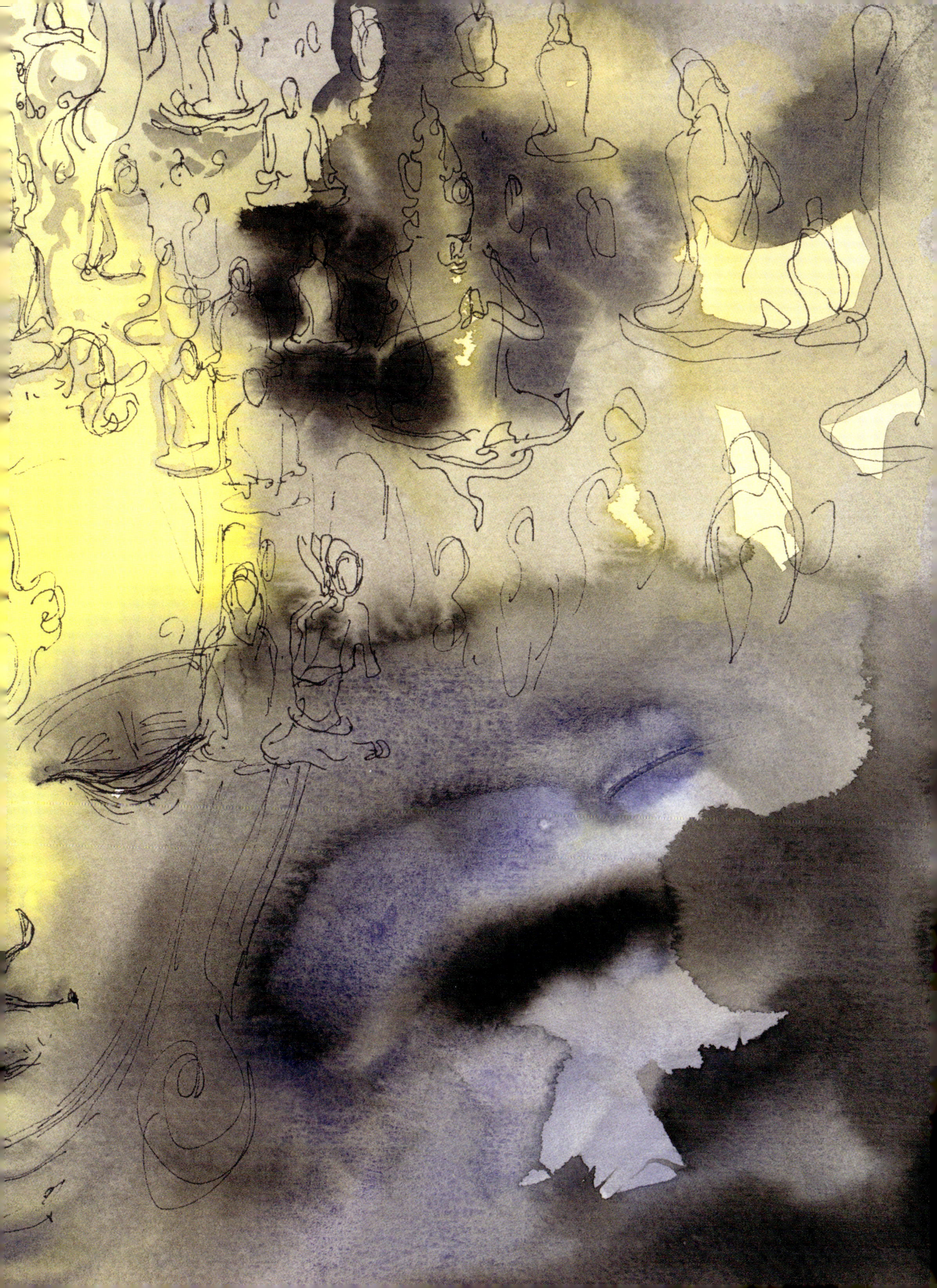

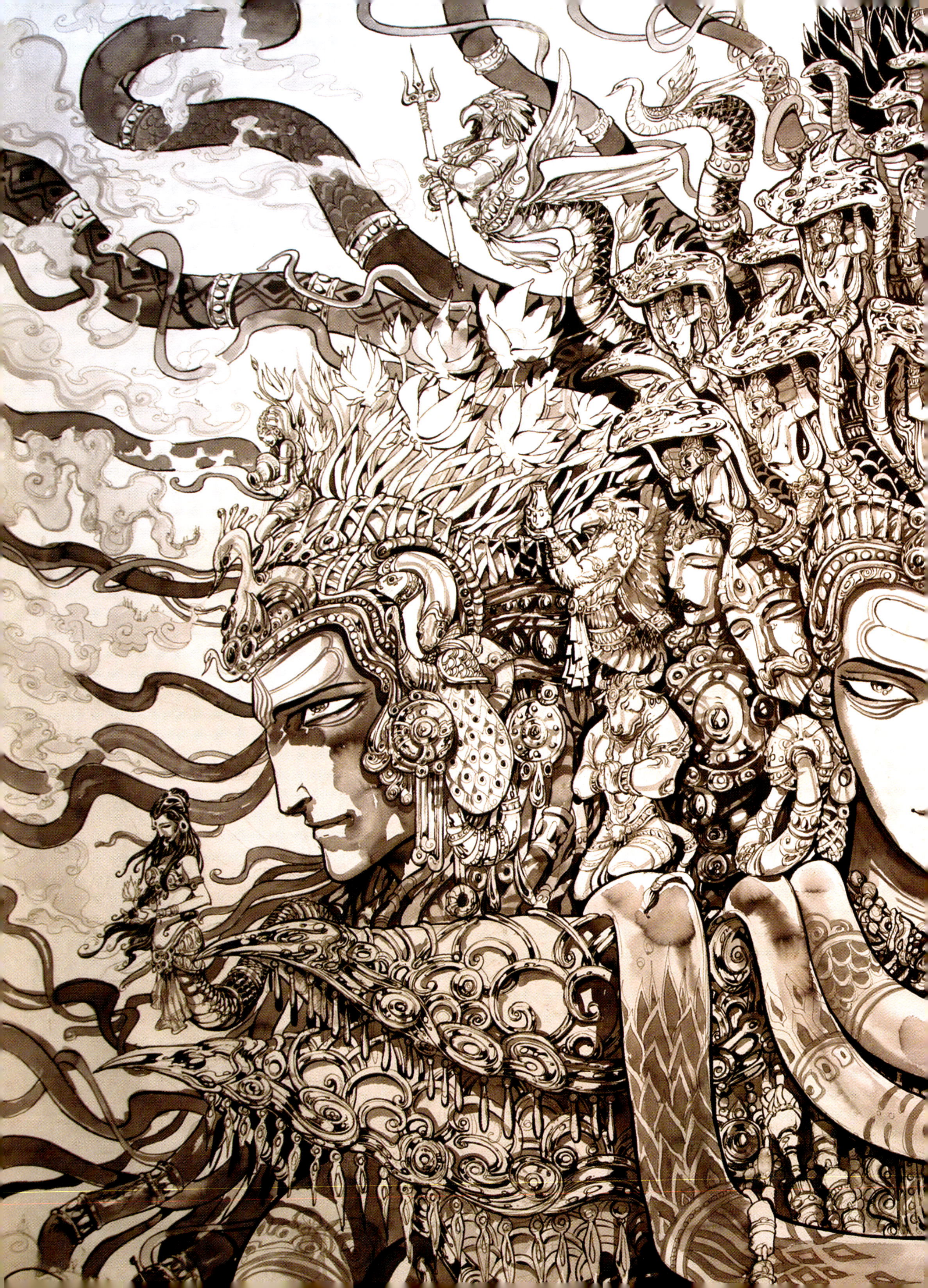

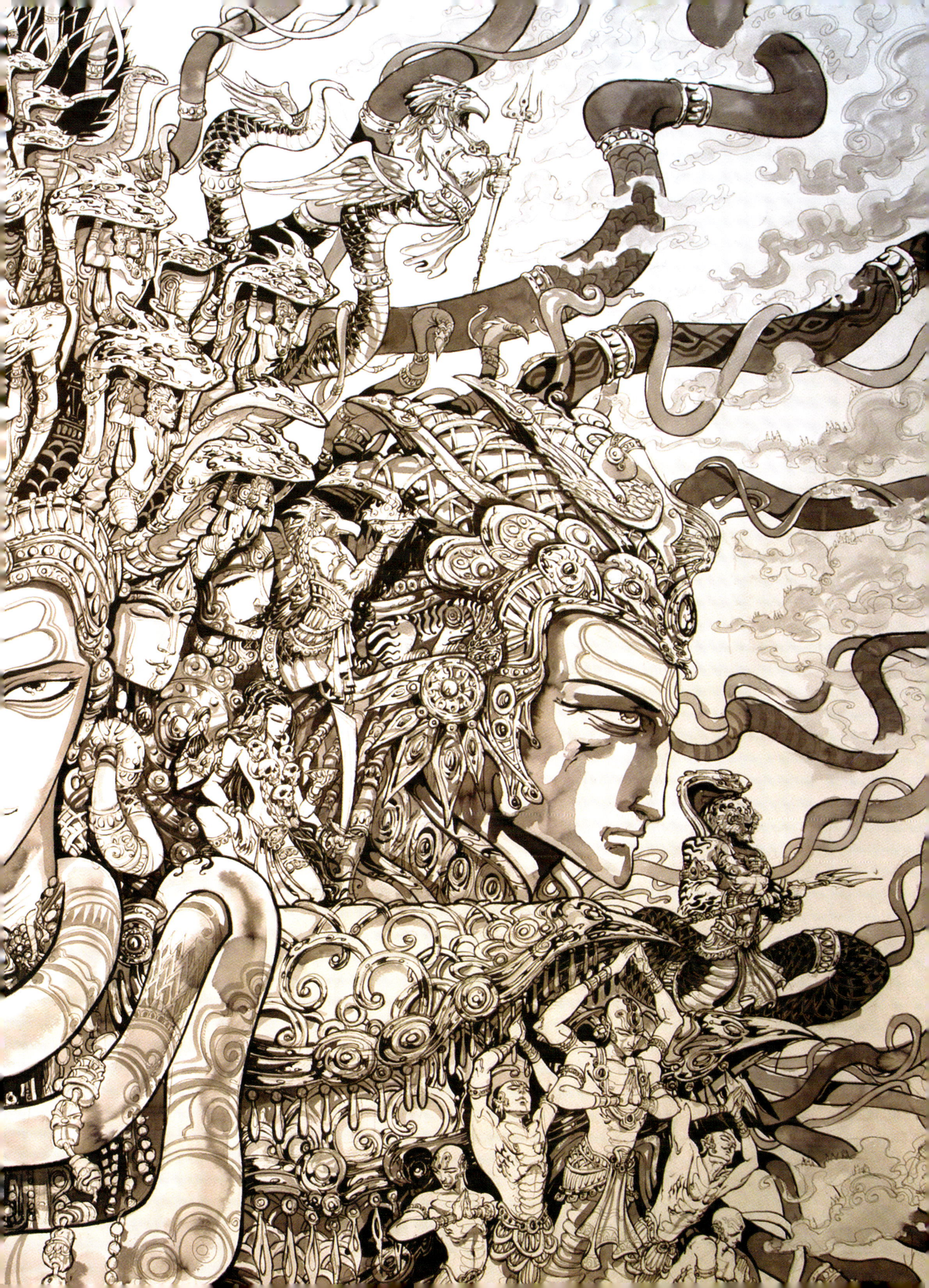

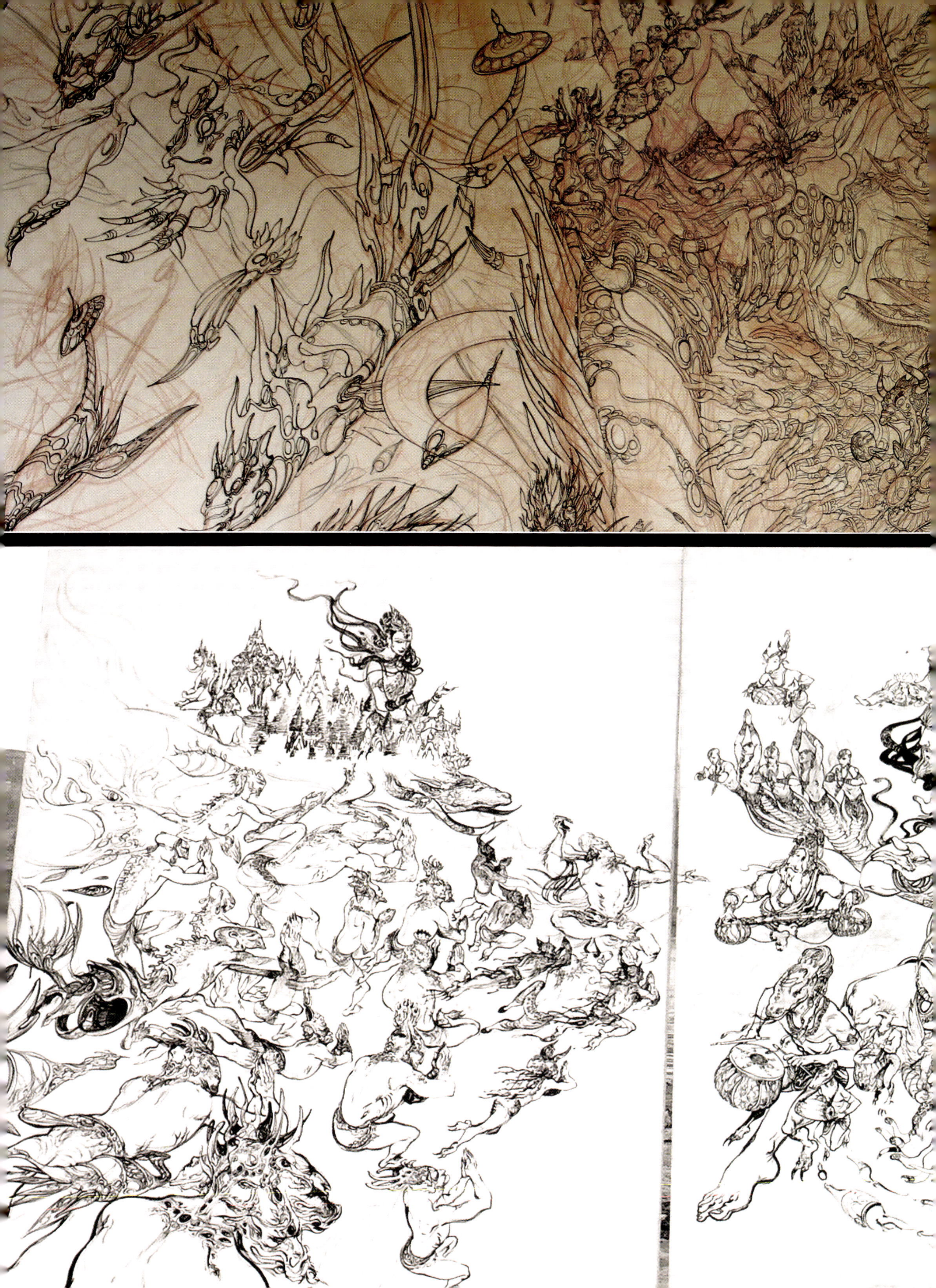

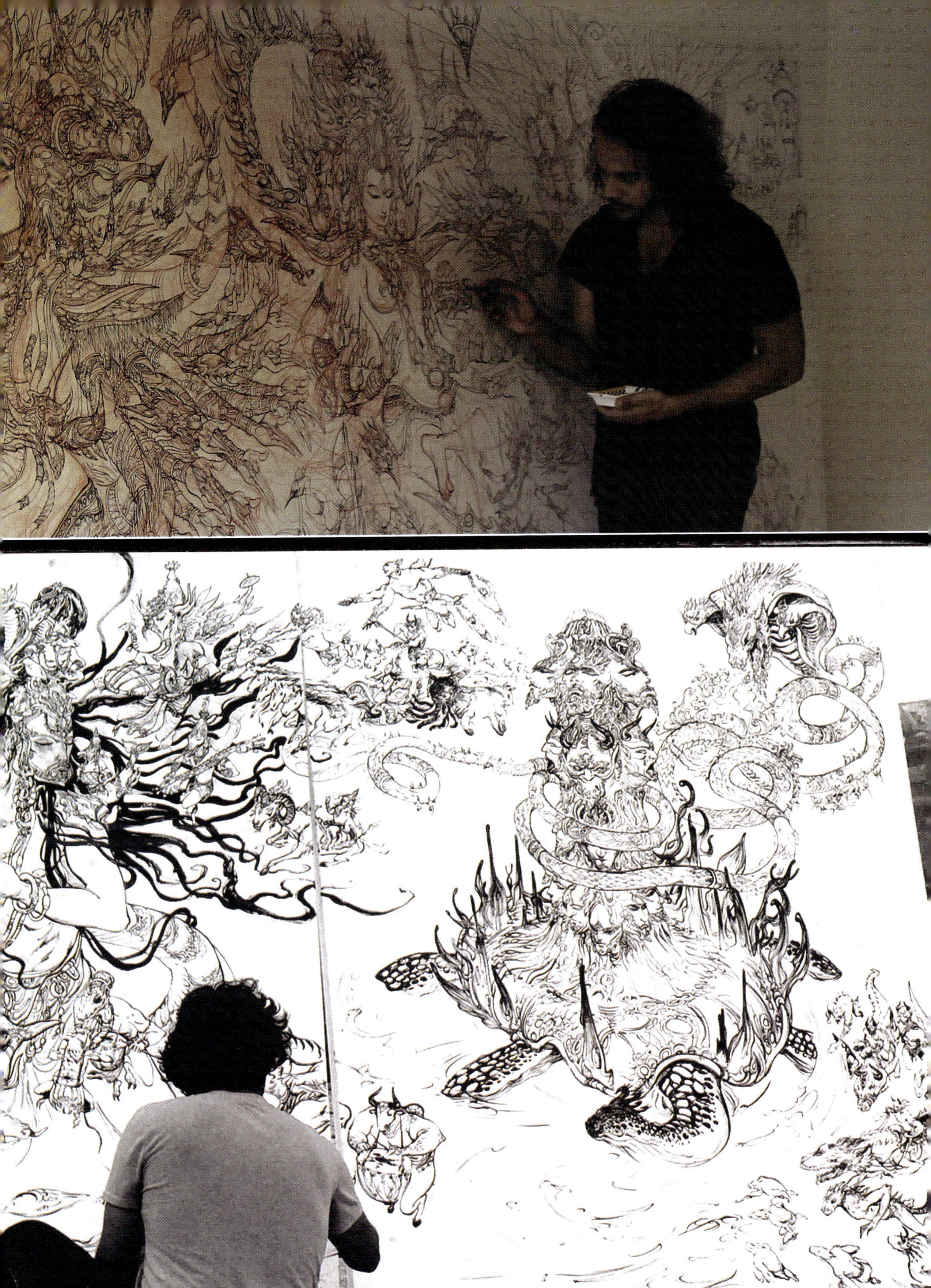

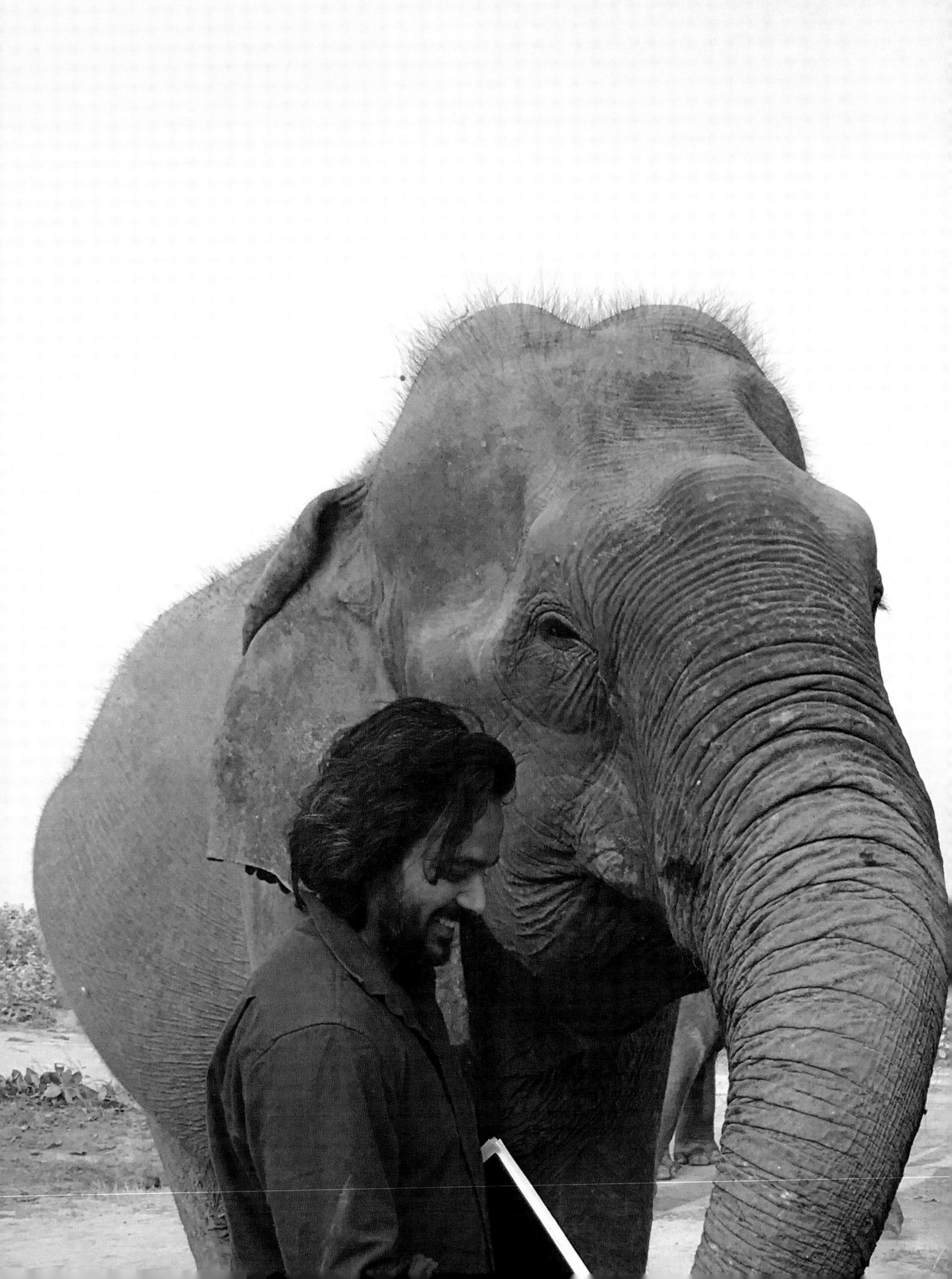

AFTERWORD

First of all, if you're holding this book, you have my gratitude.

This collection brings together personal emanations inspired by the ancient wisdom literature of India. Stories which I'd like to believe are traveling to us from a time where illuminated minds learnt from the forests and the stars. Just like our eyes cannot see the various systems of the body which govern life from within, similarly there's a wealth of subtle and symbolic systems functioning inside these stories, which are only revealed when we take a closer look.

I owe a great deal to the various books which furthered my explorations, held by the moments of love and equanimity where I truly understood their wisdom. Be it spotting fire rainbows at high altitude treks or seeing a mother mountain goat teach her calf how to jump across a stream, all revealed lessons I couldn't have understood otherwise.

The stories in the book are re-imaginations of Vedantic, Puranic, and Upanishadic texts, with an intent to take you right into the center, where a conversation is unfolding between the seeker and the source. For example, in the story of the "Samudra Manthan" , "Halahala" is personified as a character seeking absolution, while "Kevalya" is an ode to the yoga sutras. "Unmani" is a little window into the *Gita*, while "Pillar of light" is built with science and space. Some are simply personal meditations like "Ansuya" and "A thousand rainbows", celebrating a love for Earth which gleans across this book.

With the next book we dive even deeper. It's titled "Poorna - the great feminine divine" and I cannot wait to share it with you all.

I would also like to thank a few people for their tremendous contributions.

To Anubhav Nath, for his unwavering support and for creating the phenomenal exhibition at Varanasi which yielded the large painting that now adorns the cover of this book, and to Ojas art and everyone in the team, I deeply thank you.
To Kim for her immense support, for sending artworks across continents, to Snow, Maze, and Batty for their love. You guys are my heart.
To my publishers for having faith in this project and giving me room to truly create a book we all care about.

To everyone who supported the hell out of me and welcomed my work in their lives.

Love & Light
Abhishek Singh

(photo taken at Wildlife SOS, rescue & rehabilitation centre, India)

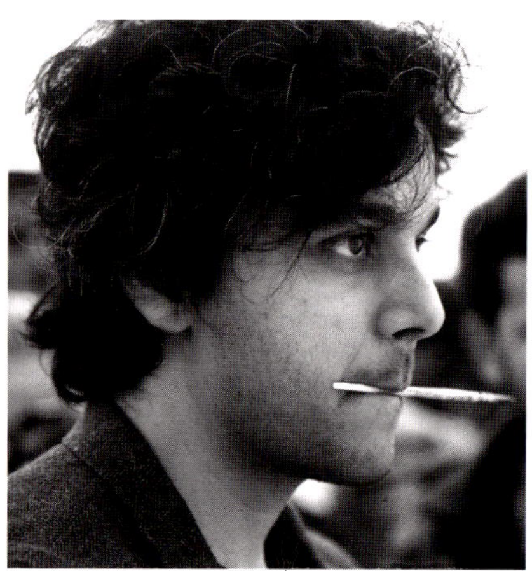

ABOUT

Abhishek Singh's work is acclaimed around the world for its unique style and storytelling and has been exhibited in prestigious places like LACMA, Asia Society, Vermont Museum, and Burning Man. He's known for his social impact projects where he blends stories of nature, myths and social themes with live artworks, like *Shiva* in Varanasi, *Vrikshdootam – Message from the Trees*, Goddess Exhibition, Budapest and JLF, Jaipur.

His critically acclaimed *Krishna – A Journey Within* is the first graphic novel by a writer/artist of Indian origin to be published in American comic book history. Spanning comic books, art direction, and VR films, some of his notable works are Shekhar Kapur's *Ramayana 3392 A.D.*, India Authentic Series and a VR film for Deepak Chopra.

Abhishek currently lives between his studios in Brooklyn, New York and Mumbai. Whenever possible he retreats for a meditation trek in the Himalayas.

abhiart www.abhishekart.com

Book Design - Rachita Rakyan
Editor - Charu Dhandia
Bio photo - Vicky Roy
Afterword Photo - Savi Kulkarni
Page 116 (Above) - Vijayakumar Armugam
(Below) - Vicky Roy

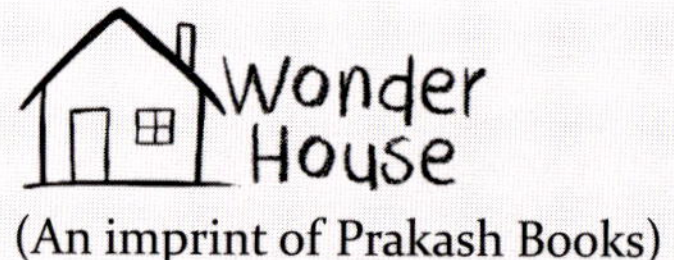

(An imprint of Prakash Books)
contact@wonderhousebooks.com

©Abhishek Singh

All rights reserved. No part of this book may be reproduced or transmitted in any form by any means, electronic or mechanical, including photocopying and recording, or by any information storage and retrieval system except as may be expressly permitted in writing by the publisher.

ISBN : 9789388810395

Printed 2025